Boston Hera/

S0-EIV-368

BY THE SAME AUTHOR

NOVELS
A World of Men

AUTOBIOGRAPHY
Grandad With Snails
In Step With A Goat

POETRY
The Silent Mirror
Voyage From Spring
Death On A Live Wire

MICHAEL BALDWIN

Miracl

MIRACLEJACK

ejack

Holt,
Rinehart and Winston
New York Chicago
San Francisco

Copyright © 1963 by Michael Baldwin

All rights reserved, including the right to reproduce
this book or portions thereof in any form.

First published in the United States in 1967

Library of Congress Catalog Card Number: 67-10943

PZ
4
.B1816
.Mi

80789-0117
Printed in the United States of America

FOR

GORDON BRUCE

Contents

All persons and episodes in this book are fictitious. There is no intended resemblance between any character in the novel and any living newspaper-proprietor, editor, journalist, photographer, priest, preacher, aristocrat, stuntman, American advertising-agent, circus-performer or anyone else. Nor are *The Post* and its rival paper intended to suggest any particular newspapers in Fleet Street or anywhere in the English-speaking world. Any slur imputed against the police-forces of London and New York, and against the Fire Brigades and Fire Departments of those two cities, must be taken as an expression of character and not as a reflection upon their reputations and histories.

*From The Gospel According to St.
Matthew, Chapter 4*

5. Then the devil taketh him up into the
holy city, and setteth him on a pinnacle
of the temple,
6. And saith unto him, If thou be the Son
of God, cast thyself down.

Man without Heaven or Hell,
Condemned to roam
Between brick and iron,
All night going upstairs to pray,
All day on the level to moan
While Nick chuckles down in the drain. . . .

From *On Stepping From a Sixth-Storey Window* by
Michael Baldwin. (Longmans, Green & Co.)

Prologue

SHE had just left me for good when the hubbub started outside. I didn't go to the window at once; she had just left me, and anyway, since it was Sunday evening I knew what the trouble would be.

It would be a tall man in black wearing dark glasses, and he would be standing on the pile of rubble in the middle of the bomb-site, preaching. Over his head a flag would be flying, and it would probably be a different flag from the one he carried last week, though it was always white on black. Sometimes it was a simple Death's-Head, sometimes a skull-and-crossbones; and I believe he also went in for an hour-glass and even a scythe. A big crowd used to come into the bomb-site, through the gate and down the cellar-steps at the other end, in order to listen to this performer; so I always supposed he was stark raving mad, since the only people who are listened to today are the mad ones, and they are only listened to to be laughed at. If I had been a member of the C. of E. and feeling secure as a part of the Conscience of England or the Convenient and Economical, or whatever those letters mean to the men and women who do belong, I might have lifted my window every Sunday evening and laughed at him too. But I had left the belonging to her, and to give her her due she didn't laugh at things, she cried, and that made it worse. The main thing for me was that the madman out there had God. It might be the wrong God—

13

how could I tell? I hadn't seen a passport photograph—but it still meant he lived in a different world from me. And if he lived in the same world as the Salvation Army band, then at least until tonight he had pleased me by dwelling in a quieter part of it. Tonight was getting rowdy.

She had made me listen once. I opened the window and he flourished his flagful of bones and said, "Crucify me!"

It was a crowd of ordinary Sunday night citizens on the way to the pub or coming back from the cinema, and they had evidently heard him say this every week. They stood there and grinned.

"You are quite right to hesitate," he said, and there was an arrogant nasal twist to his voice. "You are quite right to hesitate. It is the most terrifying invitation an ordinary man or woman can receive. Crucify me. Just those words. And yet, you see, once upon a time I *was* crucified."

They shuffled. Someone guffawed.

I didn't expect his next move, but evidently most other people did. He unfastened his cuffs with shy, rather clumsy fingers, and there were raw marks in his wrists, sharp scars I could see even at thirty yards.

A few of us were dumbfounded. We were the newcomers. The rest either knew about those holes or had some private explanation for them. They fidgeted and grinned. "Hurry up, old mate," someone called. "Show us your mermaid tattoos!"

We all laughed at this. I don't think she did.

He bent down and started to roll up his trouser bottoms, a silly gesture as any beggar knows. Even if your legs are off at the knee you won't earn money like this.

The scars in his ankles were huge and puckered, rather like the marks left by jungle-ulcers, but they were too big to be really convincing, and even if they weren't, who was going to be convinced? Nobody shut up at all while he

14

showed us these: we were too embarrassed. I found myself wondering how he had got them.

Apparently that was the end of it for tonight. He didn't roll up his shirt for us; he was probably lacking that one. He just took hold of his flag, and with his scars still showing stalked up the steps and out of the cellar. It was a tame ending. Some of the crowd jeered after him and tried to follow, as I'd seen happen before, but once they reached the road they all milled around, getting nowhere. It was dusk, and the Madman must have made it quickly to the first corner.

When I looked at her she was still gazing out of the window as if she had just seen the most wonderful vision in the world. It sickened me to see how easily they could give her this awe. " Look," I said, " this isn't the One you mean! " She caught at my wrist, but I jerked my hand away. " I don't know how he got his holes," I said. " Perhaps he *was* crucified. The First Bloke hasn't got a monopoly on it, you know. The only man I saw crucified wasn't even a Christian, he was a Burman; but the Japs still gave it to him with all of the trimmings. Not that there seemed any God around to help him."

Her eyes begged me to be silent. I didn't know why I should be. I've not been far in the world, but I've seen man do to man far worse than the Romans did to that One. Only of course He was God, and that made it all so much harder for Him to bear. After all, He was responsible for the whole bloody business in the first place..

So in spite of the row I didn't go to the window that Sunday she left me. The glass had memories for me, and there is nothing more absolute than to be left by someone who still loves you. You can't even vow to win her love back. There isn't even that.

By now there was quite a riot going on, but I still sat and

15

thought about her. I knew I wouldn't try to do anything about us, except hope that her God would become inadequate to her in some way she could recognise. Only that wouldn't work either, because even when He did she would take the blame for Him and add Him to her own guilt, instead of unloading herself onto Him as He always claimed to be there for until anyone tried.

No more philosophy, I thought. It's only rationalised tears, or so you've told *her* often enough. Now get out a bottle and forget her for a little while.

I was still using the corkscrew when the window broke, smashed in from outside. Only a moment ago I had kissed her good-bye, and now there was glass on the bed, and the violence of the thing nearly made me fold up completely. I heard shouting, voices. But I couldn't move.

A brick had done it, a hunk of somebody's long dead home thrown up in the air from that bomb-site for the second time. I remember thinking this rather weepy thought as I picked it up and put it in the waste-paper basket. The spell was broken, and I went over to the window, trying to look suitably angry. But I couldn't. I felt as if I could never have it in me to be angry again, only waspish and sharp. So I lurched there, shocked, feeling bloated with sorrow, and looked through my web of glass.

No one glanced up at me, not an upturned face. The brick hadn't been meant for this way. No one knew they had broken a window, still less the window of a man whose girl had just left him.

It was a bigger crowd than usual, and a pack of them had pushed forward and were mauling at the preacher. There were several Teds there, not the Edwardian sort but real louts and tearaways, and one or two gangs of teenagers who were behaving drunk—he must have been saying something to upset the lot of them. Or someone had stirred them

16

against him. They were thrashing and screaming and the whole thing looked ugly. The remainder of the crowd just milled around and called out for peace and got trodden on.

The Man was retreating up the big pile of rubble, quite calmly, and the Teds were stalking him quietly. One of them had a knife in his fist. He probably didn't mean to use it, but then they never do and their knives get stuck in people just the same. I heard laughter, greengrocer laughter. One or two faces were amused at his reluctance to be crucified this week, or perhaps he had said something else to amuse them. In the way of crowds they would stay amused until someone actually stuck the nails in, and by then it would be too late.

The Madman still had his flag, and he was now at the top of the rubble. A piece of greenery sailed through the air and burst itself open on the cellar wall behind him. An old wrap of cabbage, perhaps, or a sog of cloth, but there was a lot of laughter; and one or two of the women with thick ankles and big fronts to their blouses began to look for more. A bicycle tyre writhed up horizontal from the shadows, rotating in the amazing silence after the throw while everyone followed it with their eyes, struck the wall at his back, flopped along it in a springy hoop and then jerked down the pile again. A girl ran giggling to retrieve it, and her boyfriend snatched it from her and tossed it again. It struck the man on the chest, not very painfully perhaps, and there was more laughter. This could go on. Back the tyre flipped. It was like the hoop-la.

The Teds paused. They had cornered him, and could now decide at their leisure whether to rough him up or just take his trousers off. "'Ave 'is flag!" someone called. "'Ave 'is bags more like," perked a voice that sounded like the mermaid voice from a few Sundays ago, and I winced at the memory of it.

17

"It's a shame, isn't it? Poor bloke!"

"Oh, go on. Look at 'im."

"Poor little bugger, he's not doing any harm. Come off him up there—he's let us have our little bit of fun!"

"'E won't come again if you 'urt 'im, mate!" Laughter! "And I 'aven't laughed so much in years!"

The Teds paused. If the crowd weren't with them, then this was bullying.

One of the blousy women called, "Go on, Charlie: why don't yer hop it. Tell yer what—why don't yer take off 'n' fly?" They were all screaming with laughter, shaking with it, and encouraged by the laughter the Teds caught hold of him.

He didn't protest. He almost seemed to hold his arms out to them. They caught at him with a fierce snatch, struggled, then pinched him at elbow and wrist and made as if to frog him down into the crowd. The knife had disappeared, people were grinning and calling, and the whole thing looked a lot less nasty.

There were four of them, they were big chaps, and now they weren't being too rough and at least one of them was looking flushed and cheerful, the crowd was on their side. They tugged at him, grinning.

He didn't budge. He must have been abnormally strong to have stood so still while they wrenched at him, and they were jerking and shouldering him now and looking angry again; but of course he was better placed than they were: they were stood slippy on the slope of the rubble. They grunted and swore, and I noticed he was smiling. Then he pulled his hands free.

It was a slow unviolent pull which they had time to resist and resisted, but he came free all the same, and one of the Teds lost his footing and went tumbling and skidding to the bottom of the pile. The crowd roared its approval. The Man was still smiling.

There were jeers and whistles, and the Ted lay there winded. Then he stood up. There was dust all over his expensive suit, and he pushed his hands back through his scuffed hair, and his hands and his hair were white with plaster. His face was mean and white too, and he snatched out his knife again and went slowfooted back up the pile. I groped around for my phone, and as I did so, the other Teds let him come through. There was no one to stop him.

The Man glanced around him. Then, looking bewildered, he stooped and picked up the flag which he had dropped in the scuffle. It blew out beside him, entirely plain this week, just a black square which seemed horribly appropriate. My phone still eluded me, and I couldn't have taken my eyes off this if I had tried.

The Ted reached the top of the pile and began to edge along the wall towards him. The man had the Teds in front of him, the cellar-wall behind him, and above that, five storeys of blank brickwork where a house had been sheered off in the Blitz. He couldn't inch away any further because he was cornered in an angle between this and a sort of buttress of broken wall, only waist-high behind him, but rising steeply.

The Ted flashed his knife and the Man leapt onto this low end of wall. It was a stupid thing to do, because there was no rubble on the other side of the angle, just a drop of fifteen feet into the full depth of the cellar, and no point in jumping down because he could be trapped there as well.

The Ted saw the chance of this, stepped forward, and hacked at his legs, hoping to send him backwards. The Man swung his flag across himself and under his own arm, a movement that seemed totally inept, and yet the blade lost

19

itself in the swing of the material. Then with his flag dangling behind him, the Man half-turned and ran with remarkable agility up the steep, broken top of the wall. It was a move as grotesque and swift as a spider's, and the crowd let out the sort of breath that people expel at the sudden movement of an animal.

The Man went up in beautiful balance—he must have been a fellow climber, I thought, or perhaps a circus-performer—his hands just brushing the brick, and his feet placed quickly and securely with a lithe spring to each step. He certainly impressed the crowd. Someone had said " Fly ! " and he had done the next best thing. He went up this narrow edge of shattered brick until it ran at right angles against the main wall of the house, about twenty-five feet up. And then, of course, he stopped. A movement to either side meant a nasty tumble down; there were the Teds behind him and a sheer wall ahead. The Teds hooted and started to throw things. And at last I got a proper grip on myself, looked away and found the phone, and dialled nine-nine-nine.

To my horror, when I put the phone down the Madman was already scaling the sheer wall. Maniac. He had planted his flag at the top of the broken buttress and he was ten feet up the side of the house. No one threw anything now. It was bloody miraculous.

Or not quite that. There were a few bricks missing, as in any bomb-damage, and I watched him make good use of the gaps. About half-way up, there was a vertical crack, wide enough for a fist or a boot. He moved towards this, hanging back from the wall as if the whole thing were an approved route on a crag, and not too difficult at that. Fool, I thought, fool. It was an outside crack-climb just this side of the im-possible, and if he came off it he would go sixty feet down into the cellar. It made me sweat to think about it, and by then he was half-way up it. Eighty feet into the cellar. No, more: he was over the deep corner.

There was a commotion and a shouting coming up from the earlier stillness, and I saw the police were arriving. First some came in from the street and pushed people about, and the Teds made a dash, to the relief of the coppers. Then those I had called hammered in behind me—they always take an address—and cut my carpet to ribbons by treading on the broken glass. By the time I had finished protesting, he was over the roof and gone, though God knows what he proposed to do from there. "Anyway, sir," a copper said, "we'll pull this bloke in. Never mind the Teds. He was the *cause* of the trouble. We've had our eye on his little gatherings for some time." And they went down into the street to see if they could catch him. Obviously he had to come off the roof sometime, but, personally, I didn't give them much of a chance. There seemed something symbolic in this basic divergence of direction.

About eleven o'clock, when the shouting had died down and the pubs were out, I went downstairs in the moonlight to have a look at the thing. I scrambled the buttress quite easily: it was a simple little ridge climb. But there I stopped. I tried three holds on the main wall, then came back off. The crack up above those moves still makes me shudder when I look at it now, though I know quite a few men who *could* do it, and now there's Barney Molsom who has done. No one I know of could do the last twenty feet up onto the roof though, not even Barney with a lot of newspaper money to draw him. But the Madman managed it, a long time ago. Fear lends wings.

And then wings and then wings. Because he never came back, so at least his Sunday sermons could not remind me of her.

After it was all over I went to phone her; it seemed such

21

a natural thing to want to tell her about, especially her. Then I realised I couldn't phone her, especially her. I got the bottle opened properly instead.

She doesn't come into this story again. Her God did let her down, just a little while afterwards, but her Devil was too drunk to answer the phone. When they called him over next morning so they could use his key she was lying flushed and hard and the room smelled horrible. There were lots of little tablets, in the bed, on the counterpane, and scattered across the floor, and there were different policemen there to smash things with their boots. Perhaps other ways are preferable to Him, but her face did not look as if He had greeted her with any special enthusiasm.

I've opened a lot of bottles since then, to get rid of that night and that day: but it's only the Present that dies, and her face is the one that returns.

The Miraclejack

I

IT was raining. It was too dark to read the name of the
street, but everyone was looking up in the air, so this had
to be the place. I couldn't see anything; I could smell soot,
and mackintoshes, and cats. I could smell men who had
been rained on right into the dirty roots of them and from
whom odours were starting to sprout. I didn't know who
they were but they weren't the ones I wanted. I walked
round the crowd. The weather was too cold for remembering.

They still looked up.

I looked up again myself. I saw the darkness, and the
darkness falling out of the darkness, and then an eyeful of
raindrop punctured my brain with light. I didn't see anything else.

I came to a clear patch of pavement.

My foot scraped on rubble. Something fell beside me, a
wet shadow coming at almost the same speed as the rain. It
hit the ground with a noise like brick and I tasted dust.

"Watch out, friend," said a voice. "That's not the best
place to be!"

I stepped backwards just as a large piece of mortar fell
exactly where I had been standing. It was so big that it
didn't make a crisp echo; it slid into itself, and then thrown-
up particles came hissing back onto the wet pavement.

"See!" said the voice.

A fresh load of noise hit the ground.

"Never trust stucco," it added.

"Where's he got to?"

A torch came on, pointing downwards at waist-height. I saw pink hands holding a book against a yellow cycling-cape. Rain spattered onto the book, but it was covered in polythene.

"They'll be about here." A finger pointed to a place on a drawing. "They can't be any higher. The stucco runs out ᵗhere. It's brick for the rest of the way."

I looked closer, glad to be in the warm glow of light. The page was opened to a line-drawing reproduction, plan-view, of a slab-sided institutional building, about eight floors high.

"What's the book?" I asked.

"That? Oh, it's only Metson's *Architecture of Greater London*. It's as good as any for this sort of work. We keep asking Sym to do something specialist, but he tells us to do it ourselves. It's deeds that count with *him*." He laughed anxiously. His torch went out, leaving us blind in the dark. "Anyway, he gives demonstrations," he said. "It's a demonstration now."

"Pity we can't see something of it."

"You could see the first two storeys pretty well, before the street lamps went off. He's got a couple of learners up there."

There was another rumble of masonry. We gave ground.

"The last of the stucco. That'll be one of the others. Sym never sends anything down."

"Do you do much of this yourself?"

"I do a bit."

"What sort of climb does this rate as?"

"Nosey, aren't you?"

"I have to be. I'm a reporter."

"Sym doesn't like them. What paper?"

I told him.

" That rag ! "

" It's a funny thing," I said, " but you don't offend me. I like to think I'm above my profession. Anyway, what paper do you read? "

" That rag."

" That's what I like about us."

He chuckled.

" What sort of climb, anyway? "

" Oh—easy."

" Easy ! "

" Well—look at the plan again." The light came on. " It's got one of those crenellated corners for the first three storeys. Then there's a traverse along this ledge in the facing—you see it's a Classic front, with the windows inset in groups. That brings them to this column, which goes to the top of the stucco. There's a drainpipe beside it too; only Sym won't use that—he doesn't approve of pipes."

" Very interesting," I said. " Then what does he do? Fly? "

" There's a line of starbolts in the brick. The building bulged a bit in the Blitz, so they gave it those things. Then the roof is quite a simple one. Bit of an overhang to get onto it, of course."

I whistled. If this was Easy, let me have some Exclusive when he did something Hard.

" Why in the dark? "

" It's more or less illegal, you see. Besides, we don't like crowds."

" Pretty big crowd tonight."

" It's a public street, and the word gets round. The Police'll be here in a moment." There was a stir at the end of the crowd as he spoke. The Press weren't here, as far as I could smell.

" Where can I meet this fellow? "

"Sym?"

"If that's his name."

"He won't want to be met."

I stood very humbly in the rain and waited for him to take pity on me.

"Portico Road," he said. "Number 40. South-east something or other. I forget what. Only you'd better phone first."

"Thanks," I said. "Thanks very much."

As I turned away, the crowd filled my nostrils; I breathed the odour of anxiety. There was a scrabbling, far up the wall. It was also the incense of hope. I walked away coughing. I might come to be grateful to Barney after all—if the coincidence didn't turn out to be more than I could bear. If it turned out to be a coincidence at all.

II

BARNEY MOLSOM had looked at me that afternoon, corked his bottle, and said: "You been praying lately, Swale?"

"Hell, no. I've got a new woman. It was the last one who believed in that. She belonged to Christianity or one of those sects."

He smiled. "And what does this one believe in?—you?"

"She'd have to be pretty devout to manage *that*, wouldn't she?" If I looked in the large Victorian mirror behind him I could see the plump wax face with its three thin chins and its scruff of hair: me. My eyes came back to ex-Flying Officer Molsom, D.F.C., bar, and halo, the paper's part-time expert in aeronautics, and his wife's full-time husband in God. The features were healthy.

He grimaced. "You're young enough. When did you last do a worthwhile climb?"

"Up a rock or a ladder in a stocking?"

"Oh, for Christsake! You may as well have some more of *that*, then." He pushed me the bottle again. "But before you pass out completely just try and give your old friend and messmate an ear. I want to put you onto a Story."

"La!" I said. "There's generosity, Christian generosity! And judging by your gambit about prayer, it's going to be another holy one, too! What would I do with a story like that? *Me? Now?* I tell you what, Barney—if you're feeling really holy why don't you just stuff your story and lend me a fiver? Or if that's not Christian enough for a paid-up Churchwarden like you, let's say ten. You can always get it back from the plate."

He grinned at me. "That's it, Bertie. Keep talking, boy! It'll get better."

"Thanks, Barney," I said, to my face and the back of his head in the mirror. "Thanks very much. Life takes me like this." I went on watching myself to discover exactly how Life *did* take me. "You had a story for me? One of our usual stories, I take it? Because once upon a day dear Brother Bertram was a big enough prig to write up that sort of story well, and now he has fallen on hard, hard times?" I stopped watching my reflection then; it was looking too pleased with itself. "Who are you doing it for, Barney? Me, or the Story, or God?"

"None of you," he said. "And you can get any idea of gratitude out of your system. If I thought this one was really any good I'd have found somebody else."

"I'm never grateful." I knew he was lying. Any story Barney dug up for me would be a good story. It was just a question of whether I would be able to face one of his usual little conundrums in the mood I was in. He was watching

29

me with a shade too much sympathy, and I wondered if he knew that it was because of him I'd met the first one—following up one of his earlier things about Love and Re-generation and Angels of Light in the Dear Old Blitzed East End. God! what muck I wrote about it. It beats me how so many people want to read the stuff. The same sort who want to hear about dogs, I suppose. I looked at him direct, and his eye was as bright and as black as his headful of brilliantine in the mirror. "All right," I said, "but skip round the saintly characters. I don't want to hear a story with a hero in it ever again. Not from you, anyway!"

He filled up my glass. "Hence my pleasure in forcibly feeding you, Bertie."

It was a big glassful, but before I could touch it he dropped a bundle of papers into my hand. "Cuttings," he said. "They're mainly from provincials. There's nothing in the style of them to interest an expert. Just the subject."

I glanced up at him sharply, but his face was empty of sarcasm. Then I read the top one quickly, first with a stir of interest and then with mounting irritation. According to some local scribe, someone had wrenched the hands off all the tower-clocks and steeples in a small English market-town. The police, with their usual instinct for the obvious, had deduced he was a maniac. They also thought he was a rock-climber or perhaps a steel-erector. He was also a con-juror, or a sword-swallower, or wore three arms; because how else could a man climb back down a hundred-foot steeple, a two-handed job at least, with a four-foot-long minute-pointer and a yard-long hour-finger to burden him? Or perhaps he wore a crane. The police were eloquent on this subject, and the article quoted them verbatim. It was terrible.

"Interesting," I said. "I see the local vicar finds the whole

30

thing highly significant. As does the Town Clerk. You can
see what sort of sermons that one preached."

"What sort?" he asked, trying to glance over my
shoulder.

"The usual sort." I thumbed through the other clippings.
They were all on the same theme: Undergraduates falling
off towers, jerries on steeples, skulls and crossbones white-
washed on highly inaccessible walls, assorted flags flying
from factory-chimneys at daybreak.

"Hence my question about climbing," Barney said.
"There's a story here—for someone prepared to do it from
the inside. Interested?"

My face was still in that mirror; and locked in the mirror's
memory a much thinner man who wouldn't mind having a
go at all this. But long long ago. Before the invention of
Opening Time say. And only out of curiosity, as a climber.
Not professionally. "This is small-time," I said. "All right,
so small-time is my-time. But this is Local-Press stuff. Where
you found it." I beseeched him. "There's no centre here for
a story. Clever vandalism at the most."

He went on quite steadily. "Apparently a group of these
people has formed in London. Its leader contacted me by
phone the other day."

"Oh yes?" His insistence bothered me. I put the cuttings
back on the table and looked at my glass.

"As a result of some of the things he said to me, I had a
few enquiries made for you. I gather he's some sort of
super-climber, all in a class by himself. No one suggests he
does anything so mundane as pulling the hands off clocks.
But the rest take their inspiration from him."

I sipped the drink at last, and took comfort from it.

Barney paused while I did so, as if I had interrupted him.
When I had put my glass back on the table he said, "Interesting fellow seemingly. He's been a steeplejack in his

time. And a spiderman; I gather he's also done high-acts of sorts in a circus."

"Good background copy," I said. "All we want now is a story. Do we get to the story, Barney?" Dear old Barney: he'd put me onto some good things in the past—some good stories and some good griefs. This obviously wasn't going to be one of them. "Does he also swallow swords or have three arms?" I asked. "There's a story in three arms. This is a freakish age, Barney. Or what about three breasts or three testicles?"

"There's a story in this one, all right. But the only other thing I *know* about him is that he used to be a hot-gospeller. There's damn-all interest in that, I suppose. He used to go preaching around London, mainly on bomb-sites. Apparently he exhibited some very peculiar-looking scars."

I put out my hand slowly. His words were like cramp. Or time would make them like cramp; I could feel it starting. But Barney couldn't feel it.

"Won quite a following, seemingly. No one took him seriously, of course. Probably didn't want them to." He smiled. "Then I gather he started a riot or two," he added. And then he stopped and was watching the whisky I had upset soak into his tablecloth, and under his cuttings, and sogging the newsprint; I knew I had done it deliberately but I was trembling not at a mirror but a window, with her face on my shoulder and the Madman saying, "Crucify me!" God. . . . Crucify me.

I still had the shakes on when Barney helped me into my coat: he looked hurt and bewildered and there was nothing I could say to excuse myself.

"Suppose I tell you this man claims he's going to have a crack at the Shell Tower and the Vickers Building, and things like that?" He was almost pleading, and I felt sorry for his fitness and his brilliantine and his lack of grief.

32

"I shall be interested to hear he has fallen off." I made for the door, but I knew I would have to ask questions. "How does he think he's going to do it, anyway? This steeplejack bloke? I mean, there are no nice drainpipes up the Shell Tower, are there?" No cracks and no broken bricks either, I might have added. But what was mine was mine.

Barney laughed; he was a churchman and could afford his contempt. "He says it's all a matter of Faith, apparently. Faith more than fingertips." He kept his own hands thrust into his trouser pockets, but I knew they were scarred with limestone from the Dolomites. "Or so I gather," he grinned. "I've not been allowed to meet him. He says he's looking for someone quite different. As a matter of fact," he paused and looked at me, and I felt a tightening in my throat as if I knew what was coming, "As a matter of fact, he mentioned you by name. Don't look so bloody belligerent—he doesn't *know* you. Your other articles created quite a stir, you know. Once. Quite a likely request for anyone with a religious bee in his bonnet, you'd be, Bertie."

The last cramp was an invention. I mustn't indulge myself again. "Spare me! What's his name, anyhow?"

"Sym. Francis Sym."

"Sounds a faithful name. He'll fall off, all right." I hoped he did. There'd be an end to the business then. I didn't want to be bothered by any more devil-dodgers, especially this one. This was the sort of coincidence she would have taken much, much too seriously, and I wasn't inventing my emotion now. "Faith! I know one or two people who've trusted their necks to that one! It's all right as an umbrella, Barney, but it's no bloody good as a parachute . . . take it from me!"

He looked unhappy. He had spent all afternoon wasting

his drink on an unpleasant person called Swale, and I hadn't even rumbled my tummy in friendship.

"All right, Barney. I'm deeply grateful to you. Now in a few hours time I hope to be equally deeply drunk. But just supposing I'm shallowly sober, where will I find this St. Francis fellow?"

He brightened a bit.

"I don't know his address. But he's climbing somewhere up East tonight. I've got the street written down."

He gave it to me and I went away from his room and its gold-toothed mirror, and walked downstairs to the dusk. With any luck I should forget him almost at once. Inside the cat.

A red pussy was grinning at me, painted on glass, illuminated from inside with a bulb in its gut. *The Red Lion.* What an inviting name! I went in, exactly as the bolts were unbarred, and winked at the barman. He moved back sharply from the door. I had blinked, of course, or even winked. Poor man, he did not know about me, nor my new girl-friend. I would tell him about her in a minute to set his mind at rest; and whatever he said to me would set *my* mind at rest. Then I would tell him about the cat Sambo she had bought me yesterday, my pet Siamese that had already clawed my Char and nearly castrated me in the shower. "I'll have a double-scotch and then a double-scotch," I said. "All in one extra large glass." Let me continue to get rid of spiderjacks. Besides, I had just spilt one, a whiskyman all over a patchwork cloth.

"I'll have eight shillings first!" What an ungenerous man to live in a lion's belly!

"The pub has swallowed a Christian," I said.

I put my hand in my pocket. Nothing. I searched right into its seedy corners. My wallet was gone. He stood there, smirking at me; and all I could find was the piece of paper

Barney had given me with the name of a building written on it—the name of a building my Madman thought he could climb. Christ!

You might call it a sign. I didn't. I didn't even have the satisfaction of smelling them as that bloody barman poured them back into the bottle, because he hadn't poured them out yet.

So I had to go and do as Barney suggested, as I knew I should have to if I couldn't drink the memory away. But it frightened me, somehow. If she'd been alive I would have phoned her in spite of my promise. But if she'd been alive she'd have been married to somebody else and I'd have forgotten her a long time ago.

III

PORTICO ROAD was a wilderness.

Things needed doing.

That was the trouble with us: there had been a War a long way back; all the people had died and it's only their ghosts that are queueing for houses.

In a War, I suppose, you stop building for Life; you build for Death. And destroy for it, looking at Portico Road.

It had lost its iron railings. Everywhere has. Where do you see iron-railings now? I know. Round the Palace. About six million of them. But they're different: they've been looked at by Royalty; Patronage has squatted on them with the glue of flies. And you can't take Patronage, and melt it down, and shoot it at Fritz, and riddle the poor bastard with Patronage, can you?

But you can with the wrought-iron from Portico Road. Portico Road was probably in a salvo that fell short and

35

blew the balls off a Britisher. The cats keep close to the ground here.

Don't think I don't like Royalty, or quote me to the Press Council. I do like Royalty, of course I do. Until I look at Portico Road, and then I'm not so sure.

I stepped over dug-up paving-stones, looking for his house. Number 40.

Number 40 had one of those burning-bush knockers, that squeaked on its hinge. I crashed it against its anvil and heard the house echo.

The house went on echoing: it was footsteps coming closer.

The door opened into darkness and it was the whiteness of his face I saw. There were objects about him in the darkness, objects in space, a window green with dust and with leaves beyond the dust, a barometer nailed to the swirling blackness of the wall. The face in the silence was completely still. Jesus! It was older, of course; but even without glasses it was the same face.

"*The Post*," I said, after an agony of hesitation. "You remember. I telephoned."

"B. B. Swale," he said. "That's right—I asked for you."

The window was at the end of a long corridor, right at the back of the house, and without saying anything else he turned and led me back towards it. Before we reached the window he turned to his right through a door, another slot of blackness. We walked into a room with the blinds drawn. It was not dark, not quite. But the light was thick and tired, and curiously restful.

"Excuse this," he said. "I must have darkness! I shall be doing a climb tonight, and the sharper my eyes the better." He hesitated, as if wondering if there was anything more he could say. "Though it's touch that counts most."

He picked up a pair of spectacles, glinting wire frames

36

with lenses of shadow, and put them on clumsily. There was no doubt about it now, none at all. He looked like a skull on one of his own flags. Then he parted the blinds on the window. A sheet of moted light divided us, and his hands, jerking through it, seemed severed at the wrist and quite separate from the silhouette of his body.

It was the hands, seen like that, by themselves, that first told me I was onto something, something of far greater potential, I mean, than I'd seen in the cellar. After all, it might have been no more than an ordinary ability heightened by panic. Or, at least, so I argued in my rational moments. But his hands were an incredible sight, their fingers knob-ended and twisted, broken back on themselves and horrible with splintered nails. There was a frame of grime round the edges, and the grime seemed to flow backwards into the palms along the ribs of the veins. They were hands from which a man's weight had dangled by a fingertip over the abyss, and for one horrible moment the five frail points of them, the whole handful of fingers, seemed to writhe in that sunlight like a Medusa's head of worms, scarred and turned and frayed at the neck of them, punctured by brickdust at the wrist. I had seen the hands of some of the great rock-men, including the busted plumbing of Brown, but nothing like this. After one look at the holes in them I could believe almost anything he might say. One thing I was certain of: climbing was *his* crucifixion. He had torn his wrists to pieces on the holds.

He saw my noticing them, and shut out the sun again, clumsy with embarrassment and leaving me blinder than before. He gestured in some way—I heard the rustle of his sleeve—and guided me, half-pushing, until I found a seat.

We sat down by a small table and he poured me a cup of something, perhaps tea—I can't taste in the dark. It had a brown flavour, as if it had been waiting for me for ever.

37

"Well," he said. "What can I tell you?" We seemed to have been avoiding speech for an eternity in that darkness, but it was perhaps only a few seconds since we had been speaking before.

What did I want of him? More important, what did he want of me? Anything I said here was only a prelude. "Hard to know where to begin," I said. "I mean—I just don't know anything about this at all. Why do you climb— why do you climb buildings, anyhow? Why *buildings*?" I wondered if he had taken to it before or after that crowd had chased him up that wall.

"People generally ask me *how*," he said. "Not why." He went on stirring his cup, then poured something into it from a packet which grated as he touched it. Then he said, "Do you really want me to be serious about that question?"

"I hope so."

"I rather think the answer will embarrass you." He waited, as if inviting me to agree with him.

I am paid to be embarrassed, but the General Public is always anxious to protect me from my Employers. "Do please tell me," I said.

"Faith, I suppose. Or a part of my faith. I feel that creating buildings is an act of faith, architectural and physical and even metaphysical—you know, a belief that stone will stand on stone. I celebrate that act by climbing them."

It was a disappointing answer, and it did embarrass me. "Why not mountains?"

Once more I spoke into an enormous silence which swallowed my words and waited. I heard his spoon grate in his cup and go on turning; he went on stirring as if he were winding a clock.

"Men *do* climb mountains." I spoke crossly. This was an interview.

"No, they don't." He was still twisting the dregs with

38

his spoon and I thought for a moment he was going to
leave me with this ridiculous contradiction and I had all at
once the claustrophobic feeling of being alone with mania,
just the absence of voice and that mesmeric noise in the
dark room. I had always thought of him as the Madman,
and nothing in the present meeting helped me think otherwise. Suddenly he added, as if there had been no interval,
" They climb them by their cracks and flaws. Imperfections
don't interest me. Take a wall or a rock-face and crack it "—
a significant pause this time as if he wished to imply he
was familiar with forces which could smash brick and stone
like a handful of eggs—" and it's just a ladder." The Red
Wall of Lliwedd loomed into my darkness and Clogwyn
d'Ur Ardu, but I didn't argue. " As I say, imperfections don't
interest me. Take the first mountains now, the uplifted
peaks in the First Epoch—*The God-Thrusts—they* were unclimbable. I should have felt differently about mountains
then." Out of this impossible arrogance he somehow managed to bring a note of infinite regret for all that was finite
in man.

I didn't answer, and in this new silence I reached for the
sugar, trying to remember why I had come. Faith ! Once, in
a dream after the film, I had interviewed John the Baptist, a
journalist's private nightmare. As I remember, the dream
had been easier. And I had been *interested* in those
days.

He smiled. I couldn't see it, I sensed it. It is possible to
hear some people smile even if they don't hiss or breathe,
even if all they do is uncover the bone in their face. He sat
back and I knew that he was grinning at me. Then he
reached for my cup, as if he would rather do something for
me than talk to me. " Is this the sort of thing your readers
will want to know? "

" You never can tell. It depends upon the Personality con-

39

cerned. Sometimes they even want to know what he dreams about."

He put down my cup unfilled, as if I had said something profound. "I go back in time," he said. My eyes had almost conquered the darkness now. "I go back and climb the buildings of the past. Antique pharos, the first St. Paul's with its spire, the Hanging Gardens of Babylon, the ladder-buildings of the Aztecs and Incas, the Biblical Cities of the Plain. Then there's the Colossus of Rhodes"—he gave the words a special weight, so I had time to remember the Man-Tower from my childhood books, beaming its torch of light. "Sometimes, in my dreams, I fancy it's still standing. When I go up that in my mind, it's like Gulliver being lifted into the hands of his Giant. Or Man, the Flea, climbing God."

"God was a Woman." Once more the triteness of my words became lost in his immobility. I reached across for my cup, which he had still left empty, and poured tea into it. It was tea—I could taste it now. It was stewed and strong. "And just where does The Post come in?" I asked irritably. "I mean, I gather you don't normally grant interviews." The sarcasm didn't hurt him; he seemed to find the phrase appropriate.

"I've decided I need the publicity."

"Money?"

"No. I wasn't looking to publicity for that. But it could lead to opportunity. Publicity does, I believe." Sarcasm was returned quietly. "If I have that I can do some wonderful climbs."

"What have you in mind?"—I wanted to whisper. I could sense endless possibilities and the walls were listening. And what was the purpose of it? Something dark and manic and destructive perhaps that I preferred not to think about.

"I could make the opportunities myself, of course, but it would take rather long." My question was going to be ignored. "I can provide you news—if you are prepared to write it up." Before I could confess the snags he said, "I don't require any money, just the coverage."

"There is no money in *The Post*. Just coverage." *The Post* is the best fish-and-chip wrapper in the world. "What will you climb for a start? "

"I said I was going out tonight, if you remember. I thought I might commence with the University Building in Malet Street."

Impossible. The Senate House may be small by American standards, perhaps a dozen floors high, but how could he climb a piece of modern architecture like that? It wasn't like Victorian Ornamental, with knobs and pimples that could be climbed by even the drunkest student. . . .

"Later this week I hope to go onto Shell-Mex House and Tower Bridge. Then there is the new Vickers Building. . . ."

So Barney had told me. But hearing him say so himself in that crazed, matter-of-fact voice, I felt numb. "How about Big Ben? " I believe I was joking.

"I've already done it. So have several other people. It's a badly flawed tower and not very interesting."

I wanted to disbelieve something. But there was the evidence of his hands, and of what I had seen last night, and of his fantastic scramble on that evening I preferred not to think about.

"Why plan so much? "

"There is no moon, you see—and I make the most of moonless nights." Again the faint hint of mania, almost of necromancy. And yet it was reasonable not to want to be seen.

I stood up. "I'll be in touch with the Editor right away. See what he says."

As I put my coat on, his hands brushed against me, helping me. "You'll get your job back," he said.

I felt my face redden in the darkness. It was common knowledge in some quarters I was downgraded, but how did *he* know?

As we went down the passage I asked, " Why the urge to do so much in London? "

" Before the Fire."

" You mean Ban The Bomb? "

" No—Beat The Fire. It's an insurance neurosis. It's all going to burn sometime." We shrugged at one another, outside the range of understanding. " The rest is just a prelude," he said.

Then I was outside in the sunlight, looking at a closed door and remembering the feel of his peanut fingers and the pattern of his scarred handshake on the roughness of my skin. I still didn't like him. He had once made her cry, and he was one of the whole holy class who believed in preaching tears, whatever their sect.

As I walked away, she was hurting me again. But I tried not to think about her. It always led to drink, and this might be my very last chance.

IV

WE paid off the taxi near the British Museum and walked round the corner. It was pitch dark, November dark above the street lamps, and there were no stars. Paul rattled his camera-sling against something in his pocket; it sounded like a tobacco-tin. He grunted. " Seems a good story," he said. " With any luck he'll kill himself, and then you'll be a a star-reporter. Who've you been sleeping with? Lord Dultie? "

People didn't like Paul, quite apart from his tendencies, and he was never given to anyone worthwhile. But he had been known to take a very good photograph in his time. "It could be the making of us," I said.

He walked on thoughtfully, as if he were discovering an insult in the remark.

A small group of figures—four of them, when I separated them from their shadows—huddled by the courtyard gate in Russell Square. Sym was there, standing taller than the others, and he was the only one who saw us arrive. The rest of them were arguing with him, or arguing around him, and it was impossible to tell what about. I looked up into the brick-built darkness and waited. She was married all right. She was upstairs in bed with All Three of Them. And why did I think *that* was different?

When I looked down at the group again I recognised my friend from last night—the Man with the Torch. He saw me and came over, leaving the other three to argue.

"What's it about?" I asked.

He jerked his legs and his breath smelled of beer. "Bloody novices. They want to follow Sym up the wall. Both of them. Up *that*!"

"Heroes!"

He looked at me morosely. "He let you in on it, then? He let you come, and your paper come, and your camera come?"

"That's right."

Paul got up and sauntered over to the others.

"I told him not to," the man said. "But he doesn't listen to *me* any more."

Paul took some flashes, Sym shielding his eyes in his hands, and came slowly back, humming sadly. "Cute," he said. "And brave, too."

43

"Jesus," said the torch-man. "A nance! I might have known the Press was here."

Paul smiled at him, then clenched his fists.

The others stopped talking then, and Sym came towards me, shrugging his shoulders. It was a gesture that jarred.

"I tried to dissuade them," he said. "It will be a very hard climb." He glanced upwards into the night, and laughed shortly. "Almost impossible, in fact. Well, if they want to try, I suppose it's up to them. I wish it weren't!"

"Just how are you going to do this thing, anyway?"

He didn't answer me.

The other two started to change into plimsolls, and I noticed they both wore belts and a fireman's attachment fixed to their waist, like a butcher's hook.

There was nothing like this in Sym's outfit, as far as I could see. Our Man handed him a bag, and he took another pullover from it and shrugged it on, the man pulling it down for him, and then he tugged out some rolls of cloth, stiff stuff like hessian, and between them they wound it round his knees and thighs, on top of his trousers. He took off his shoes and socks and we helped him bandage his ankles, and then add a layer of hessian, it was hessian, I handled it. He left his feet free. "Bare skin's the best," the man said, slapping his ankle as he knelt on the pavement beside him. "If the weather will let you!"

Sym mumbled something I couldn't hear. I noticed, with a sort of horror, though of course I already knew and should have been prepared, that his feet were as scarred as his hands, groined and full up with shadow. They had long strong-looking toes that flexed, almost autonomously, at the grooves of the pavement. He took a few steps, testing the flexibility of his bandages.

The Man with the Torch produced a bunch of keys, and we waited while he rasped at the gate. No one seemed to

44

worry about the other two, but I noticed they were ready. Sym appeared to dismiss them from his mind, and probably us as well. "It takes some of them like this," said the Man. "They climb with him once and they want to go on climbing." He nodded to where they stood sullen in the background. "The same pair that went up with him yesterday— *you* remember."

The gate came open, it was a new gate and shouldn't have kept us, and we were in the forecourt, under the weight of the building. We couldn't see it, but we knew it was there; it leant on us, heavy with night, the stones seeming to tumble outwards in the darkness. I started to sweat. Several hundred feet at thirty-two feet per second squared on square paving-stones with hessian round his thighs and his ankles —how would it be? As a climber myself—a climber, not a maniac like this—I knew the sensation when one's personality slips scrabbling off the stone; but there had always been a rope to hold me, and daylight, and the bright buoyant faith of the spider. We had spent half an hour before coming, Paul and I, studying photographs of the building; they had all made it look the same: square, intellectual, and completely unclimbable. It wasn't like last night's climb at all. There were no porticos or pillars, and no starbolts. There weren't even any stars. Nothing stuck to the sky, no bright lights bolted it up; it was around us, all plastic and mystery. And in the centre of the mystery I found only myself, wearing the mantle of another man's danger and feeling the hollowness of height in the tube that joined the draught of my bowels to the taste of bile in my mouth. On the way here I had said to Paul, "Whichever storey he falls from it will be a good story." The joke didn't console me now. "Cranks," said Paul in my ear, "I always have to do with cranks. Yesterday I had to photograph a man who thinks he's only got to unscrew his navel and Khrushchev's back-

45

side will fall off!" He spat, and I had the feeling he still wanted to punch someone.

I went up to Sym. He was standing by himself, in the shadow of himself; as if waiting for me. "Good Luck," I said: it didn't seem like Luck anymore; the premonition was enormous. We were surrounded by the pathetic fallacy of a night well suited to dying. You could smell it, as Paul had said. Last night's rain lay in the sewers, and the odours of death seeped through the fragility of the pavement. There was no luck here; I wanted to give it up, to call him off it, but I was saved by the knowledge that it wasn't up to me, or *The Post*, or Paul—not yet. He would go up this building, and live on it or die on it, whatever I said. There was also the sly possibility which Paul had offered me, and I couldn't put aside: Sym's bad luck might not be mine. It would be a good death for the Newsroom. If it weren't for the other deaths in the world.

He didn't say anything and I couldn't search into his mind at this moment. There was a torch flashing in the courtyard, up and down the side-walls, like a streak of whitewash. It was the other two, questing at the long square drainpipes which go up to the wings. But the torchlight was blunted before even the top of that shorter wall. No pocket-torch could shine up the tower.

Sym went into the far corner, right under the tower, and I followed him. Nobody spoke. None of us wanted to betray ourselves to the world, especially to caretakers. The suicide has a similar anxiety as he creeps out onto the bridge.

"Well!" I held out my hand.

He didn't take it. Perhaps he didn't realise what I was doing in the darkness, even though I nudged up against him. Or perhaps it was a gesture he saw no need to answer, any more than when I'd wished him luck: he saw through it all, and knew how little I cared for him.

46

I looked round for Paul. He had been frugal with flash-bulbs as if respecting the moment. Perhaps he remembered what I'd said about Sym's eyes. He is one of those rare newsmen who is reticent before the living but who will take loving close-ups of the dead. Anyway, he didn't seem to be near, not even by the clink of a tobacco-tin.

"Right," said Sym. It was his first word since coming into the courtyard.

I stood back to give him room. To my surprise he crouched down, and I thought for a moment his ankle-wraps were bothering him. Then I realised he was kneeling. At prayer. It was a good job *that* crowd wasn't here. Then he stood, cruciform. I nearly puked. "Good luck!" I said again. Would she have wept at *this* pantomime?

He felt up into the darkness of the night with one hand, and rested his other hand lower down against the black of the wall. The mumbo-jumbo was completed. Then he lifted himself quickly with a sort of push and a pull, getting his toes to the stone, and disappeared upwards. I saw the white-ness of his bare feet dangle for a second and the sudden blur of his face as he glanced downwards, then the patch of skin was hidden, and I was surprised at how quickly he moved, for in that moment of whiteness I saw him shift foot and hand several times like the stalking of a white-footed cat. Then my eyes lost the movement and even the glow of his features went out like a reflection dying in the distance. It was uncanny—just a scraping, the quick note of his breath-ing, and the held silence of his breath. Soon one of the intervals of soundlessness became permanent and he was too high to hear. His first climb for me and I knew as little about it as that! I felt against the stones. They were smooth, with good pointing. My hands told me nothing. It was a slab-climb, tilted back to the vertical.

This made it impossible. What would Barney say to *that*?

47

"Fingertips!" probably. Faith is limited to members of the Club. I thought my thoughts and waited.

The dust of London fell on me from the air and I tasted soot in the darkness.

I looked up for about five minutes, searching for a silhouette. Sometime or other I should have to phone some of this back, but I couldn't bring myself to move, even though there was nothing to see. I think he climbed into an inside angle, there was a tiny hump in the dark, and once I heard something like fingernails on the stone, nothing else. Someone was mumbling somewhere. I couldn't tell if it was the others behind me or whether it was Sym up there, talking to the holds, his voice being cast back by the stone. I hoped it wasn't. Most of the rockmen whom I've known climb aloud haven't been very good. It's a sign of nerves. I listened upwards. The whole story was going away from me. It was just shadow. I had to do it all in my head. Still, I put together sentences, soundlessly, for Ericson.

They were short sentences, with the words nailed together with brass. I composed a lot of them, one by one, five minutes of them, then I turned away from the building to look for Paul.

He was a long way back. I found him by his breathing. He was sitting on his heels behind a tripod, with a camera-clock ticking on a time-exposure. "Not much hope," he said. "Anyway, so far—so good!"

I knew what he meant. He wasn't talking about films.

There was a shriek.

I ducked and looked up and saw nothing but heard the long breath of him falling, a voice growing downwards.

God!

There was a crash on stone, a moistness as if the stone melted, and the sound echoed round the forecourt. Then a smaller thud, little, inside the echoes, like a hand turning

48

over onto the paving or an arm flopping outwards from the body's limpness, or a leg jerked upwards by the shock in its trouserful of air, then axed down too.

Smaller pieces hit the ground, a stone, bone, teeth drawn from the building's face.

And then silence.

Only this time the silence was flat; it had no height.

I walked over sickly. I walked twenty yards over the spinning stone, and as I walked I heard the fall again in the ringing ache of my skull, the lungs revolving, the bowels bursting, the breath coming out at differing angles, and then this crushing of itself into the pavement.

"You've got your story." It was Paul's voice, disassociating itself from it all. I had a mouthful of coins and spat.

Here it was—I felt it on the slime of my feet. I touched it accidentally in the darkness with my boot and imagined the blood of it inside my boot and in between my toes like a small boy wiggling them in the mud. Then I knelt down.

Sym lay smashed underneath. I touched him and my hands were sticky.

I heard Paul fumble with a flashbulb.

There was a wailing noise.

Then it focused into a voice, and the building, the whole unseen face of it above our heads, started to scream. We froze under the gaping cry as if it were a ghost. And it *was* a ghost, a scream with the dead man blind at our feet but the voice still above us. I looked up into a blackness with lights coming on, and the wind grinned in it.

"Jesus," a voice said. Then it began to laugh hysterically.

It was the Man with the Torch.

"Right," said Paul.

I shuddered. It was normal to have people fall out of the night and die, men with bent fingers, and leave their voice behind them. There it was again, screaming inside me. It must be normal; friends, acquaintances, faces around me, men who would otherwise be masks of tears and moving in a mist of woe, could pause and giggle, and say "right". We stood there in the normality of it all, shivering together in the night, looking upwards, seeing nothing, wordless.

There were voices beyond the railings now, nasty voices, Bloomsbury voices. I heard footsteps coming in and treading together. Where would people come from? Trying to think, trying to be responsible and involved as a man, and detached, as a reporter with a story to protect, I looked around numbly and saw light go on, all round the square, and doors open full of light and coloured shadow, their knockers pattering, keys being checked before doors were closed, some weren't closed, and people shouted. Feet knocked little segments of pavement. Then there was the silence, expectant like the silence of horses, feet shifting, or like the trees of the square breathing, and I heard them leaning in on us. Invisible spectators leant in and looked at us, blindly.

The screaming was a whimper, a soul held to its flesh by a memory of skin.

The body grew light at my feet.

It had a cone of torchlight on it, shone by the Man Who Had Only At Last Found His Torch. He didn't giggle any more.

A young head, the eyes open, looking straight into the torch, lying on blood like glass. The eyes were unblemished. Eyes are resilient, made of gristle, and do not crack, even on square stones. It was not Sym.

It was not Sym.

The murmuring beyond the railings increased. They saw what we saw in the glow of the torch.

"Now what?" The Man said, quite calmly, and put it out. "The other one's up there screaming his guts out!"

And of course, there had been two more. But they had seemed so totally unimportant to the moment that I hadn't even realised they were on the wall yet!

A gate came open, to the shushing of feet. We had to think fast. I had suffered for this death. That meant it was mine and exclusive.

With pictures. Paul took one now in a gout of light.

"Where's Sym?"

"About six floors up." He spat. There was too much spitting tonight. We were still near the dead. I heard the spit strike.

"Leave Sym out of it, then," I said. "There'll be enough for the police in this and the other one."

Paul spoke sourly, "And for the other papers. We'd hate to give it to them, wouldn't we?"

"We've got to keep quiet about him," said the Man with the Torch. "It will be dangerous for him, if they try to make him come down now."

"That decides it," I said.

Paul didn't answer. I heard the rattle of a tobacco tin. Then the rush of feet.

We were surrounded, barged into, pushed. There were lots of them, plebs, God knows from where, and pukka voices all taking charge of one another. They tried to take charge of us, ask us questions, but they lost us in their own noise, swallowed by the crowd; no one was important enough to be found or intelligent enough to find us.

The Police were here, it was a ratepayers' area, and they found us at once. They shouted at us and the crowd shouted our answers before we could speak, and the pukka voices took charge of the Police. I didn't count how many; they were the solider shadows and their hats shone. I was watching Philips of the rival rag whom I'd smelled out by instinct, I mean the rival rag that is everyone's rival rag. He smelled

51

me in turn, and caught hold of my policeman. How soon all the scavengers arrived, the idle parasitic bastards!

"What's it about?"

The copper didn't answer so he turned to us.

"How should *we* know," I said. "We were only passing."

Paul looked green in the moments of torchlight.

People trod on the corpse, kept on treading on it, and sometimes in the dark they apologised to it, and then tried to help it up, and went on trying, and they didn't give it up, it is surprising how many times you can touch flesh and not know its brokenness. All this time, Paul and myself, and the Man with the Torch, who told someone in a loud voice his name was Bunch, did a kind of circular dance with a policeman, and I saw Philips moving off to a phone-box. Lights came on in the building then, lots of lights, and he didn't move far. The crowd thought he was escaping from something, and this was a very self-righteous crowd, a crowd that had been kept back from disaster by railings, and Paul suggested to them that they should stop Philips and they believed him. He was persuasive like all the great queers of antiquity.

We heard the screamer again; Bunch had put down his torch and was retching in the corner. I found myself suddenly able to tolerate him, the callous bastard, now he brought up his beer in the opposite corner from death. I remembered his hysteria—that was in his favour, too.

"Christ! . . . for Christsake *get-me-off*. I'm coming down! Please!" Till I heard his voice up there I'd forgotten him again. He sounded ridiculous as people do sound when they are going to die in a panic and you are not going to die at all. "Please!" He was on a windowsill suddenly, several floors up with the lights being switched on behind him, pushing his humped form outwards, but it hunched back, still screaming. He didn't go in through the window;

52

either he couldn't turn or it was on a stairway. He sat there dazzled with panic, dangling on the edge of night, and we were unseen in his night below him.

The crowd moved backwards and outwards in case he came down. A man laid down his mackintosh for him, a magnificent gesture, seventy feet down onto a damp piece of plastic, but a woman told him to pick it up, even more magnificent, his wife or some other woman, and with a half-glance of apology up at the man screaming Christ he did so.

A fire-engine rang in through the main gate. It arrived as fire-engines do, into the middle of a tongue-licking night-mare, by instinct. The firemen were still getting dressed, fastening tunics with glittering buttons under shadowy hands.

They rattled their noise under him and he screamed once more.

They put up a ladder for him, two of them going up even as it trundled and traversed round, sounding on hard plank steps above the careful whir of the motor. Where was Sym? Sod Sym. Let's have this bit of story first.

Paul took pictures, composing out of instinct. There were rungs and angles and mirrors of light; someone had a flash-light steady on the window, holding the poor sod up by the pressure of will. The firemen broke its beam into grappling shadows as they reached him.

Paul shuttered them as they brought him down. I saw them treading on the rungs of spotlight, wading knee-deep in illuminated dust. He came down the steps of time upside down with his trousers undone, falling out of his belt with his slim waist, and terror hanging through his teeth; he was half-dead, with his boots off too, like the classic falls of history, relaxed and boneless and gutless at the ankles. Who could blame him?

A roar of anger. The crowd were manhandling Philips,

53

the pukka-voiced part of it. "Bloody *newspaper*!" they said. "Jammy sods!" said a single tinny voice. And Paul took loving pictures of that. Then the police got fed up with us and manhandled the crowd in turn, and Paul got pictures of them, he could make pounds on the agencies tonight; and he still had film when two men beat into a policeman, the corpse still lying in front of them, with its face softening; and still more film, juggling a spare camera, when the coppers got someone, a student in a scarf, and twisted him all the way to a van. It's always a student they catch in the end.

What was *he* thinking about it up there, the only one left in the air? I looked up the wall of noise.

I didn't see anything. When I looked down, the corpse had been moved, occasioning silence, a shuffling of feet back behind us, and much more shouting. Paul started to fight for his camera.

There was a white gush of pain on the walls, and we all went down, pummelled by water. The fire-engine finding itself nothing to do had hitched up to a hydrant and was now piddling all over us with its hoses. It was a free country, too.

We all died down in an instant. Even the lights went out. Paul and I ran out and back round the corner, still looking up. There was nothing to see. We ran wringing-wet among people still walking in to find out what had happened. People hung out of upstairs flats. Bunch had gone.

How was Sym getting on? What sort of hell was it for him, spreadeagled up there and hearing the other one come off?

Did I care? Paul had my arm and was for some reason grinning; he was pushing me towards a phone and hailing a taxi.

In the phone-box, then in the taxi, I didn't care at all.

54

There was Ericson and the Newsroom to consider. I felt for my bottle for the first time since breakfast. With Paul pressing himself white and sniggering in the corner this one story was quite enough. Only what would *she* say to my leaving him up there? If I drank just a little, there was no need to remember her voice for a long time to come.

I must remember to thank Barney.

V

SAMBO the Siamese Cat clawed along my leg, his footsteps puckering me through the counterpane. He reached my stomach and his fangs went in. I threw the whole heap, bedclothes, hot-waterbottle, whisky bottle, and screaming cat to the floor. In a crash and gurgling the cat hissed to the windowsill and sat behind its bright blue eyes snarling at me. It wasn't the waterbottle I was hearing now. I was vomiting. It took an age to get better.

My head was still aching when the phone rang.

I picked it up and recognised her voice. "Who is it?" I said. My stomach was so clenched I only managed to whisper.

"It's Mavis."

"Mavis who?"

The voice grew tighter. "You've been drinking. You know Mavis who. Who gave you Sambo."

"Sambo?"

Pieces of me stuck to Sambo's fingernails. I lifted my pyjama-jacket, as if she could see the pain that was prickling me.

"Sorry. I don't know you. I'm successful now."

"You've been successfully getting drunk, you mean."

55

I put the phone back onto its cradle. Eleven o'clock. My watch said so, strapped to my short-sighted wrist, ticking in my tousled ear. I lifted my pain from the bed.

I still felt warm with my clothes off. But I was successful now, I had just said so, with a future to consider. Let me consider it carefully, a step at a time. I went naked into the hallway of the flat to fetch in the papers and came face to face with my Char.

"Good morning," I said. I was too ill to care.

"Morning Glory more like," she grinned. "All right— I'm not watching. I just got you these." She pushed newsprint into my hand. "I thought it was about time you came along to borrow them."

I padded on bare lumps and the hardskin patter of my feet back to the door. I felt sick again: it was seeping out through my skin.

"What you think you are—anyway?" she called. "A sprig of parsley?"

I lurched onto the mattress, the spring jangling inside me. As I'd sunk down, the bombsite had shown me a few dirty flowers, and God! this was the same bed. The waterbottle squeezed in me. Was it worth it, was it worth it, this trying to forget? I heard grumbling, and there was Sambo with the smashed face watching me. I reached out to him, but he avoided me. I picked up the telephone and dialled. Then I dialled again; my finger kept jabbing the wrong holes.

The voice in my ear was angry, a man's voice.

"Is she there?" I asked. "Is she come back yet?"

"Who, for Christsake? If you're the bloody joker——"

"She used to live there. She used to live in your room."

"I've told you before——"

"She died there, too."

"I don't care! I don't care! She isn't here!"

"Promise me you'll——"

"I'll call the police. Who the hell *are* you?"

"I loved her," I said. I was crying. I wasn't talking to him any more. Or to Him.

"For Christsake! *Who* the hell *are* you?"

I was dialling again, missing it and dialling.

A woman's voice, uncertain. If I gave her time she would be angry. If I give them time they're always angry.

"Mavis?"

"Yes."

"Mavis, it's me. Don't fool me, Mavis. Don't say you don't know who I am." I was still crying. "Tell me, Mavis, am I real?"

She hesitated. She didn't know. It was a simple question. I picked up the bottle from beside the bed. It was empty.

"I'll be round right away," she said suddenly, urgently.

"Tonight!"

"No. I'll come round at once."

"No: I've got to get better. That bloody thing I've got inside me."

She was laughing, crossly.

"That bloody hairy thing. All that fur." I was choking.

"The other girl, you mean!"

It wasn't laughter I heard. She was weeping. I felt the claws start to go from inside me. It was pleasant to have a woman cry for me. Even this one.

I dropped the phone onto the bed.

Sambo, real Sambo, came back along my naked legs. Not even my imagination could invent this fire. I kicked him off. He rolled, mottled, brown, yellow-bellied, steel-pronged, on the carpet. I picked up the phone again. "It's all right. I'm better now."

She was still crying, deliberately into the receiver for me to hear.

I held her crying against my bare chest. My stomach

57

belched at her. I took her voice over to Sambo, who spat in her ear. Then I hung up. I mustn't weaken. "I love you," I said. But the phone was down.

The cat started to claw up the newspapers.

I opened the Rival and sniffed it. I waited for my eyes to focus. The headlines were too big and too black and they jostled between my hands.

Philips had a quarter of the front-page—he always had at least a quarter of some page. He was tucked under the main headlines about the busmen, *Busmen Say No*, in forty-eight pointed caps; but here nevertheless he was: *Death Fall In Bloomsbury*, thirty-six point caps above *Double Climb Spells Tragedy*, twenty-four point lower-case and caps. His own name was written so big that it might have said Rape in Regents Park and not Hector T. Philips; and half his copy was written in letters as big as tadpoles, with fullstops dissolving in frogspawn. I was unfocused and drowning again just to look at it. What did it say? Never mind what it said. Let's see me.

I unwrapped the front page of *The Post*.

Triple Climb Sensation. It was poor; it was like *The Post*. But it scooped Philips. I had put Sym up that building and brought him down again. *Climber Goes On After Death Fall*. It was ambiguous, too. Someone would be on the carpet for that about now. Perhaps not, not on *The Post*. Then here they were, my lovely words, front-page words, going on and on in the best type-face in the business. At least a *Post* page always *looked* good. I had put it in and said a prayer against international crisis, rail-crashes, multiple murder and rape, and here I was, without real competition.

There was just one snag, and it would teach me to stay around the Newsroom longer and not get so drunk in future.

Where was *me*?

The News Editor had signed me as "Our Own Reporter".

It was a lie anyway; I had almost left. Someone had died for "Our Own Reporter", and Swale hadn't benefited. It was as stupid and remote as dying for God.

I lay there cursing, my indolence resting on my belly like a tired plum. And then I dragged on my underclothes and looked for the rest. I should have to get across to Portico Road at once. Before Mavis came to cure me of ambition. I daren't even write her a note, in case she came before I'd finished.

I took the short cut to the bus across the bomb-site.

Up in the road the sunshine was unbearable. I wished Our Own Reporter were here to suffer it for me, and the Death. God God God God God, I was ill. And calling on God hadn't done *her* any good either.

What He gave me now was a bus that shook me slowly apart.

VI

A CHILD was following me, crying. I had trodden on its doll in the gutter. Go away, you silly little bastard: I want to knock on Sym. I want to ask him a favour. And he can't say yes now someone has died.

Number 40.

I knocked. I knocked hard. Something fell at my feet. It was the doll with its cracked face.

When the door opened there was a light burning, a shade-less bulb, and someone was singing. It unnerved me to see light burning in the daytime, electric light in the sunshine, just as much as it had done to find darkness by day on the previous occasion. The singing was strained and lonely, and happening among other men's silence.

A shadowy face stood by the door. I nodded to it. It wasn't Sym.

The child went away from my back, still crying. It had clutched in horror at the half-crown I had given it, and I felt cold as it left me. Its doll still lay on the doorstep for me to step over.

The door closed. It had been held for the child too, as if she belonged to me. I made a gesture, to say No, to say Thank You, to . . . "I broke her bloody doll," I said to the Shadow. It nodded sympathetically. I went away from its speechlessness to find Sym.

Where was he? I walked along the passage to the back room, brushing past a girl with her back to me, being climbed by a man's hands. Let them not be Sym's, O Lord. I shall be cheated. Sym's hands must not climb any woman's darkness. I shall be cheated of the image I have built of him for her sake all the way here. Illness is a great maker of images, Swale; and so is the death of love. It is only a newspaper image, though. You must not let yourself be pollinated by Molsom. Not cross-pollinated, anyway. God, how even an atheist prays when he vomits. God, I have said God between every gasp.

Where was he?

The room became still as I entered it. Tall silent men, like a family of Syms, turned to me eye-sockets of glittering shadow. I was baffled by a circle of dark glasses. Evidently they all took the sunshine seriously, but, whatever the reason, it was momentarily sinister. Then I wanted to laugh at them. Rockclimbers do nothing like this: suddenly it all seemed bogus. I smiled, trying to judge their expression. . . . Sym was not here. There was no one tall enough, still enough, smelling enough of prayer. There was no Ego. There was just a cold waiting, looking at my intrusion. I became unhappy again.

60

Someone gave me a glass. The Shadow had followed me down the passage, but he was a real man, real and pallid, breathing peppermint now. This real man's hands were without wounds, without punctures, almost without veins. I sipped gin, sadly. I knew exactly what I felt like. I had identified this feeling that outlasted illness. It was infatuation. You dread to see her again in case she isn't worth it. Well, I dreaded to see Sym. As I would dread to see *her*. How much was my memory of both of them true? The glass, as always with a glass, steadied me.

Then I noticed Bunch. I was no longer daunted by spectacles. He was hunched up over a coloured guitar. He caught sight of me, nodded belligerently, and started to sing. I remembered the music I heard as I came in. Other people turned to him, shushing him, embarrassed and trying to make him keep quiet. But he wouldn't keep quiet and his voice rose about us. He was singing a hymn-tune, fingering it out on the guitar, and his manner was nasty. Bunch had spent five minutes in the presence of Death, so now he sang a parody of *Holy Holy Holy* to show us how tough he was. I swallowed my gin. I knew I wasn't tough at all. If he didn't shut up soon I should start to cry.

He finished with a wide-fingered scratching on the strings, and snarled at me direct. "Not enough Will and you fall off the Wall, eh, Swale?" His speaking voice wasn't as controlled as his singing had been.

"Is that it?" I asked. "I wondered."

"It was a good story you wrote, anyway." His voice was soon going to disintegrate completely.

"A good story writes itself," I said. "Sorry it had to end like it did."

He looked at me contemptuously. "You belong to us now, then? 'Our Own Reporter'?"

"So *you're* the newspaperman!" A girl was standing

beside me, and her voice had that old note of awe in it, a belief that the world was good; but she wasn't similar in any other way. She wore a pullover with darned elbows, and jeans with patched knees; and her clothes had the fusty smell of soot and brick. I studied her over my emptied glass. I wondered what the Art-Editor would make of a girl in a bikini stuck on a steeple. "You'll give me away," I said. "And to all these people."

"To all what people?" She sniggered. "There are only the Twelve."

"Twelve?"

"Spiderjacks. Plus Him. Sym."

Him? Sym? Spiderjacks?

"The Miraclejack. That's what Bunch calls him. You want to really *see* him!"

Twelve. The Ego of it. What would Molsom say to this? "You mean he keeps a sort of coven?" I asked.

"Something like that." She grinned, delightedly. Then she said, "But you mustn't poke fun. You should see some of the things he does."

"Oh, I hope to," I said. Indeed I did. "What got *you* interested, anyway?"

She looked uncertain for a moment, and then she said: "I got myself taken up one time for a dare. . . . Well, it's no dafter than doing a ton on the back of somebody's motorbike, is it?"

"No," I said. "You can't get much dafter than that."

She gazed at my faceful of chins and coloured. "I went up with Sym, you see." She looked at me intently. "You *can*, you know. You really *can*. If you *think* long enough."

I hated him then. Who was *he* to inspire all this? Even in just one person. I remembered that time by the window. That made two people. Then I recalled how I'd once taken

62

her up on the Milestone Buttress, and her blasted God had deserted us both.

There was a stillness, a draught. The conversation stopped, and people stepped back from the centre of the room. The dark glasses flashed as they turned. Was it ordinary curiosity behind those lenses?

The door from the garden had opened a moment before, and now Sym came in. He was dressed as he had been the previous afternoon. He hesitated, and then came towards me, moving through the stillness with unusually light strides. His face was enquiring, pained perhaps; and he was without his glasses. Yes, they were mad eyes.

"A good story," I said.

The pain became too much for them to bear. "The climb or the killing?"

"The climb would have done," I said.

"The newsroom made rather more of the killing, as I remember." It was Bunch's voice, thick and tired.

"It wasn't Sym's fault, anyway," the girl said. She was watching him with glowing eyes.

"Nor yours," he said. His fingers crawled on my jacket. "Nor yours, Swale. They *would* come up. I'll be responsible for people I *take* up, but I can't do it all the time. They have to *give* themselves on a climb like this, and I knew they wouldn't have enough."

I watched him. I can't pretend I liked him at that moment.

"Still, it *has* put a blight on things," he added. "I should have done more to stop them. As it is, I shall have to call things off for a while. Especially if people think they want to follow me up."

I smiled at him. My main interest at present was in keeping a newspaper public following him up. "Of course," I said, "there's the Inquest to consider."

63

He looked at me sharply. "I rely on your paper to keep my name out of that."

"Oh no," I said. "We don't break the law. Not *The Post*."

The sharpness gave way to amusement.

I went over to the window and pointed out a tall, towered silhouette that pushed itself into brown haze by the river. "Do that small thing for us tonight," I said, "and I dare say we could say something gentle to the Coroner. After all, we're quite a bit of help from time to time."

He scarcely glanced, and his smile had disappeared. "Sorry, Swale. There are some people I just won't climb. Christopher Wren, for one. *And* Sir Giles Gilbert Scott. I refuse to climb towards heaven on that man's architecture. Find me something built by someone else."

But there were only one or two really big towers, and I didn't want him turned onto *them* yet, even if he could. This story must build slowly or there wouldn't be enough in it for me. I took a long sip of gin and it was almost as if I saw the answer in the glass. "*Crucify me!*" I said. "*Crucify me!* Do you remember saying that, and they followed you with knives and bricks and you went up the wall?"

His face didn't show any emotion, but I noticed that some of the group who had joined us by the window looked puzzled.

"Yes," he said. "I remember. I don't do that now, you know. I've moved away from it."

"So've I!" I said. "She's dead now."

Did he know what I was talking about? If he even pretended to know, I should wring his neck.

He smiled again, fully this time. "Look," he said. "I'll do this climb for you. As an act of friendship. Only *sign* your next article!" My face prickled with heat, and they all saw

64

me blush. "But I want you to make me a promise . . ."

I nodded vaguely.

"Promise me you'll do a climb with me soon. You do climb, rocks I mean, so you must have a head for it. I'll pick something easy. . . ."

What would Mavis say? All I could think of was the other one screaming on the buttress the last time I had ever gone up.

The little girl was looking at me. "Go on," she said.

"All right," I said. I couldn't say No to a little girl; besides, I'd drunk too much to think of my future. "Do you mind if I use your telephone?" I pushed my way to the hallway.

No one was very excited with Our Own Reporter back at the paper. I gathered between snatches that a filmstar had just lost her cat. Then I got Ericson personally: I never knew why I was allowed to do this, but I think he had a soft spot for me. I tried to mention the Inquest. "We put the police onto *you*," he growled. "So tell them what lies you bloodywell please. After all, it's your funeral, Bertie. No one here will miss you!"

VII

IT was raining in Battersea, but perhaps that didn't matter; I was reinforced by the bottle. The rain was full of the Power Station smoke, and the dust of Five Continents, and the atomic grit from the navels of The World's Statesmen, but a man was going to go up into it with goggles of rain on his forehead and the monocle of sweat in his eye, hand over hand, in the dark. I had confidence in that fact, even though I didn't know how he did it.

The Power Station looked impossible to get into. Beyond the first wall, which was difficult, there were trucks moving around; we watched them, and men manhandling in the yards, swearing at each other and putting their smell on the night. I breathed old tobacco, even in the rain, and nosed it again as Paul's tin and camera case knocked together loudly. I cursed their clanging voices. I'd never been so close to it before: Sir Giles' snoot, the two fingers of each hand that London cocks at heaven. God, it was ugly. I began to understand Sym's reluctance to climb it.

We waited. Paul picked some sky from his nose.

Sym fidgeted. "You could have used your influence on my behalf," he said, as we crouched by a shed, listening to the rain fall into chalky mud with a hiss like unslaked lime. "I thought papers could do things."

"When papers do things," I explained, "they do things as papers. They get official permission, and you'd be surprised how quickly official permission leaks to other papers. That's why papers don't do things. Except *The Times*, of course. None of the other papers wants what *The Times* wants."

Paul sighed and patted my shoulder. Then he yawned. "Here we go," he said abruptly. "Follow me!"

A truck was coming past untended, sailing down the rusty rails on the weight of the gradient. The others darted out and sheltered behind it, crouching bent for a few fast steps into a pool of darkness, then veering their shadows across the knock of its buffers. I followed them. We ran wildly, our footfalls hidden by the clang of the truck. I skidded on slime and tripped over sleepers. There were cinders as well, soft and then sharp. It was a ridiculous thing to be doing half a mile from the West End. It must be doubly ridiculous if Sym thought it was.

I finished up among some zinc containers against the wall

66

of the building itself, and thinking of Mavis. I should have kept my date with her. It might have got her out of my mind. Or my something. The truck swerved away further left, where voices were shouting.

"We've made it," said Paul.

Sym said, "You two have made it. I've got to start."

I looked up, past the bulk of the building. The rain was lulled, for a little at least, and this part of the brickwork was dry. There was a big breeze, and an upcurrent created by the height of the wall. The chimneys nearest the river were putting out smoke, and the smoke glowed at the base, a red glow reflecting furnaces or the accumulated lights of London. If Sym climbed high, against that dull light, Paul could get a time exposure on a telescope, or at least see how to fake a picture. Just the same, Ericson was right. This night-climbing was weak: there would be too many faked pictures and too much dishonest copy. After another quick glance around, but the noises were still loud and un-suspicious, my mind started to wander. What could I get him to do next? What would he do next? I couldn't black-mail him twice. Holiness is not the same as innocence.

He finished with his hessian; there was no Bunch to help him—I thought Bunch or someone would be a permanent part of the scene. But then perhaps his disciples weren't to see him climbing Sir Giles and betraying his tenets. I saw he had some white nylon cord round his waist, yards of the quarter-weight stuff that climbers use only for slings and waist-lengths.

He reacted to my curiosity. "I shall abseil down. It saves time, and the climb's unimportant to me."

"Abseil? On that stuff?" I was so horrified that I didn't say any more, but my fear was there, at the front of my face.

He shrugged. "It's not a rock-face, you know. There's

67

nothing to fray it. I can use a far lighter-weight nylon than a climber would. It's brand new. I only use good stuff." He smiled, and added, "I have faith in it, anyway." He spoke as if Faith was more than scientific. It needed to be if he was going to use that.

He hesitated. He was disturbed about something. "Look: I'm not interested in this building, I've told you that. You don't care *how* I do it?"

"Providing you don't use a ladder," I said.

"What I mean," said Sym patiently, as if we had to have everything straight here and now, "is that you don't mind if I use drain-pipes and things? See this pipe—according to the photographs it goes nearly all the way to the roof. The stacks may be a bit more interesting."

"Drain-pipes by all means. These drain-pipes were part of the original design anyway."

"There's something infernal about a drain-pipe." He smiled. "If there is any truth in the idea of an Underworld, you can imagine the devils down there using them to grin up at the stars."

Oh yes?

He knelt down. Paul hadn't seen this before, and we watched Sym intently. It wasn't a posture of prayer exactly, more of concentration. But then, what does Prayer look like?

He stood up for his cruciform act.

"Spare me!" muttered Paul.

My thoughts exactly.

Sym became brisker. He scuffed his feet several times in the cinders to dry them and then he put his hand on the pipe. "This won't take long," he said, over his shoulder.

"Good luck."

He brought his feet up, into a balance position, and shifted his hands rapidly. He went up out of sight. There was the same dragging, and clenching, and scraping. The same rapid

68

progress into nothing. It was sensational, of course. The trouble was I couldn't see anything. And even though a good cat-burglar would have done as well on the lower reaches, there were the chimney stacks to consider. And the pointing on these wouldn't be loose.

I looked back at the workmen, but we were a good way away, and among the bins and the shadows no one had noticed anything.

"Lousy," said Paul. He had a night-glass to his eye. It was the paper's only night-glass. We were a daily paper, of course.

"What about *me*? You can at least get something with a time exposure—he's bound to get into difficulty long enough for that. Just a few still seconds. I have to fake the lot."

A fruity mumble. "He doesn't get into difficulty. Not according to this. He's at the top of the pipe already, and *that's* all of a hundred feet. It's incredible, you know. If only I liked the bugger I could get interested in this."

"Never mind you. This is a case where the reading public wants details," I said. "Faced with the impossible it needs to be told how it happened. And what do you say to that?"

"Tell them it's Faith. That's what he says. Baffle them. Intrigue them. Next week the grand competition. 'How does he do it? Can any *Post* reader tell?' You know the line."

Suction-cups, I thought. Suction-cups, fingernails, teeth. Faith. What about skyhooks? Man the Flea on the prick of God. *That's* the trouble with Faith: it always happens in the dark. Then it struck me—the world's First Four Journalists had it easier: there weren't any reader's letters in the Book. Much easier: they didn't even have to be there. . . . But these were dangerous thoughts and I come back to Mavis. Only her face was too recent to remember. Perhaps holiness *was* innocence, and my aphorism should be that innocence wasn't the same as gullibility.

We moved backwards, out of the real shadow. We had stopped worrying now he was on the way up; and anyway some sort of teabreak was in progress, so the apes had disappeared. We moved a long way back; by the rails, now there were no more trucks.

"He's *up* there, anyway. He's going up one of the stacks."

I felt I should have the glass, but I didn't want to spoil the chance of a picture.

"Try a time-exposure!"

"No, thanks. I've faked up some shots of this one already. We've got a model down in the darkroom, and some candle-wax. Not that I know why I trouble."

And *why* do we trouble? Innocence? We are gulled by the slimy fact of being born. . . .

A crunch of footsteps and we were dazzled by light. My heart thumped and stayed thumping. Being in the Press was not a privilege any more, and we had to take the story out soon. If it was a story.

"All right," said a voice beyond the light. "Take it easy!"

"We are!"

"Doing what?" The heels ground on coke, and the words crunched. I smelled vinegar, and sweat, and onions. One of my own kind.

"Birdwatching," said Paul.

"Oh, yus!"

"Yus!"

"What sort of bird, mate?"

"Up your chimney."

The torch didn't look skywards. "Up my spout, more likely." The light kept itself into my eye. "Can it," he added.

Paul giggled.

"You cutie," the voice said.

Paul stopped his giggle and breathed sharply. "I'm warning you," he said.

"Such as?" said the voice, embedded in muscle.

"I'm just warning you."

I looked upwards wearily. What was Sym doing?

There was a laugh and for a fraction of time I thought we had been joined by someone else. Then I realised it was the same voice, changed by laughing, a big voice, fuddled by toughness. It thought it could laugh at Paul in a torch-beam. Paul was panting. He couldn't stand this sort of thing, and he was a lot tougher than he looked.

"Right," he grunted. He jumped his silhouette ahead of me and kicked upwards at the torch. There was a curse and the torch moved flinching, then Paul's bootful of sea-leg hit the black mass of man beyond, full in his pronged centre.

"Run," he said. The voice fell into the swirling thickness of the ground, and Paul kicked where the ground swirled, and kicked until the swirl subsided. "Next time I'll hit you," he said to the ground. "Go on, run," he said to me.

"What about Sym?"

"Never mind him."

But I didn't want to establish any further precedent for leaving him up walls. There was even then at the back of my mind a feeling that, if I did, he might disappear altogether. We worked at the body in silence for a few more seconds and I tried to think. All I could think was that Paul had been a sailor doing natural service, and that this Paul would have kicked the Burning Bush.

There was a scraping by the building, a sort of airy twitching, and I saw a faint white loop of line vibrating in the darkness, catching the reflections. It ran like a scratch up tower and stack, straight up above and swinging below, and the weight on the straightness was Sym dangling back on

71

the dazzle of it like a spider, coming down in a walking abseil that was more of a run. He dropped the last hundred feet in a breathless swarm in a matter of seconds.

"What's the trouble?" Sym's voice, no smoke, no steam, no panting, almost conversational—with the merest heightening of excitement.

Even allowing for the abseil he had been fantastically fast.

The voice we had kicked shouted up from the ground. "Help!" it called. "Someone g——!"

We ran. Sym didn't want to run but we grabbed him and went. We stumbled over the man at our feet and he gasped as the studs struck. We ran over rails, over rails, over a wall, over dirt, over rails, in between trucks, rails and rails and ruts, until we came to a high wall, myself half into it, hurting my hands as I stopped my rush with a slap against the wet sting of brick. I staggered back, too tired for the height of it. It was difficult with night.

Sym was up in a lithe jump. So was Paul, balletic and agile, numbing me with his ease.

I cursed and jumped.

They pulled me up by the wrists and scruff. My scruff tore. I grated the knobs of my knees on the stone, and the truthful sensation as I grappled there feeling the moistness of pain, went beyond bottles. I shouted, but where was the sympathy?

We dropped down and ran on dirty lamplight covered with bananas and old sandwiches and people's feet tripping us; we ran through the anger of voices and the hard bones of shoulders, till we came near to Battersea Dog's Home, which was not designed by Sir Giles Gilbert Scott at all. Then we stopped running.

I leant on my knees.

Paul took deep breaths.

Sym breathed normally. It was easy enough in its way.

There were drain-pipes and concealed buttresses on the first part. But what about the chimneys? I was dazed.

"Ah," he said, and smiled. "No news value?"

"Not much."

"I thought not. What a feast of waste you thought up for me. All in the wet too." He put his hand on my shoulder, a curiously repellent touch. Affection touched me, with the peanuts on the end of its arm. "Now it's your turn."

I shook my head and shuttered the image of a fish-and-chip shop I could now focus quite clearly.

"They want to know how it's done, don't they? So do you."

"So do I. Yes."

"Then you're coming up tomorrow. As you promised. Something very elementary, to give you some atmosphere. We'll use ropes, I can promise you that. And window-ledge hooks, like the fire brigade." He grinned. The fire brigade amused him for some private reason of his own.

The boy who had fallen had a hook too. But then, of course, he lacked the Faith. It was this I had to learn, as the little girl said.

I pretended to smile.

"Well, that's settled then," said Sym. He turned, and started to walk away as if nothing of importance had happened this evening. "I'll be in touch tomorrow," his voice coming back breezily and athletically and freshly between the old decaying walls. Someone came out of the fish-and-chip shop and stared. I swayed a little. He was gone. All my stories go away from me.

I waved down a taxi. Paul was morose again. "Sod all we've seen, sod all we've been," he muttered as we climbed in.

The driver glanced at us sharply as if we were drunk, realised we were the Press, and latched up the meter on extra charges. We sat in his expensive box of patched leather and turned rattling for home.

VIII

AFTER dark in Fleet Street there are two sorts of newspaper offices: those with too much light and those with not enough. *The Post* was one of the latter and I knew we were going to lose our headline in the dark. The story looked depressed before it started; read in yellow light, printed on yellow paper in grey ink.

One of the night men grunted, "It's a centre-page quarter-column, that's all. You know, Wall-Man-Does-It-Again sort of thing. It may keep the interest going, but I don't see anyone caring very much unless he kills himself soon." He was right. "Your copy's a bit purple, isn't it?" I saw the blue pencil working. "Anyone would think it was a bloody Coronation."

A Coronation? He hadn't even put a jerry on top of the chimney! "What's on the front, anyway?"

I looked at the file. I went away and asked questions. Nothing. The News was dead. The Paper was dead. She had found her dog. Nothing. Apparently her maid had been taking it for a walk; it had walked all over the Front Page. Something about a Bishop. Since when have Bishops been front page since they stopped getting burnt? Not even with actresses.

At ten, the northern editions already running-off, we heard the Police were at Battersea. The Power-Station people were puzzled by white guide-lines running up the side of the building. I was surrounded at once—by the malicious more than the friendly.

74

The joke was on the Police at the minute—it could well be on me tomorrow. The paper wouldn't like jokes that only ran to a quarter column. . . . After screwing at me hard for about a minute, the News Editor phoned Ericson in the upstairs flat. Ericson refused to come down. Trouble for me in the morning.

At ten-past we heard the other papers were there. Philips was there. That meant the Rival was prepared to regard it as important. Our Own Reporter said on the line—Our Other Own Reporter that is—there was a drunken workman there claiming he had been beaten up by a Gang of Toughs. People patted Paul on the back, and I hoped he was going to remain a Gang by himself. How much of a story were the other papers seeing in this? The News Man tugged his conscience.

At ten-twenty he phoned Ericson again. I was worried.

"Ericson's coming down," he said. *He* was worried now. I was scared stiff.

Ericson at this time had to be seen to be believed. I was suddenly left alone, looking at the News Editor looking at the telephone. It was surprising how empty a newsroom could seem to get.

Ericson's face, very red, very still, appeared at the far door. People met him, talking, deprecating me and Paul with their hands. I waited for the explosion. Ericson *loved* the public explosion of rage. There was a moment of total stillness and then he burst out laughing. I relaxed a little, but not much. This laugh could mean anything.

He came across and spoke to me for a moment. "It's news to them, those bloody white lines. They've got the story— well, we've got the answer to it! They're all there now, the whole bloody gang. It's a good enough story as Our Man says it, and you can bet Philips will say it better. Just those white lines going up a tower and a man knocked out: if they're talking about bombs down there it's a hell of a story. Well, we're going to blow the mystery sky-high." It became borne in upon me, from the flurry around us and the sudden dredged-up look of people fished from the pubs, that we were remaking part of the paper! Ericson glanced about and then said sadly, "It'll be one of *The Post's* bigger laughs, and we're not allowed to have many." He looked at me sharply. "*You* didn't do any knocking out, did you?"

"No!" There was more than an element of truth in the remark.

Then we all got busy.

We took the Bishop into the centre-page and cut him down to size. We threw away his picture.

We set up Sym in Swale. We set up me.

We were going out, in the absence of Rape, Murder, War, Actress's Dogs and Royal Weddings, under our biggest headline for some time.

"MIRACLEJACK DOES IT AGAIN!!"

B. B. Swale. Five of us wrote it, but they let me sign it. At this time of night I was the soberest man among us.

Paul had vanished. I found him smearing white scratches down a negative.

The early editions were coming off now. All the populars had the Battersea Mystery front-page. Philips had gone for the bomb and was also talking of a helicopter, which spoke well for his inventiveness.

A bomb! What a bang *we* made.

It was only when I was on the way home, with my reputation in my pocket, and cats still licking the dawn, that I realised that I was going sky-high today as well.

IX

As I came down the steps from the road into the bomb-site, there was a sick smell of methylated spirits and I noticed a pair of old men asleep by the embers of a small fire. That's where the real stories lie on their folded newsprint, I thought, and not even the cats read them. I saw a cat prowling now, it wouldn't be Sambo, towards a tree where the birds still stuck asleep; and then there was a woman's voice, sharply. . . .

A couple having it off in the bushes by the pile of rubble. Lucky man, I thought. Then I saw her face, looking at me, a hard old professional's of fifty; her voice had been wounding and high like a young girl's. But any image of girlhood would have been wounding then, in that place, at the beginning of dawn.

The cat paused at the foot of the tree, its tail swinging angrily, scared I would frighten the birds. It *was* Sambo. I wondered who had let him out or failed to let him in. Someone had gone to the flat. My bloody Char, I supposed. He was *her* penance, not mine. He gazed at me spitefully, divided from recognition by his instinct to hunt. I sided with the birds, but I tried not to rattle my keys, and hearing the breathing of the lovers and the sleepers I went indoors sadly. The cat didn't follow, and I was in no mood to call him. Or chase him when he didn't come.

Upstairs I didn't bother with the light. I was too tired to pull the blinds, and I didn't want to appear naked in front of the inhabitants of the bombsite—not that they would have noticed or cared. There was a slight noise at the window, and I started at it. There it was again. I relaxed. A branch, almost too black and old to notice by day, scraped

77

at the glass, and on it a pair of pigeons fumbled, ruffling themselves in the breeze. I watched them for a moment, two pale silhouettes above my bed, and then, hoping the cat wouldn't climb to kill there, pulled the rest of my clothes off and climbed into my pyjama trousers. For some reason I turned my back on them, or on the other eyes beyond—it was ridiculous, but I always turned my back on that window when I undressed, whatever the state of the light.

The branch tapped a second time, a slow eerie drag and scrape, and I had to force myself not to be startled into turning round again. It was only a bed's breadth away, and then the thin glass of twilight, and I almost felt it as a physical presence in the room. Once more it sounded, dragging over and back, and I walked away from it, going towards the bathroom to find myself some water. I remembered the evening, and being blinded by light, and Paul landing his kick on the Burning Bush. God, how he had grunted!

A movement, so real and close that I felt it rather than heard it, halted me like a blow. It was behind me again, it struck panic into my chest, and I stumbled, tasting fear. As I jerked round, cringing, almost hoping in my nerves for something as tangible as violence, there was a long shuffle of cloth and the dryness of breath in the dark, but I couldn't separate sounds, the beating of my own fear in that room became too much for me.

Then I saw her.

She was lying quite white on the bed as I had seen her that last morning, only her eyes were open and alive and looking at me. I tried to make her a shadow, a bolster, her eyes some crooked focus of glass, but it wouldn't work; I was stone cold sober, I knew I was sober, and I was being watched by the grave eyes of a girl I had loved a long time ago on the twilight of that bed, and who was now dead. The fear all ran away, nothing to do with her could be fear, but my spine still tingled with the mystery of it. If only there were more light, more contact, but I daren't try the light, it would all go. " Why? " I said : it was my voice, I could hear myself speak. " Please, why? " There was a stillness then, almost a mockery; and whatever she meant, or whatever my mind meant in making her here, I hated her for it at that moment.

She sat up, and the light came on.

In the flash of the bedside lamp I cried out. I——

It was Mavis, her face shocked and angry, Mavis who never stayed—what the hell was Mavis doing? I tried to take it off my face, all the anger, all the fear, and most of all the awe. What words had I spoken to the other one, aloud, for Mavis to hear in that darkness? Why? I had said. Please, why? . . . Mavis was still fully dressed and I could see why for her. She had curled up on my bed which was my couch by day in order to wait for a little while, and instead she had fallen asleep.

" I didn't see you there," I said, the beating of my heart making my voice breathless and unnatural. The clock on the window-shelf by her face said nearer five than four when I looked at it, and any minute now she was going to glance at the time on her wrist. I walked over numbly and kissed her. She let me, I suppose she let me—my chest was aching with cold. I lay down with her on the bed.

Then I remembered the uncurtained window and put out the light. " You'd better stay," I said. " You can't go out at this hour ! Please."

I saw the alarm in the shadows of her eyes, because whatever she ultimately wanted from me I knew this wouldn't be how she would have wished it, but I lifted the bedclothes up round us quickly. " Let's go to sleep," I said. " I'm bloody tired."

79

She relaxed a little then, and I went on tucking clothes around us, but she undid all this by sitting up, and I thought she was going to leave me alone with it all for ever. Instead she started to take off her dress. There was something defiant or unhappy about the way she did this, and she was suddenly clumsy with her fingers, but when she lay down she slept, or pretended to sleep, almost at once.

I watched her for a little while in the growing light of dawn, and then I went to sleep myself until she chose to wake up.

X

No hessian this time. Sym looked at me with the beginnings of curiosity. He had already knelt in his little heap of prayer, and I'd felt like squatting down too, but I didn't. An Army Padre had once told me that all men pray before a battle and before a parachute-jump. Oh no, not this one!

I had put the rope on. I had been drinking a little, under the rope; and I still felt bemused from Mavis, and totally alone. Why had I thought *she* could cure me? You're alone, but you're yourself. Then you give yourself to a woman in bed, and your manhood's gone: and then the two of you lie there, both of you women now, more alone than ever. Afterwards she gets up and leaves you with nothing left to face the coming day. I was alone, all right. Especially now, at this moment with Sym. I wasn't even clear where we were.

I was surrounded by friends, of course, several Pauls for instance, but they were all too distant to see. They were in another area of the intelligence; they still lived in the horizontal dimension, whereas Swale had already stepped into the palace of fear.

Flashbulbs hit me. Or they hit Sym, but I was the one they hurt. I was blinded by bushes.

After Sym had watched me a little longer I knew there was nothing to wait for. I nodded brightly. It would be novel to climb after concupiscence. And stranger still drunk. As I nodded, my eyes pricked with thorns of flame.

Sym took hold of the wall that the car had parked us in front of and started upwards. I waited for the rope to pull, as if this were Tryfan.

I also looked up for the first time. It was a skeleton of sharp light, a modern building suspended by light, a pain in the retina, like climbing ice. Drink had made a lens of my feelings. Lust had drawn out the telescope of my spine. . . . I had dangled on the scaffold of coming.

The rope tightened.

There were corner ridges, nurls, crenellations.

Easy. Protruding ornamental stone standing proud at the angle.

I eased up, then came back into balance with my hand round the corner, backside well back, Swale on Tryfan. Now the rope dangled between us and Sym moved higher. When he paused I started to follow. . . .

Then there were long ridges, excrescences, concrete bands, builders' blight (how I praised them), getting quite high now, at least twenty-feet, not all buildings would be this easy, you bugger, cantilever floor-platforms, the third, that meant I was up fifty, was there *any* other building, there were plenty of rockfaces harder than this. . . .

How I praised all architects who hang knockers and knobs and knuckles and jugs on the wall. How I praised impurities. As the little girl had said, it's all quite easy, up the right sort of wall, with the right sort of boot. With the right sort of Sym. . . .

Fifty feet up a wall, stone cold drunk in the morning. Sym dragged me up after him on his hank of faith, nylon, three-quarter weight faith, coming down between his legs straight to my stomach, an umbilicus of unreason stretching between the knot of my navel to the asterisk of his arse.

The wall moved.

We were already, I believe, quite high.

But then I have been high before, in my heady time. The wall moved again, that sensation of sag when the earth yawns. I nudged up tight, vertiginous, gripping my fear to the stone. Rationalise, Swale. As a rockface this would only be V.Diff. As a building, Swale, it is only a beginning, a beginning.

A rockface has unevenness and flaws and heather. It has the inquisitive nesting birds. I saw my face glower in a glass, a golden eagle. This climb has nothing: a scaffolding of light, the thin tubes of sunshine snapping at my back. Nudged up, inching, clinging to the wall with the prickle of my flesh, *tell me*. I started to blubber.

Sym turned and looked at me, cracking at the rope with a free hand.

We went up.

The rope, what was the rope for, no one was belayed? He couldn't hold me; he would scrab off too. Don't trust Sym, Swale. That rope is only his trust in you; and *you* know what *that* is worth!

We went up.

Packaged together, down we would thrash, lashed and parcelled in our yards of gut.

We went up. We went up the unfilled brick, we went up the corner, ledged on edges. Plenty of half-inch footholds, plenty of shrimp-humps, bubbles like snails. No jug-handles exactly, but we went up, me gasping, and I saw Paul grow smaller and the crowd get bigger. I shouldn't have looked down.

Certainly I shouldn't have looked down. I was too high now, even for hope.

Sym was resting easy above me and I came up through my nasty breath under his feet.

Two black heels with a man-hump above. He was bringme up.

"Is this the news you're after?" Had the wall-face spoken? Sym's voice came from the air. His voice undid me.

As he spoke, one line of stone above me, I saw the slack of his trousers flag in the wind. I had to get out of this now. While he was speaking.

"I've got to get off this."

"Don't be silly."

All those words had been an effort. How could he say that?

"I'm scared. Look, I confess it." An airless voice, I had gone back inside, trembling in the caves of spit. "Get me a belay. Whatever you get up there. *Tie me on!*"

"Control yourself a second. You'll be in no harm if you don't move."

I shuddered, racked between toes and fingers. I spoke well. After a long time I heard my voice.

"Christ, I've had my lot, Sym. Get me to that window. I'll knock my way in."

He laughed. "*That* window?"

"I'm finished here."

"It's a pity. You're spoiling the tactic of a good climb. Just as I was growing fond of you. As a climber, I mean."

The crowd, like pinheads seen past my crotch, in the blowing frame of my legs, altered their position a little on the

83

pavement. New concrete, new shapes of concrete, appeared and altered like the tension of water.

Why were we climbing the daylight? With a crowd? Past my crotch? The police had arrived too, under brittle helmets.

My foot went, suddenly.

For the second it dangled and my weight sagged, for the second I nearly fell, I wasn't afraid. Then I got my foot back and knew how near I had been. I was afraid.

The crowd opened beneath me. Nothing in my vee now. They were making a space to fall on. It would be nice, hugging here, to let go, my strength gone, onto the cushion of silence, onto this warm blowing air, and go down to that piece of cement and rest. A small piece of sick, a tomato-skin, blew through my teeth, rested on my lip, and dropped through me. I swallowed the rest.

"A good recovery. Don't hug the wall."

"Do I have to spew my ring?" Mountains are comfortable. "Get me the window."

He didn't answer. He looked at me until I relived the sound of my voice in the long silence, the screaming castrated syllables, the cheap words of panic I had cheapened myself with by uttering cheaply.

"I'm a bit rattled."

He nodded.

"It's an easy move to the window. I'll go through and wait down below till you're finished." I had said so much, and calmly.

No word.

"Increase the value of your own climb," I said. I was brave, so near to safety. "Having me give up, I mean."

"Not *that* window won't. I'*m* leading."

I was pleased he was speaking at last. His trouser-legs were banging aloud now, as if he would take straight off into space; just perched there, clawed to a crack by his hands, the rest of him flapping.

"You go across to the window, then. It's an easy move." He spoke as if unhappy about something. "I'll cover you from here." He put the rope over a starbolt, his first concession. What was a starbolt doing on a new building? You learn things high up. He put his rope over a star.

Why was he making me go alone? I knew it at once: *he was scared*. It was an easy ledge, but he was scared of the traverse. Else why was he making me go alone in the state I was in? The man could be scared. I felt almost elated.

"You lead me off," I said. I couldn't die unless my fingernails tore off, or my toe-rubbers unplugged.

"*Think* about the window," he begged.

"I am," I jeered. I knew that it was a move well within my ability. "If that's the way you want it I'll go it alone."

"I'll not be seen leading you there."

"Yeh!" I sneered. I was very close to safety.

"Look: try this window. The one above me. I'll go first and bring you up."

"No thanks!" I'd found *his* little weakness. He'd rather do something difficult than traverse. It's funny how many men will never climb sideways. To crab needs its own kind of pluck.

I started along the ledge. It was less than a Difficult, except for the exposure. I could manage the exposure if my stomach would let me.

He played out the rope. "I said *think* about the window, remember?"

"I am. It's got an easier sill." I was half-way there. It invited me with nine-inches of concrete.

"Let's talk a bit."

"With a hundred feet under my heels? You're bloody mad."

"About news. I still haven't finished about that."

"I'll write you up," I said. "I'm not that blasé." I got a hand to the sill, up above me. I was safe.

He laughed.

"You hero," I muttered.

"Take a good breath before you pull up—you'll need it."

Telling me!

I put the other hand on and shuttled underneath. It was as wide as I thought, a bit of dirt on it, one greasy bird-dropping which I smudged clean with grit as he'd told me, but otherwise fine. Coarse concrete like rock. I was feeling too secure to be patronised. I'd take the bastard on Lliwedd someday—I knew a nice traverse there. "Thanks," I said. "Thanks, I'm sure."

I did a full mantle-shelf heave, head down, guts to the bar, eyes closed with effort, left foot on, straightened my arms, right toe on, and up in one shuffle, standing erect, face to the glass, hazy now with breathlessness.

"Classic," his voice said. On the wind there was admiration.

"Thanks again." I opened my eyes, standing easy on the sill, and took a good breath for my eyes' sake.

It came out of me like cold fire. I was sick, panic sick. It sloshed the pane in front of me, I heard it run off the sill and hiss into nothingness, as a cloud hears its rain hiss into earth. I gouted, and clung there, a vertical vomit, trembling against the long glass.

There was nothing behind it.

Nothing except a reflection of me, and my fear staining the glass, being pecked away by the wind, just a few bubbles on the nothing, and my eyes looking at themselves.

A great big tube beyond the glass, a depth, stepping into the side of a well, a rat, stepping into the mile depth of my own emptied bowels. The glass on which I leant, embraced now, fondling my shadow, sagged inwards like chewing-gum.

I screamed. I screamed properly. I got my emptied voice out onto the wind and waved it around like paper. As I screamed, the air went past. I saw the sky move.

His voice came to me.

"Now you understand?"

I blubbered. I spoke little pieces of wetness onto the window, tatters of wetness onto the glass. Everything I spoke dried and disappeared.

"I told you not that window. Learn your building! It's basic." He gave lessons, Bunch said.

A bird from the depth of my belly flew out, up, up my mouth, scraped itself from my head and splashed flapping into the gravity outside me. The wind blew up my trouser-leg, up my rectum, after the bird, beating words, bleeding my agony through my mouth torn with vomit, eaten away with bile, as I ached on the bending glass, the rigid glass that was silica trembling in putty, supporting me.

"That's the stairwell. That's why we climbed this side. You'll learn."

I died. Oh I died.

The stairwell was rational. But I could fall into Reason and break my neck.

"Can you come back to me?"

I didn't answer. I had learned my lesson, all right. How long did I cling there? I knew I couldn't move, not even my hand to implore assistance. . . .

"I can't wait while you pull yourself together," he said. "This was a discipline."

"My story," I started. . . .

"Be your own story."

He chuckled.

He went on chuckling. He had left men out of his life

before. He went on chuckling as I screamed. Yet it was an entirely humorous chuckle, quite without malice. After all, I was safe enough. Could I sit down?

"Stay on that window much longer and you'll be someone else's," he said.

I didn't move. The taunt was meant to move me, but I couldn't move. I knew how much of a coward I was then.

He took off my rope.

He unpinned my Faith.

He left me with no joints, no sex, no me, no anything, and climbed out of my focus.

I waited for the Fire Brigade, fastened to the cracks of space by the crumbling nails of my fingers.

XI

I WAS in bed, very ill, when Ericson rang.

"Well done."

I mouthed.

"There's no summons pending, either. We've taken care of that."

I looked for words.

"Don't contradict me. News isn't what you want: it's what you get. You wanted to be the hero—well, you're the heroine. Make the most of it. The readers will love it."

The readers? "I would prefer . . ."

"You're a sympathetic story now. The whole paper's a sympathetic story. From Lord Dultie down we dare do what we encourage others to do."

"Officially we do not encou——"

"Officially there has been a change of heart. The whole

88

world is in love with your suffering gut. That's why we're having you moved into hospital."

"Not into hospital. Have a heart, Ericson. I'm a man. I've got hair on my chest."

"Congratulations."

"It will be playing right into—— Philips will love it if I go into hospital."

"Well, you had your chance to be a hero. Believe me, this will be better."

"I could have fallen. I nearly did."

"That would have been much appreciated. It shows the sort of dedication we require. However, the next best thing is a private-room in a hospital. No more bulletins from Our Own Correspondent—bulletins *about* him instead. You know the stuff—agonised heroics with bandages and grapes."

"Look here, Erics——"

"We've booked you in somewhere, I forget where. The ambulance will be round in a minute. Remember to smile bravely at *all* cameras." He rang off. Or being Ericson he probably had a secretary to instruct a junior secretary to instruct a typist to type a letter to a telephonist to ring off for him. I lurched out of bed, and the room did a slow diagonal swing, the floor twisting up and over and hitting my shoulder, then going on turning with me.

The conversation had perhaps been pre-recorded. Continuous creation was a doctrine dictated by God onto a long-playing tape. He has since died.

I crouched against the swinging gunwale of the fender while long black waves broke over me. Then I stood and rode the pitching cockleboat of the mat.

Mavis was coming over this evening to help me get better. Meanwhile she was out and I couldn't contact her. There was no excuse I could make, my pen felt as heavy as an oar, she would have to arrive into nothing; it was always happening like this. She lived on the fringes of my story. And I owed her more than this since she'd come into my bed.

The doorbell rang. It was my Char and a Fireman. My Char gazed motherly down at me, then burst into tears. "*Mister* Swale, sir!" she said, and left her mouth open. I heard a clock ticking, and wondered why she had swallowed it.

"Mr. Swale, sir," the Fireman said, smiling in space. "I'm the ambulance, sir. Feeling a bit dor and totley, eh?"

I tried.

"Half a mo, sir."

I stepped across a fathomwide chain of height, and he caught me. What was my Char doing, up so high? She was real, too—I could smell the sourness of her.

The firebell rang, as they backed her in. The Fireman stood looking at me. I picked up the telephone in case it was the telephone, and Ericson said, into my ear, "This Steeplejacking is attracting attention."

"Good." Either myself or the ambulance-man spoke. He was now two Firemen, with a stretcher. My Char had gone away to her weeping, and taken off the smell of cooking and cat. Only Mavis smelled clean. My memory smelled of death.

"It's a good scoop. Plenty of people are doing it, of course. There was that undergraduate who fell off in Oxford the other week, you remember?" Someone had been doing research for him while the Firemen waited. "In fact, undergraduates are doing it all the time. But you seem to have hit upon the one man who is capable of doing it sensationally. He has his following." He chuckled into my sick ear. The ambulance-men were assisting my devotion to duty, supporting an elbow apiece while I stood on the bobbing sky. "We've got the big news, the others only get the crumbs," he was saying. . . . "So many crumbs that we're sending you into hospital for a good long loaf." He laughed.

I struggled to keep the receiver against my ear. . . .

"We'll need his photograph, of course. You know, the face. Full-face. Complete with eye-horns and fangs."

"He refuses." I gyrated above gravy, hooked at my elbows.

"We'll send Paul round to him. We've got his address in the file."

"For Christsake, Ericson, he's not to be pestered. Play it smoothly. He'll go to another paper!"

"That's my worry. Not yours."

Oh yes? My breath hadn't tasted like this since I'd been in love. While she had been in love with me I had always smelled of fear.

He paused. What came next would be an order. "Ask him to come and see you in hospital. We'll catch him there. He can't blame a cameraman for an honest job of work in the open-air."

"I'm sorry, Ericson."

"You refuse?"

"We'll do a Sporting Profile of him. *You* can write it."

I was ill for some time. Today had been a greater fear. To my surprise he was still on the line—Ericson waiting for me to finish being ill. Lord Dultie must be keen on this story.

"I don't think I'm up to calling him," I said.

"Don't worry: we've had him called for you."

When he rang off I nearly made the call after all to Sym, to warn him, but the ambulance-men had waited too patiently for too long. And I might conjure up my Char again, or my angel come back and begin her weeping. And add yet another smell to my fearing.

XII

I GOT out of hospital three weeks later, about twenty days later than the paper had expected of me. I had been a bad case of fright and all my moving parts needed oiling and resetting. I smelled indelicately of carbolic and peppermint and chlorodyne, and once I was back in the Office I was in worse odour still.

They had lost Sym. I prowled round moodily and picked up the ends. Forty Portico Road was closed up; the Disciples had disappeared. We had done the Sporting Profile, we had suggested big things, and now the whole story had died. It was only to be expected; Sym needed nursing; he could have been a good stunt for any paper with a little bit of imagination. Well, The Post didn't have imagination: it had me, so the story had died.

Even I had died. Philips had seen to that.

"A man who has done difficult things on Clogwyn D'ur Arddu is not going to be frightened by anything in Acton. A put-up sob-story by The Post? I doubt it. The answer is rather more simple: whisky. Swale has been a prey to that sort of weakness before, as certain sanatoria up and down the country could testify: The Miraclejack nonsense can be safely left to bury itself. As for the drink, when will some of these newspapermen learn it is dangerous?

For those who doubt my reading of the matter, let me put a simple question: what sort of fright is it that will put a man in hospital for three weeks without visible injury? I would suggest that it is a special kind of scare that comes only to hunters, and only one hunter at that: the hunter of hangovers and pink elephants.

All in all this has been a rather sordid piece of sensation-mongering—with a death thrown in, readers will remember —which reflects no credit on a certain section of Fleet Street."

"Forget the possibility of libel," said Ericson, not unkindly, when I'd finished looking at the file. "The Legal Department say that with your record it's not worth trying. Especially with your symptoms thrown in."

"Fair enough," I said. It was never any different for me. It was only a matter of time. My Past was always present at moments like this, and my Present was numb.

"Well, it's done no one any harm. And, of course, it's done Paul a bit of good. He's Second-Senior Staff photographer now. Go and look him up for a word or two."

I stayed where I was. I imagined her face, looking at me sympathetically. Only it wasn't looking at me sympathetically.

"You better have a few more days off, Bertie. Then we can discuss things. After all, we ought to be able to use a man of your talents somewhere."

"Thanks," I said. "Thanks very much." I left him then. It was a sad little knell.

Stories do die, of course. Papers don't mind. Ericsons don't mind. Lord Dulties and Circulation Managers don't mind, even after paying the hospital bills. It is men holding on to jobs who mind, men like me, little dying men with dirty thoughts and no Happy Hope For Tomorrow.

Outside, in a corner of the main office, I found Morpath writing his two-minute prayer. His job was safe, even though the knees of his trousers were glossed a little. I wish I had taken it when the chance was offered; there are always the odd few readers who want to pray. I should have taken it three years ago and asked her to help me. It might have

93

kept her alive. I couldn't count on her sympathy, though: she had only sympathised with herself when she had left me.

"You're getting thin on the benders," I said. "Been at it again?"

Morpath glanced up, devoutly. "Praying? Again? Christ, no! These are my copulation trousers." He looked entirely pious, and held his heart like a real clergyman with photographs of choirboys in his wallet. "But, Brother Bertram, I envy you."

"Me?" Nobody else was envying me. I was one of the lowly who were going to inherit the earth. A nice little plot at Twickenham, six feet by eighteen inches. No flowers by request; just plant your wife beside me. "Me?"

"Yes, you, Brother. You don't mind if I call you Brother, Brother? It says in this column I write that we're all equal in the sight of God—the Myopic Old Bastard!" He spat in his inkwell. "That's what I write my prayers with in there —gingivitis, gonorrhea and catarrh."

"You were envying me?"

"You're a newsmaker," he said. "A man in the headlines. The man who was the girl the fireman rescued. Paul was terribly jealous, you know. You don't mind if I twist the knife a little? I'm only a poor bloody Christian!"

It was a long conversation by my standards. But what could I do to interrupt it? There is never anything that Failure can say back to Success.

"Do you know," he said, "there's an actress just had a model of herself made in gold? You know—a cast. Full size. They wrapped her up in plaster, took her out, and poured in the ingots. . . . It's given me an idea. I shall do the same, one day, when I'm rich, with my own mortal member. My pocket wouldn't stretch to any more of me. I could

94

leave it among the wax-fruit to surprise my guests. How much do you think it would cost?"

"In your case, next to nothing." It was a cruel blow, but I have my patience.

I went out towards the sunshine, wondering about Sym. It would teach me not to put all of my eggs. . . .

The sunshine was rain, there were no bright eyes, and I doubt if there was a single mortal member flourishing in the entire space of Greater London. Except for the ones in Parliament, and, as Burke says, they flourish all the time.

XIII

WHEN I got back to my flat it was empty. Obviously. Even Mavis hadn't waited for three weeks. There was a little note pinned to the table-cloth in the kitchen, but I went to the living-room first. No: she hadn't waited. She had taken herself away, even her hairpins. I sniffed for a lingering scent. There was nothing.

I went back to the note on the table-cloth. I unpinned it and picked it up. My eyes were still fuzzy with anaesthetic from the hospital.

Darling (that was encouraging) *Bertram* (no man called Bertram is real; that is my problem: Bertram Benedict Swale, born without love and christened without compassion). *Darling Bertram,* she wrote on the scentless sheet, *Breakfast is in the oven. Phone me when you've eaten it. Love, M.*

I opened the oven and saw a plate of three-week old mildew, the decay of a love-affair, and wondered how much it would hurt. I closed the oven; I would clean it out later. The kitchen now stank like a gas chamber. It smelled like the other one's room that morning, and even now I had to go beyond that smell to remember being in love. But being in love was always a smell. It was the smell of fear.

I picked up the phone, thoughtfully replaced by a fireman, and dialled.

A woman ages in three weeks. Her voice was tired and without hope. "It's me," I said.

"What the bloody hell do you want with me *now*?" As if she hadn't known I was in hospital. She *had* known, Swalc, be your age; but everything was so vile you hadn't wanted to be seen.

"I've eaten it," I said. I put the phone down wearily only to feel it ring under my fingers, and vibrate like a pain up my arm. The bitch, ringing back at me like that. I picked it up.

"Are you better?" it asked. I recognised the nasal twist, and its reassurance was incense in my ear.

"Where the hell have *you* been?" I asked him.

"Resting. Like you. Are you better?"

I shuddered. His voice pulled me up walls. "I *was*. Till you gave my paper the slip!"

He laughed so long that I nearly hung up from weakness. "Don't be silly; you were ill!"

"Wouldn't Henderson, or Jackson, or Brown do just as well? They can all write English."

"You would have lost your chance at me. Besides, *The Post* needed a lesson."

His ego was as enormous as his generosity. They both pulsed down the wires into a head still aching with the ringing. I didn't tell him that it is impossible for a piece of news to educate a newspaper; our bond was a little too fragile for truth.

"You're very kind," I said.

He laughed again. My stories may laugh at me if they wish. I am not Lord Dultie.

"I'm sorry about the hospital business," I added. "It wasn't my idea they should photograph you, and give your name. . . . Where are you living now?"

"Ah! You'll have to take me on trust. No addresses! With a paper like yours it will be safer for both of us."

"Yes, of course."

I started to wonder where Sambo was. Who fed him? Had Mavis taken him away?

"Now look," he cut in, "I may have something for you tonight."

I took a big breath. I just wasn't fit enough, and it was time to stop this night nonsense once and for all. "There's absolutely no news value in doing this sort of thing by night. We can't get good pictures and it's too close to the editions. It wants care, unusual photography, lay-out. This is really feature-stuff, you know."

He chuckled. "I've still got to make my mind up about this one; but if I do it I promise you it will be news all right."

He rang off. Not tonight, please God. Not so soon. As I stood listening to the silence and wondering about the cat, Sambo my bloodcurdling Siamese, the phone drilled my arm again. I thought how he had looked at me once from her lap.

"All right," I said at once. "Your apology is accepted." It was a live lap, after all. Warm but not burning.

"Nonsense. I'm phoning about your cat. The sooner I bring it back the sooner I'm rid of it."

"All right. Apologise later."

The phone was already silent. After a moment I put it down. I couldn't listen to the silence for ever: there might be those other sounds in it. The other one might come on the line and I wasn't sure I wanted her any more. Or I might find myself listening to God. Who would smell of Morpath!

I went downstairs and hoped Sym didn't phone while I

97

was out; and preferably not for a day or two while I was in.

I walked once, very slowly, round the shortest square of roads I could manage. I didn't want the pubs; I didn't look. There was also a Church, but it wasn't opening-time and I wasn't tempted. I tottered back home to the flat.

Upstairs, she was waiting for me, with the cat in a basket.

"Sorry," I said. I was being weak, but I couldn't act any more. Why pretend I wasn't sorry. Or happy, which was the same thing. It was wonderful to have her after the Syms and the walls and the upturned wilderness; it was wonderful to have her after three weeks alone with the one I couldn't remember and my own face in a mirror. I kissed her. I wanted this woman who had come across London in buses and taxis, who had ridden in the bowels of time on the dark grease of escalators and who, carrying our cat, still smelled of *her*. "Sorry," I said. "Sorry, sorry, sorry!" And I took her in my arms. Here I was, only at the beginning of darkness, and I really was sorry, too. She smiled at me. She started to look happy.

I was happy, too. I knew what bush it was the Voice spoke from, and why it blinded Paul, that old homosexual in the desert—the Features Man of the Bible.

Then it rang.

The bell was jangling in the tooth of my smile, and I couldn't smile any more. Modern Man is Man equipped with a Modern Telephone. I knew who it was.

I let go of my sounding brass and looked at the tinkling symbol. It was, of course, doom. I paused while she looked at me, listening to the note my smile made dying. The telephone, good black baby dragging its cord from the loins of life. Lie on your cradle, baby. Die there and let me live. No more oracles with the voice of Sym.

"Aren't you going to pick it up?" she said. Women feel

the need to instruct in the business of living, and I must remember that even Mavis belonged to the sex which had given birth to God.

It was Sym, as I thought, still joined to me by a cord. "Hallo," I said, in the voice of my normalcy.

"Remember Gavestons?"

What was my interest in burning buildings? What was my interest? The fingered bush. "I'm trying to forget it. It's been on fire thirty-six hours. Yesterday's evenings, this morning's, tonight's. What's in it for me?" What indeed? It was regular front-page.

"Probably nothing."

"So?"

"There's a traverse there over a fake Classic three-quarter front, and then a hundred and twenty-seven feet of outside angle. Steel frame. Finishes in a pylon flagstaff three hundred and twenty-five feet above ground. Sorry to be technical, but that's what there is."

"It's burning!" My watch said five forty-five.

"That's right—I've not got much time. It'll be gone in the morning. I'm going to get it pure, before it starts to buckle."

"But, it's——" I was nearly shrieking.

"I'm starting now. It's my best chance. I needed to look at it and think about it, you see. I'd been planning Gaveston's for weeks, and now some fool with a cigarette-end!"

"It's the Fire," I jeered. "You said it was coming."

"No, it's a part of the Fire. I thought it was down, then I read in the papers it was only lightly damaged and under control, and now, of course, it's flared up again."

"Where are you?"

"I'm in a phone-box there. I'll be on the building in five minutes. The firemen are doing damage to it all the time

99

with their hoses. Some of the façade's fallen, and there's glass everywhere. I want it pure." He rang off.

Pure.

I dialled.

Pure.

Ericson, tired as old tin. I told him. "Good boy," he said. "Get some photographs, of course. I'll send someone. It's a pity the other papers'll be there covering the fire. Still, we've got an exclusive on the body —you're almost related."

I rang off and dialled a taxi. Then I looked at her.

"Not again," she said.

"Sorry."

"You're standing me up?"

"No, stay," I said. "Stay as long as you like. Stay all night." Her eyes flickered defensively. "I won't be back, anyway." Was I being nasty to her just because she loved me? Or was it because Mavis was becoming this taste of fear?

I left her and went downstairs for the taxi. A sign in the butcher's said: "Nice legs. 9/6 each." There was a smell of old blood and new sawdust. I looked in the window, waiting for my taxi. There were no nice legs, nothing as nice as the legs upstairs. A few chickens hung in a row, naked except at the neck. They reminded me of my aunts. They blushed as a neon opposite flushed on, and then off.

The taxi's engine was knocking beside me.

"Gaveston's," I said.

"It's not there any more."

"I'm a shareholder."

He looked at me respectfully and drove fast.

I was a shareholder, all right. In the ten stone of live red meat climbing the burning tower.

XIV

THE papers were telling the truth, and to a newspaperman this was reassuring. It *was* burning. All up one side the steel frame—the bones of the place—glowed like brass; and the granite slabs between had gone translucent with flame.

Flame! There was flame into the bowels of it. I could see the spiral stairways twisted like guts, with hot gusts of sparks rumbling up and down in them; the zig-zag escalators, one flight a floor, running with drops of molten metal— obviously the holds were starting to melt; and the lift-wells stood there like stovepipes, red-hot from the inside. Even from where I was standing I could hear the flame roar in the flues of them.

Round the side it was cooler. Perhaps it was the way the wind had set, perhaps it was the construction of the place, but the heat held itself in. The great furry monster of fire was pacing in there like a lioness in a cage. I prickled with the nearness of it, just as if a lioness had flexed her claws on the wire netting.

Sym was here somewhere.

Or up there. Climbing with a cinder foot, fighting like a singed fly, his blood boiling.

I looked around me. There was no special crowd. Nobody knew or would believe. Men do not climb the hot wall, even by the cool brick. It is highly probable, Swale, if you rationalise this moment, that Sym is just a bubble in a bottle. He doesn't exist, Bertram; he is only your private neurosis who drags you up towers on the telephone.

There was the crowd. It stood further forward and to my left, silhouetted. There must be something for them to think they could see. Some hero or hot disaster. Couldn't they wait to read about it in tomorrow's papers? Weren't we necessary any more, the cold gospellers?

I went nearer. There was nothing to look at. The warm air rose, tinged with red.

He might be up there now, sticking to a hot brick with his own glue. Dead, or dying? Hanging in fire with the flames killing him an inch at a time. Hearing his hair burning. The whole world of pain becoming sound, unbearable frenetic noise as the wax melted in his ears and with the raw nerve of reason exposed to the quick he could hear himself bubbling, hear his bones stretch, and even hear the intaken breath of God smiling, a long long way away.

I shouldn't come out on these jobs ill and sick and three weeks in need of a woman.

Where in Christ was he? Where *was* he?

I blunted my eyes on the high embers, the towering sparks. I imagined him crucified up there, spread out on a traverse, nailed by his own fat melting, tented by heat.

It was cooler here in the shadow of the fire. I uncorked a bottle.

Up on the second-floor, which still had a virgin window, polished and counter-polished every day then rinsed by water at night, a lewd tongue of fire came like a brush among the brassiere display, among the wire frames that wore corsets, the plastic and plaster nudes dressed in the season's sharkskin, sealskin and sheepskin, and the few that were dressed in their own skin as well. I watched, my mouth drying with fascination. It was like Pharoah's tomb; the fire rose priestlike and pried among a hetacomb of mutilated women.

I hugged the dream. Sym wasn't here. I could hug the dream. Standing so close, the whole world was on fire; the puddles were reversed in fire. I threw my bottle into the air and it filled up with the focus of flame, then burst in reflected sparks. My throat was full of embers.

Up went a nylon nightie, leaving a wax figure bare and screaming. Now she was melting, now she went up in yellowish puffs of smoke, naphtha-like flaring at the knees, flames gnawing at her fork, the nipples glowing their hot cinders. Only her hair, horribly inhuman, was inflammable. I watched it perch unburning on the very pinnacle of the flame of her, the flame that was her, still unburning; I watched it perch, minutes later, on her black, negro-woman cinder. Then the cinder disclosed embers within itself, bulbs of deep radiance as the wires glowed at the socket, the cinder's belly became a great cave of light, the cinder expanded, the cinder contracted, leaving a tree shape with filaments of white ash. The cinder collapsed, and the ridiculous hair floated on a long upcurrent, sideslipped towards the floor then disappeared behind the sill.

Would a man burn like that?

I was drunk. I could have danced there on the burning floor among the burning women, the scarlet women, the women who were red-hot twists of metal. I would have locked myself in the long embrace of those great iron maidens. While Sym climbed above them you could have wrapped my singed manhood in the guts of them.

Flame came up through the floor. Even as I danced on the image of it, the carpet must have been burning all unseen by me. Skirts billowed on the rising heat. One wore hers round her face; I watched it rise inverted, her legs better under flaring nylon than any mortal woman's, but when the last inch of ecstasy was revealed she was nothing but the gap of an artificial groin; her pants fizzed and there was only the dark vee of doll's legs stretched on their elastic away from the body. I saw flame through their shadow. Wherever he was, this window was me.

One by one the models were collapsing, the crowd tittering at their nude death, dying down gently, going to white ash or flaring with strange chemical smoke, or standing there glowing, their hot wire filaments as pure and radiant as the whitest veins of lust. I almost screamed for them; it was the very nerve of beauty. The crowd tittered. All this beauty, watched by the brash shyness of aunts at the monkey-house.

God, how I wish I had stayed with Mavis for an hour.

But I was here to write about Sym, not back home with her to think about him—only there would be nothing to write about, nothing seen; there never was. He would clap me on the shoulder and call the climb off. There must be something steady I could do, steady and simple, like proposing a marriage and just settling down.

The fire was back, properly now, in the brassiere display. The nylon bags were gone and now it was the big bay breasts themselves, the very personification of the Great God Breast that the fire had to deal with. That such things should be: the mouthless mute oracle of the disembodied Breast, the Number of the Breast which is Sex Sex Sex, as St. John said. Mavis was waiting for me three weeks on a bed. There were other men here, gaping with me. I have seen us standing by a window, American sailors, Teddyboys, me, when a plastic model was being undressed. Now it was the truth of the world denuded.

The beaks of flame went pecking on the great tits of tin, the tits within tits, the foundation of the fantasy. The foundations of the foundation-garments of the fancy. They turned white-hot and dripped like the wax from dead ears, where was he now? like the ripe gold from corn. How the pillows of fancy slumped in their slumbers and melted their blossom.

It reached the hat display.

The wire hats of owls, the latest crowners of wisdom, wagged on their stalks, but presently all fell, down moulted

104

the wise birds' lids; it was even more horrible to see the hats burn.

Men shouted and jostled me. A woman trod back and screamed. I was aware of them all, bloody people! Then I saw there was glass falling. A window came down.

Most of it went backwards, sucked by the vacuum of flame, and cut all the corpses to ribbons.

Some fell outwards.

Outwards. Heads gasped, ran jerking in circles, knocking into their fall of glass, and then grated and fell, some of them fell even where the police kept us at bay. . . .

I staggered my moment of pain.

The horror caused by those little squares and triangles of shrapnelled glass.

Here, in front of my pain, was the head all in blood.

Here was the bone in the smile. Consider how in the infant the skull shows itself early by growing teeth, and the same teeth grin in the grave.

I saw a policeman's helmet sliced in two. The top of his dead head smiled at me.

I caught my own scar, fifteen stitches, into the shoulder. A single star, raw round the edges, opened and floated. I saw Sym.

I saw him one hundred and fifty feet above me, just above the glass upper fangs of the tongued window.

He was up there on an outer angle of cold brick, or it looked cold: his hands were ordinary, dead white in the glow from the great surge of sparks and stars that rose about him. He seemed perfectly cool, still chilly round the crotch, and looking for a move. I noticed he climbed easy on a ridged corner; there were inset bands of brick.

I saw Sym just as the crowd went to its knees with its legs cut from under it, its tongue clicking the dice of prayer round its spotty teeth, the crowd with its great open eyeball out and dangling on a stalk.

Someone went past me coughing quietly, just as I have described, with his eyeball out and dangling on a stalk.

He paused by a man who stood among misery and still looked up at Sym.

"What shall I do about it?" he asked, pointing to his eye. He waited with an anxious socket.

"Just don't touch it," said the man. "That's all. Just don't touch it. Find a policeman."

"The policeman's dead. I just asked him. There's a lot of people worse than me. I just asked them."

"You'd better hang on." The other man shuffled around. The glass was ankle-deep in some places and the flames cackled.

Fire-engines changed station. They had to keep it cool. So it would burn longer. So it would last. All they could do was put steam in the sparks. Gaveston's was gone: this was just to save a second Great Fire of London.

It was, as he said, a part of the Fire. Had anyone else noticed him at this moment of falling tinsel? He moved upwards into pink smoke. I found it hard to focus. I watched without emotion while he moved towards death.

The man with the bolus eyeball was gone. He had gone howling off, dangling into his destiny.

My shoulder started to ache impossibly. I shrugged. Glass grated in me. I was a cut-glass wall. No cats would mate on me now. I sat down in my own red puddle. It was me; it was my life running away. I could be emptied of myself, I could feel my saliva go dry, even my bladder bleed, but how could I lift a hand to help me? Or others? I was bleeding to death and Mavis was in bed and Sym was up in heaven and nobody cared at all.

I cried.

106

Other people cried. I realised how badly I was hurt. A plate-glass window, drifting on the wind, anchored by gravity into my shoulder.

Other people. Lumps sitting on the ground. Shadows going among us.

A bell, a bell at last, an ambulance with white women with needles. A vanload of stitches and lint for my shoulder.

The ambulance went past.

"Sym!" I called. "Sym!"

Another ambulance went past on the other side of the road. Where was mine?

The firemen were busy with my brassiere display. A lovely phallic plume of water, a feathery fiery phallus worth its weight in sparks, burst among them. How are my poor roasted girls, my dear little ducks? I wept through my teeth now, and blood was coming out of my eyes. I lifted my hands; they were defiled. It was a voyage into great weariness, surrounded by all the breasts I have ever known, each one as big as a pulpit, and from all of them Mavis was preaching, and who was the shadow tugging at her shoulder? I was emptied of life. Sambo tore me apart with his claws. I was the great burning building giving off stars.

I wrestled suddenly. Something was dragging my wallet from my inside pocket. I was losing seven-pounds-ten in cash, my Press Card, a picture of the forty-seventh position.

My wallet went into the air. I cursed, I cursed God.

"All right, mate," a voice said. "You won't need a wallet in the Waterloo Hospital. There'll be someone along by and by."

"You bastard," I said. "You Great Bullying Bastard."

My wallet slapped my face.

"Naughty," said a second voice.

"I'll remember you," I said. "I'll remember you both."

They started to kick me.

Thieves.

An ambulance, another one, went by on the other side of the road. A disembodied bell. An ambulance or a nunnery on wheels. I rolled over and tried to bite. There was laughter.

"Poor boy—he's hurt bad."

"He's got a bloody great wound in his pocket, that's all!"

"Only seven-pounds-ten, and a dirty picture."

"He must be one of us."

"Look at it! Dirty bugger!" I was kicked again.

They didn't leave me. They disappeared. The fire grew bigger. I was burning inside me, and people moved to and fro in me. I was gravid with movement. Let me be delivered of them.

Then I noticed Philips.

I looked at him sadly. Poor Philips.

He was lying flat on his back in a pool of lamplight, and they were kneeling round him and shaking their heads. There were firemen as well. Poor Old Philips: He'd gone too close in the line of duty. A damned good Pressman. I'd fought with him. A good man lying there. I'd once lifted my knee into his groin.

I felt better. I got up. Seeing him there brought me outside myself. I had lost more heart than blood. My clothes were ruined, I'd lost that much; I was a pint lighter, but I would get to Poor Old Philips.

They took a photograph of my first lurch.

Philips was still flat, dead and flat, but Cullen got me. "A great pressman presses on," he sneered, and the flashlight pierced me. I throbbed with the lack of blood. I slumped by Philips on the pavement. Glass, a matchstick, a woman's stocking, blood, me.

"I'll be all right," Philips' body was saying. "Get that silly bastard down, though!"

I looked up with dehydrated eyes. It was Sym. He stood on the roof, above the diagonal drift of smoke. He stood there, and therefore I had not imagined him. I had been doubting myself for some minutes now, especially after the glass falling. The whole world was created five minutes ago with a history of lies and a memory of what never happened. Now here was Sym, about to go up the flag-pole.

The flag-pole was a pylon of metal struts. Even from here it looked hot. A great glowing pylon with the stars for insulators. It hummed with heat up there. The crowd hummed, too. The crowd had really seen Sym now. Or the seeing crowd had. Some of the crowd was being helped with ribbons on its eyes. There was a blind crowd lying.

Oh, the sheer naked guts of the man. He wouldn't manage, of course. But the cool beauty of it. Hand over hand to the glowing top of the night.

The building might go any minute. Let him fall *this* way.

"Get that silly bastard down!" said Philips again, hysterical with loss. A fireman nodded.

The clear spider pylon ticked with a million volts of impossibility.

Sym started to climb.

Impossible.

Women screamed, as if he were trapped and was losing his way upwards. The men held their breath; his movements were too deliberate. He was already ten feet higher, with the bone baking.

My eyes, drained of fluid, were longsighted suddenly. The nearness splintered. He had great white gauntlets on his hands. Asbestos gauntlets.

He was still going up.

And that is what is meant by miracle, my friend Philips, those asbestos gauntlets, and the goggles on the face he half-beetled backwards—he was wearing welder's goggles and a helmet. There was miracle also in the great booted foot. It didn't matter that he looked like an ant up there; even Man was Myth enough. Christ, the Great Thing was happening, and how could I ever write it down? I could only put down the horror of it, and not the beauty. I mean the beauty of a calculated idea, of a white asbestos gauntlet masking the leaves of blood. Those irons weren't glowing hot; they were oven hot at the most; but they would have the skin off him slowly, and what was under the skin slowly, until his grasp crumbled. Now the Idea, the Invention, the Formula, protected him.

He went up.

That was what was wrong with Icarus, Philips, his place in history. If his wings had been welded instead of stuck together with glue he could have reached nearer the sun. Instead he fell out of his myth and pickled himself in a pane of water. But Sym went on; look at him now: it was easy climbing, swathed in asbestos, up easy struts—then it was easy, technically, to get yourself crucified too. Just the wood and the nails. It's the trimmings that count.

I had boggled in Acton, but I would have given anything to have been up there above this pockfaced crowd and this poxy Philips. I should have piddled the benediction of Jove, and the earth and water of me would have evaporated in the fire and air.

Police whistles were blowing—the old accompaniment. I couldn't be too far gone.

And my wallet had been lifted, too. Yes, I was fully conscious.

I lifted up my eyes and they turned into telescopes.

All the blood drained and focused through long tubes of distance. A long-sighted skull, even when dying. I find only mean things near to. Eyes only rest on the hills. On the mountain of flame, the shifting sierra, they now loitered.

Sym stood on my apex at the top point of the climb. He stood there secure at three hundred feet plus. Add to which the linear coefficient of expansion of metal. He had reached the top of his pylon and left us voiceless. Nobody dare shout lest he stumble on an upborne lung.

What about it, Reverend Who? This, and this only, converts me. Three words convert me. *I have lived.* To hell with *I have prayed.* Come off there you ripe silly bastard I adore and worship, before the nine storeys fold and you break your neck in the ashes. Come off.

A movie-camera was whirring behind me. I took endless snapshots in the lenses of fear.

The supreme, superb, cocky bugger. He stood there on the flat metal disk on top of that hot pyramid above swaying burning London; rushing on the Earth's rotation at a thousand miles an hour through the cindery sky, he stood there holding nothing and stuck his gauntleted hands in his pockets: And the crowd roared at him, ankle-deep in death, as if it was a circus they had come to see. They applauded the magnificent mad gesture. With so much confidence in him how could it be possible for him to die?

How the hell would he get off, though?

There were flames under him like the nine rings of Hell. Jump, said the Devil. I saw him incline his head there, as all men incline their heads from on high, considering the cushion of space.

Philips suffered hallucinations beside me. They'd got him onto a stretcher at last, but all I had received was a cup of tea. I felt weaker but better. The Unseen was going among us dispensing cups, the hot steam rising like angel's hair. It was a snackbar proprietor, coming back anxious in Italian for his crockery.

I dropped mine in horror. *They were going to try to rescue him!*

Firemen, urged on by the damned diabolical Philips, now demented, and by black-helmeted policemen, and women misunderstanding the moment with screams, put up a gigantic extending ladder with a platform top like a crane-grab. Then two firemen wearing coal-scuttle hats making them look like supersonic angels went up it. They went up it while it was still elevating. The humiliating bastards! They went up on official steps, moving in time, the trellis still moving.

They thought they were going to rescue him.

He stood with his hands in his pockets doing a slow circle on the top of space while the foul great grab grew nearer. It's a betrayal, Sym, but you've done your climb; you'll have to come off that way or you'll die.

What a come-down, to be escorted back by men who trod merely on steps. Philips called a camera to him. They got ready for a wasting-the-tax-payers'-money sequence.

Sym appeared to notice the firemen and stand for a second undecided as they rose beside him.

They drew level.

He laughed at them, stooped agilely, caught the flat of the pylon-top in his hands, and knelt backwards into space. The ladder overshot him, foolishly.

He chuckled down the buckling girders, but only a second! He was mouthless, then whitefaced with fear, for the girders were buckling, starting their rivets above him, then under him. Twisting, sagging, the beanstalk was collapsing. Snapping from heaven it wore hot leaves of flame.

The ladder shortened and came in again. It was lost for a moment in a dark vomit of smoke.

There it was, within a foot of him. Everyone silent, the ladder quivering on the rattling gusts of hot air and the twisting thermals of flame, the pylon swaying, folding into itself moltenly from the top.

It was the end of him, I saw it.

With the top collapsing onto him and the bottom falling under him he clung for a second to the illusory stillness of his own piece of trellis, suspended in time. Then he leapt.

He leapt and landed on the ladder platform, and they snatched at him with bleached hands.

The whole tower was over them in an instant, snap-snapping like a conjuror's ladder and fanning its heat cherry-red in the swift rush of fall. They steadied each other momentarily and then collapsed under tumbling flame.

When I opened my eyes it was still falling. The tower of smoke was spiky with spars, the spars falling, the smoke standing.

Then everything went. A corner of building fell away; it came slowly and as it fell a corner broke off from the corner and came cascading down the ladder now a ladder of hot rubble. I saw firemen figures lower down walking into the sliding rubble, walking on it, wading against larva and scree and stones and melting pitch, screaming in treacle, fighting off head-high cascading blocks, and then one of them falling like a torn rag plucked down a chute of coal. Then the ladder bent stick by stick, twig by twig, aluminium girders hunched into nothingness, and at last came the noise of it, the rumble of flat weight striking through the tearing note of the flames. People screamed as the noise rose and settled and then there were only the stones rolling, the heap smoking and the fire lulled, not a sign of life, not a roasted limb even, on the surface of the huge pyre. *Movietone* was there, with Man's whole fall printed for ever.

Suddenly the building was smokeless. The play of water and this downdraught of falling calm seemed to suck it away. And in the silence and the clarity there was a great ragged cheer.

I turned over.

On a corner of the roof jutting out beyond the fall, a man stood, basted black. It was Sym, moving tiredly, gasping smoke, grasping smoke, and weighed down by unseen weights as if the sky still fell on him in hot fragments.

He tested a drainpipe from above, leaning over, dangerously over for ribs full of smoke, and rattled it with a gauntlet. Not a noise now, they waited. He turned back from the edge and disappeared.

He was gone for a long time, and it was almost as if I had imagined him. Surely he was dead. Or if alive this second time then dead again on that smashed roof. The smoke blew back.

A hump, a vast antlered spectre appeared in the torn gouts of it, a huge man-monster, in the drifting sparks; I couldn't focus.

Then I saw. It was Sym, turning backwards off the roof, carrying a figure over his shoulder. Lashed in some way, feet lashed to hands in an ungainly triangle of man. He was out on the pipe now, holding it between his gauntlets, Christ, don't let it break, and hunched out into space, his feet flat on the wall. Stooped and clenched, with the other man's weight on his back, he inched down the hot surface. The figure he wore lifeless was black with smouldered serge: it was a fireman.

"Get this," I shouted to Philips (they were all shouting to someone, the thousands of them; or shouting when he stepped away from the foot of the pipe); "Get this, you bastard!"

And I shouted again as Sym put down his load and turned weary back to the wall.

But Philips was gone. They had taken him away from his small tin puddle of blood, and I lay there with my eyes floating above the triumph of this moment all by myself.

False Prophets

I

My pyjamas were moist and crumpled. I must remember this was my sickbed, as all beds were. I lay there, my hands moving idly, till she rolled away from me and switched on the light. Then she shaded my face with her shadow until I could focus her. I still blinked weakly.

A woman by lamplight is slightly less satisfactory than by dark, but only slightly. I was much less satisfactory than she was; her look told me so. I realised there might be a later ghost: I had my live woman now, but I didn't deserve her. I wondered how wholeheartedly I would want to have her—until she didn't want me.

She leant over and fingered my collar-button. She was thinking. Or she was pretending to think. Sometimes she had already thought; but she put on that look until I asked her what her thoughts were, and then she could tell me with the right tone of seriousness.

She gasped.

I glanced down and saw that my collar had come open at the neck, exposing my scar. The plaster was only just off, and it was puckered and raw in the features of my shoulder. "Bitten in the course of duty," I said. I had to say something.

She kissed it. I was a man with a scar to kiss, so she reprieved me.

Then she kissed my mouth and said, and I knew this was

119

one of the thoughts she had been saving for me: "Is journalism usually such a dangerous job?"

"War-reporting," I said. "And Royal Weddings. Not otherwise." I yawned.

Her mouth kept on pushing itself into the beginnings of words. I buttoned up my pyjamas again and waited.

"If it's not the job, it must be you then."

"Very likely."

She stared at me and I wished I hadn't said it like that.

"You could try laying off the bloody bottle for a bit, couldn't you?" she snapped.

I was angry then. "I've tried laying off the bottle for lots of bits. You're just one of the bits I've laid off it for."

"I know," she said. "You even talk to her in your sleep!" She started to cry. "Oh God, why do I keep coming here?"

I leant up in bed and lifted the curtain and stared out into the darkness. What did I hope to see? The Preacher? I saw the lamplit reflection of two transparent people on a bed: they were drawing further apart. Why *did* she keep on coming here? I couldn't go on being her magnet for ever. Or her maggot.

"Anyway," I said, "I can't lay off the reputation of the bottle for you or her or any other bit. That stays with me in Fleet Street until I die."

I had spoken too cheerfully.

"So when Sym goes you'll be finished?" she asked.

"Very likely. Of course, I may do well enough out of all this to stay in the top-line for good. But very likely. I know what I can do. I can carry snaps for the Art-Editor. I can make tea. I might even be trusted to look up entries in *Who's Who?*"

She sat up and started to pin up her hair. "Anyone with any intelligence would have been looking for another job *years* ago. You're fighting a losing battle, aren't you? Even if you make it they won't let you stay. And even if you give up the drink you'll stay branded as a drunk."

"I'm still fighting."

"No virtue in that."

"What would you have me be? Tea-boy with Shell-Mex? Look at me a minute, Mavis." She didn't look. "Well! What *am* I good for, anyway?" I pulled some pins out of her hair.

"Lots of things. Schoolteaching, for example."

I laughed. It was only when she finished doing her hair that I realised that girls who do their hair aren't staying any more. And I knew, quite suddenly and anxiously, how much it would hurt.

She looked at me and said, "If you got a job with prospects we might . . ." Then she looked startled. Even the best girls think aloud. Even when they do pretend to be leaving.

"No we mightn't!" I was angry, bloody angry. We glared at each other, me in crumpled pyjamas, she in her underclothes and slip, her hair pinned tight as if she were going to a party.

"You bloodywell listen here," I said. It was ridiculous, kneeling face to face on a bed, *kneeling*, and asking her to listen. I pulled her hair down again. "You listen to this. Stop pinning it up, sod you! I'll tell you why I'm staying. This man Sym—he's not a story for *any* reporter. He's not for Robertson or any of those. Or bloody Philips across the road." I held her and she beat at my fingers.

"Jesus, and what is there in him for you?" she sneered.

"Look," I answered, and I knew there was no satisfactory explanation I could give, somehow I wanted to explain to both of them, "I don't care whether I write straight or crooked, whether I'm sober or stark raving mad, but that man's special. . . ." Her sneer made it impossible to find any words I wanted. "He's terrifying in one way. Conceited, and there's something like madness, like a priest but not so bloody cosy. But I'd follow the bugger—I *do* follow him. Perhaps it's just an instinct for sensation, perhaps it's because I can't do it myself any more . . . what he does on those walls means something to me. I know half of the character I give him is a lie, half of what I hate and half of what I love—and Christ knows what *love* means. But I get the feeling that if I watch him long enough I'll find out something."

"That's right. And you get the other half from a bottle."

"Half of what?" She had lost me. Anyway, I wasn't listening. I had said my say and she had said hers, or I hoped she had. And what she said had reminded me. I let go of her and got up from the bed and padded over to the cupboard.

"What you hate and what you love," she shouted out behind me. She was crying again.

I picked up the bottle and hunted for a glass, and I realised as I did so that I was only looking for one. I was getting good at these things and my finale was always private.

"Please," she said.

I turned back to her. "And there's another reason," I said, and I could hear my tongue thicken and slur with anticipation. I could do it without there being anything in the bottle at all except emotion, and I always had plenty of *that*. "He used to be a preacher, and before you say 'Since when did preachers interest *me*?' let me say what was special about this one: he used to preach outside that window a year or two back."

"And *you* used to listen?" Her eyes became round and sharp. She had noticed the single glass in my hand, but that

122

wasn't why she was angry. "You used to bloodywell listen all right. And you listened with her!"

"Very likely," I said. "Very likely. I did lots of things with her."

"With her or her halo?" she was crying again.

I didn't answer.

"I said: did you make love to her or to her halo?"

"I'm sorry," I said. "I didn't. I didn't make love to her the way you mean."

"Oh yes, you did, Bertie. Just like I mean. But it was to her halo, wasn't it? The woman didn't matter!"

She didn't cry any more—why should she?—and somehow I wasn't being heroic enough for anything else. She started to laugh at me instead. She laughed at me, sadly and then hysterically. And then she said, "Oh, Bertie, what a poor, sad, bloody turncoat you are. You're in love with this God you don't believe in, aren't you? Is dying all she did to convince you?"

"Oh, bugger off," I said.

I poured myself the one I had been holding for too long and started to swallow it. Not happily—it was my need, far more than any need to answer her. As I drank it, I heard her finish dressing. I knew all of the sounds, and there weren't many. Then the door closed. But the door was outside my head, a long way outside.

II

"ALL right," said the Features Editor. "I dare say we can use it. . . . Some of it, anyway!" His pencil was working, but there were no blue marks on the bits I thought were important. I watched him wreck it some more; and

123

then I turned away feeling reasonably happy. A small success, but it made her seem less indispensable.

Then Ericson called me over. He sat in on the Newsroom quite a lot. He rarely started things; he stopped them—after all, it was his Kingdom. To my surprise I noticed my feature in front of him. Then I remembered that he asked to see all Miraclejack stuff. Probably because it was a Swale story. At least there was no more blue pencil on it.

" 'The Crucifix Climb'? " he snapped, his fingernails putting scratchmarks on one of Paul's better negatives.

"That's right," I said. I looked down at it: all angles, and sky, and perfection. "That's what we called it in our story of the thing. This is just a gentle piece of recapping. Sym is good feature-stuff surely?—plenty here for a feature."

"Sorry," he said. "In fact, I'm not even sorry. It's bloody bad taste. We'll keep Religion out of this story *if* you don't mind!"

I looked at him in amazement. "You'll be lucky!" I found myself gazing at his empty desk-top and realising in bewilderment that the proof had already disappeared. He had tossed it or dropped it somewhere, but it was out of the conversation for good as far as he was concerned.

He pointed his white finger at me. "Leave Apocalypse out of this, Bertie boy, and keep your nose out of the crystal. Or I'll take you off the story and I'll take the story out of the paper. It's Policy. All over the Country there are people with normal ideas about Religion. *The Post* does nothing to offend those ideas. Get that."

"All over the country there are people like me, with no ideas about Religion at all."

"You'll offend them. That's Policy too. God is not News."

"When the rest of Fleet Street is hawking the Second Coming what'll *The Post* be doing?" I jeered.

"Laughing up its sleeve and waiting."

124

"That's what I'm doing over this story," I said. "And I suppose *The Post* will be doing the same on the bloody Day of Judgment, too!" I walked away.

"That's right!" he roared. "And we'd *be* right too! Because we've only got one reporter who'd think of coming here with a twit story like that. And that's you, Bertie!"

I went among the cross desks with my ears buzzing. He had a voice that could build up like a bull's. All the Newsroom was gloating now. "Go and have a drink," he called after me. "And leave Religion out of *The Post*. There's no bloody God in Fleet Street."

"There's Religion everywhere," said Morpath as I passed him. "Even in the mating of dogs, Brother Bertram."

When I got downstairs and outside I was overtaken by a messenger-boy. He was about sixty and he had just had a hard run. "Editor wants you," he gasped. He turned away, winded. Even so, I went back up more slowly than he did.

Ericson grinned at me. "I've had a little idea," he said. "Me and the Lordship. And we want *you* to go and break it to His Holiness. *If* you can lay your hands on him."

It was a long time before I left the building a second time. The bastard hadn't thought this one up in five minutes. He'd let me walk all the way out just so he could have the pleasure of calling me all the way back again. Mavis was right.

On the way out I passed the messenger-boy. He was still out of breath, and looking old and reproachful. But I didn't sympathise too much. It was probably the first time he'd had to run in his forty years of tenure. Nobody on *The Post* has a bright idea that often.

III

THERE was fresh scar-tissue on his cheeks and the raw marks of burns dusted with powder. Without glasses his eyes were strained, and hard to meet, especially now I was back asking favours.

"Isn't there enough news in the world, without newspapers *inventing* more? " he asked.

He was trying to be sad, rather than being genuinely afflicted. It was the difference between a Saint and a Clergyman.

"What about you? " I said. "What are you but a bloody invention? " It's funny how right a woman can seem when she hasn't been to bed with you for a few days.

"I *am* news," he answered. "And if you're wise you won't alter me."

I smiled. I always felt better when he started to talk. His conceit diminished him. The First One was probably the same: a modicum of deeds and a maximum of words. He knew if he went out and healed any more lepers they would forget he was divine and think he was merely a doctor. And it's the reputation that counts.

We were in his old room in Portico Road. Either *The Post* was to be trusted with his whereabouts once more, or he was less inhibited about the broader sorts of publicity than formerly. Fame makes everyone human. Once famous there's no point in pretending any longer. I let my eyes wander. . . .

This time, with no nights contemplated, the room was bright with daylight, and there were birds singing. He was keeping canaries. Paul would have made something of that, a sad head among cages. Meanwhile, I had my message to deliver.

"What about Chalk Hills?" I said. "You know—the radio-tower."

He smiled. "I'm sorry. I'm finished here, Swale. You know what it must be next." He looked at me, but I didn't answer. "I don't mean I've finished everything *worthwhile*. There are lots of things, delightful, unflawed, particularly churches, and some of those new cantilever office-towers, and of course I shall keep them to please myself. Later. I want to *know* these buildings. But I've done everything that is news. To you."

I was glad he saw the need to justify himself. "It's Ericson's idea, not mine. You might bear that in mind. Ericson could have quite a big say in your future!" Or in the part of your future which is mine, I almost added.

"I don't think so."

"It would be excellent practice for the next thing."

"No resemblance. It would be like going up a ladder. I expect there is a ladder."

"No, there isn't. Not on this one. It's too high for normal inspection. They are going to use a helicopter when the installation's finished."

"I'm not interested, Swale."

"It will be laid out on the ground, all twelve hundred feet of it, and then jacked up to the vertical."

"A negation. That isn't architecture. It's just making a bridge and lifting it up into the sky."

"It will still be good practice," I said. "They're the same height."

"Height doesn't frighten me."

Lucky man.

"You'll be up there with the winds and the weather." I had to persist. My job depended on persistence.

"Different winds and a different weather. A different climate, a different country. There's even a different feel to the sky."

"How the hell do *you* know?"

He looked at me quizzically. In a second we would be back to the old game of silence.

"It doesn't matter to *me*," I said. "I've got other irons in the fire now." I had taken her words to heart, though perhaps not quite as she expected.

"Milocz?" His contempt was increasing.

A man named Milocz had just done a statischute jump off the Clifton Suspension Bridge, and I had dabbled with that one. "Yes," I said. "He's another fool. Newspapers see fools come and go." Well—Milocz was alive so far. Let him keep on coming!

He looked at me pityingly. "Milocz!" he said. "A parachute is only a device. Either it opens or it doesn't. Where's the striving in that?"

"The world doesn't care about striving," I said. "Only the sensation. Take it from me, Milocz is sensation." Better sensation than you, I might have added.

A miracle's greatest requisite is wit.

He went into the kitchen and I heard him opening birdcages and feeding them. St. Francis Sym, with his fingers diamonded with dung and encrusted with canaries. Why not Golden Eagles, and Hawks, and the other sharp birds of high places? Why not a cageful of bishops, those even sharper birds of higher places still? Why not a bleeding dove?

He came back and said. "It's ridiculous, a ridiculous wastage. He's going to kill himself, this Milocz, and then you'll have *that* on your hands."

"So will Ericson; so will Lord D. So will two million readers! Why single out me?—I've got to live. If he wants to kill himself, he wants to kill himself. Nobody's been stopping *you*."

"I don't intend to kill myself. Not yet. I'll do this Chalk Hills thing, but it's my last. And I'm doing it for you. I'll do anything to keep you out of the hands of some of these people."

"Thank you," I said. "Thanks very much. At least they *are* people. They eat and they sleep and they fornicate and their guts are full of . . ."

"They're people," he said. "That's all. Just people. That's their weakness."

"Not yours?" I got up to go.

"No, not mine. Not quite. Not in the same way. I'm not letting you destroy me. Nor am I destroying you."

"That's a bloody nuff," I said. "Enough. This is a partnership. Not a marriage. I can have this sort of quarrel any day or night with a woman."

"Oh, it's a marriage, all right," he said, following me to the door. "All the worthwhile relationships are. Talking of marriage, you ought to marry that girl!"

I turned on the step to the closed door. The brass fire grinned at me from its black hinge.

I stood on the step for a long time. I had never mentioned her to him. The Snooping Bastard. Anyway, if she gave me half a chance I probably would.

IV

FROM our chauffeur-driven car, the Down looked like a Fairground under country-column sunshine. The entire landscape was dominated by nearly a thousand feet of illuminated girder, the bottom two-thirds brittle with light, the next third a spidery shadow, and an unseen hundred of feet hidden in cloud. The new Chalk Hills radio-tower dangled from the motionless mass of vapours like a beanstalk, one set of support wires tense, the other set, on the sunny side, sagging with the lean of the wind.

"The miraclejack," said Paul, "is morose." Sym didn't answer. He had taken a single glance at the tower through binoculars as we caught sight of it over a ridge in the A.2. and then had put them down quickly. Now he said nothing. Paul was a person he rarely found time to answer.

"What's up with it?" asked Paul. He was taking some moving film of the vista, with the tower perched spiderwise on its cowpat of shadow. He didn't need a reply.

"It's technically very easy," said Sym. "Very, very easy. As I said it would be."

"But it's news," I said. "Look at them!" I spoke excitedly, but I had just noticed. The Down was swarming with figures. What I had taken to be distant acres of glasshouses throwing sun at us were in fact immense parks of cars, blinding us with the weather reflected on their windscreens.

It started to rain slightly, a storm-rain with the sunshine still striking through. We drove on through falling lenses and crystals and clock-faces of light; and as we went forward the green freshened with rain, and the trellis of the tower grew brighter as the beads of water lit on it.

Sym muttered something, so we looked at him. "All those people," he said.

"Your next climb will have people," I countered. "You won't do *that* one unseen."

He waved the comment away angrily. Always before climbing, it was the here and now which obsessed him.

We swept onto the Down now, along a hedgeless road between wire and posts. Then we turned off along a chalk-track, sticky with rain and the hurry of feet. Sym became silent.

The crowd was immense. It was a newsworthy crowd; it covered an area as big as the cloud that pressed on the tower, and looking up from its fringes I saw that the sky was alternate bright blue and black thunder cloud. The metalwork of the tower had turned a sick green. We had reached the point before a storm when the air becomes motionless and generates darkness. I turned to Sym anxiously. Should we call it off?

"What do you think?"

The car bumped over grass between knots of people.

"I don't think there's any problem."

"About the static, I mean." The air, divided by bars and wires, was hissing with it.

"I don't feel it."

I looked at him and he collected himself for a further patience.

"That is—I feel the static, but I don't feel there's a problem. I see no reason why the lightning should want *me* in particular. Not yet, anyway."

"You owe it for Gaveston's," said Paul, still taking pictures.

Sym thought for a moment, and then said, "It doesn't strike at birds!"

Birds don't join themselves to the earth with girder and wire, but what could I say? There is always the luck of disaster. It could even happen to me.

We passed St. John's Ambulance men, and refreshment stalls, and policemen on bright silver motorbikes with radios. We passed flags saying *Post, Post, Post*, banners saying POST, posts saying *Post*. We passed placards saying *Special Edition . . . Souvenir Edition*. We passed cheap paint on damp paper, curling on slings of string. People pressed to

131

the window, more and more people, but Sym acknowledged no one. He sat in his old, black, woollen track-suit, looking morosely at the floor of the car. There were expressions on those passing faces, eyes to meet, but he wanted none of them. Eyes full of hopefulness and money, eyes coining curiosity, eyes inviting looks from him, who kept the slots of his own to the floor, the stuck-up, remote, peculiar bastard.

Paul took bootblacking from his fingernail with a knife "It's wonderful to be official," he said. The car hooting us from behind was Dultie's, and though the sun was gone, the sky dangled with banners. "Anyone would think *The Post* had built this tower."

"I think I shall use rope-soles," said Sym. He was chewing his fingers, but deliberately, inspecting each one in turn to make sure he had taken the nail past the end. I was startled. I had thought of him in terms of bare feet and miracles. Where did rope soles fit in? Not into the same pattern of divine inspiration as fireproof gauntlets. He had concealed his techniques for so long that they were now irrelevant. We stopped.

The car was either stuck on a gradient or deliberately halted. We got out.

The other car had pulled in behind us, and Lord Dultie alighted under an umbrella, making me notice it was no longer raining. He moved towards us, quite brightly, and Paul and I smiled deferentially, encouragingly. I inspected my creases deprecatingly but when I glanced up again he had turned away. No—he had been turned away by Ericson, handed off, guided. Philips had been loitering, and Cullen with a lens under his jacket, waiting to catch an encounter like this. Dultie and Sym shaking hands. I glanced at Sym, hoping he wasn't slighted. I needn't have worried.

He hadn't noticed.

A faint smile altered his lips. He was looking at a fire-engine. Suddenly he said very bitterly, "Do they think I'll get into a predicament *they* can rescue me from? Is it likely? "

"We *had* to have it," I said.

"A pity," said Paul. "Look at that Gaveston's bloke. Never recovered consciousness. Whenever you buggers show off, somebody dies." He turned away. He could afford to turn away now—he had a reputation to turn away into.

Sym said. "One day I'm going to jump off. One day when I'm really high. Not *come* off. *Jump* off. And if one of those imbeciles catches me in one of their little nets. . . ."

I turned away too, hiding my laughter. Then I remembered the photographed cinder.

We moved towards the loudspeaker van, between damp white ribbons. "Good luck," Paul mumbled as an act of contrition. After all, Sym belonged to *The Post*. He was our own piece of vulgarity. We followed in deference. We followed him close to the microphone. Paul wanted a picture of this, the Oracle with the megaphone. I knew his lens would find an angle from which to sneer, a pimple or a dimple, and Ericson would snigger but not publish it.

Philips, close by, looked guarded. Sym represented moral fitness nowadays. He had made a big impact on the wireless, so even Philips must wait and smell out his moment. He might even find himself writing this straight. Better write himself straight than write himself wrong.

Sym stood in front of the megaphone, under microphones and with others beyond him, with the shrivelled stillness of unconscious pride. They all grow a saint-trance, these orators. A television camera traversed onto him. Ericson had fixed it with the I.T.V. company we owned a slice of. *Movietone* was here as well, a cameraman nudged up on a truck.

The television announcer wore a dark glossy tie and a black moustache. For an awful moment of silence I pitied him. I pitied Ericson and Lord D. for having to place their affairs in the hands of this tie and moustache. Which meant I pitied me, who would suffer if Lord Dultie suffered if the announcer suffered. How could he interview the Oracle? If I choose to speak I speak. If I choose not to speak then I am silent. A Pity. I did not pity the crowd. They would hear wisdom, perhaps, and see sensation, which are all that crowds ever hear and see. Words aloud, wisdom. Agony, even that public stiffening on the garotte, sensation.

The Announcer spoke over their vast sea of permanent waves and hairy ears. The words went away at the top of the tower. The cameras recorded. Paul, in a bright gust of breath, took his picture and said, "I should hate to be handling a thigh on the television couch, and come face to face with Sym in the wavy lines!"

I looked at him, with more of my pity. But discovering Sym in a darkened room was like any other meeting with conscience, as I could remember.

The Announcer was saying, "Mr. Sym—or may I call you——?"

"Call me Sym. It's simpler."

Paul sniggered and the Announcer said hurriedly, "Mr. Sym, may I ask you a few questions about your climbing technique?"

Sym appeared to relax. "Any questions at all."

I drew nearer. The Announcer had reached the nub of our dilemma. Only there was no need to draw nearer when there were microphones, tape-recorders and fourway loud-speakers roaring across a groundsurge of transistors. I could feel the whole interview vibrate in my bones. Ears were unnecessary.

"Good. Well then. How are you proposing to get up that

134

radio-tower in a few minutes' time? That is—if you *are* still proposing to . . ."

"Will."

"I beg your. Sorry. Oh, I see . . . Well, I certainly *hope* you will."

"You misunderstand me. *Will* is what will help me. Will is my technique."

"It's largely a matter of will-power? "

"No. Entirely. Not largely. Entirely."

"Will-power? "

"Not so much that. I stick to my first word. Will."

"Excellent. Would you like to . . ."

"Will in a religious sense. "I *Will* because *I am Willed.*"

"Well now—comparing that remark with what Sir Edmund Hillary said . . ."

"No. Take someone else. Take someone else."

"Not Ed. Hillary? "

"No. Not appropriate. Take Billy Graham."

"Well, if *you* think he's . . ."

"He is. I assure you he is. Think about him. A sort of latter-day John the Baptist—a professional Holy Man."

"I don't see . . ."

"Now wait a minute. Don't interrupt. Wait a minute. I'm coming to me. I believe in Will. Will will get me up this piddling little tower in just a minute. I believe in a *physical* affirmation. In fact, that's what I am: a——"

"Could we——"

"A physical affirmation of man's moral capabilities. Not merely vocal. That's where I differ from Graham. He's just a mouth. Like the Pope, you see. Or the Archbishop of Canterbury. Just a mouth in a funny hat."

The Announcer, who was by now the same green colour as the storm, said desperately; "But what about Hillary? "

"What about him? A bad example. A very bad example.

He depends upon techniques."

"He—er? Oh, I see. And you *don't*! I mean, you—er—don't depend on . . ."

"Oh, well. Of course. I mean, over the years I've evolved techniques. Many techniques. Reinforced by Will. The Will in itself reinforced by the techniques of sustaining Will. Prayer, for example. But here and now, on this silly little tower, it's just Will. Will by itself."

"Er—the top's hidden in cloud, I see."

"Yes. Make it cold up there."

"Well, thank you very much I'm sure. Now . . ."

"Very cold indeed. I tell you what——" I felt myself shudder. An awful clarity was coming. "This Will thing. Let's put it to the test. How about that?"

"W——"

"*You* follow me up the tower. How about it? Do the climb with me?"

"I'm sorry."

Sym had him by the arm now. "Put it to the test. Why not?"

Paul did something with his camera. The Announcer's face was worth the trouble. Several people peppered him with flashbulbs even though he was being telecast and the notices said flashes were forbidden. He tried to laugh it off.

"No, no—I'm sorry, but——"

"You wouldn't be the first, you know." Sym was hynotically persuasive, his face the still centre of a whirlpool of storm. No, he wouldn't be the first. Swale, even Swale was drawn forward; and Paul with the leer sucked away. "And you won't be the last. There'll be plenty of other people here."

He took hold of the loudspeaker microphone as if all the others were redundant and said, "I'll take anyone who wants to come up that tower with me. This is an appeal to

136

all men of good will." His voice in the loudspeakers came with a great hollowness, and the vibration of dust in the dark acres of mind. " Such men need only keep close behind me. They will have nothing . . ."

The Announcer plucked at him, mottled with light.

"Don't interrupt. All right, *switch* me off ! *These* are the people I'm talking to. A private demonstration of the Conquest of Fear. *You* may be afraid. These people aren't ! "

I was so appalled, so drawn in, that I ignored the crowd altogether. A murmur came from them. His voice, leaping from wires, had taken effect. I heard it wheel and bristle, spiky under thunder. A line of birds came off from the hedges.

"Jesus Christ," said the Man from *Movietone*.

" All over England," said Paul. He passed something else into his camera, and caught Sym from underneath with much more nose than was godly. I was being jostled.

When a crowd gets ugly it gets ugly. And when it gets enthusiastic that's very ugly indeed. It was hard bones that struck me. I was being jostled even though I was on the calm side of the fence.

I leant back on the sharpness of my elbows, shoving against blows or stumblings. There was a silence. I became aware of a silence. It went on. The echoing voices had stopped; there had been a breakdown, someone had trampled a wire. Paul said something, his face full of importance, arch. But it was too late to stop them; there was only the pressure of Sym looking out on them, and I heard the voiceless shuffle of their feet as they leant back, swayed on ranks of joined hands, tried to hold themselves in.

No murmur this time, no shout, a great surge forward, the screens and fences straining, stirring, the stakes going, and the Announcer saying nothing audible, the microphone dead or the loudspeaker dead, Philips climbing quickly on top of a truck, a white canvas latrine falling over like a pack of cards, mercifully no queen or joker installed, Dultie undecided on his clear patch of grass, Paul with his camera raking the sheep-faces, the murmuring eyes, the ruminations. The Announcer talking his bland silent talk into the fireside, deprecating, smirking, one of the cameras doing a slow traverse of the base of the tower, the other a vertical sweep, someone a long way away in a glass box picking what he wants—as if anyone could still want the Announcer's face or Sym's, professional's or prig's, the crowd raving. Ericson was mouthing, tipping me a signal, and Sym was saying words I couldn't hear.

But the crowd could hear. The crowd hears most when it most hears nothing.

They roared at him, brandishing hands. They snatched him a cheer.

They surged forward, bursting a snag of wire.

Paul, with head down, his eye in a lens of ecstasy, caught them as they sundered it, caught them tossing the stakes in the air as they came, caught them dragging the whole tackle down like string; he got the whole yapping pack of them.

There goes my job!

A riot at a *Post* function, organised by B. B. Swale. A riot moreover that was happening quite simply and suddenly as riots do. Not a special riot, not a *Post* riot. They were even cheerful about it. News should take itself seriously.

They came round the truck in a wave of hands; Lord Dultie sank in them, they snatched like elephants' trunks at the shocked buns of faces; they beseeched Sym down into their fingers, they wanted to chair him, to have him upborne to the tower. Dultie came out of them, rejected, almost unharmed, except for his pride. No, he was smiling. He still had his ears and his flybuttons. He struggled through a

138

cluster of girls impressed by his shaving-lotion. He walked
away from them, smiling from among his popularity. The
cluster growing around Sym pushed Dultie outwards from
the centres of his importance. He stood beyond the sphere
of his influence, nudged to the periphery by a thousand
backsides.

Sym stood above them and laughed meanwhile, the
Announcer still pecking beside him. They paused, undecided. I waited for the real trouble. After all, a crowd does
what it wants to its heroes; the bobby-soxing factory-girls
have off the pop-singer's bollocks for souvenirs, which
accounts for the pop-singers, and likewise Sym could go
down in their sharp wail of love and flounder up naked,
dressed only in his popularity and scratched in a rash of
crosses.

His laugh stopped them.

They paused, agonised with proximity, so he laughed
again. They laughed back, and seizing his chance he waved
them on. It was magnificent timing. He waved them on
towards the tower—without him. They hesitated for a
moment, and then some broke away in the direction he
was pointing. They cheered in acknowledgement, surging
about him, and then they all poured on, their shout going
up and echoing from the thunderclouds, their cries bouncing thin and tinny from its base. . . .

Incredible—here was a man who could talk into the deaf-
ness of a crowd with his hands, the leprosy of his scars as
influential as a policeman's gloves.

"Here goes your story, chum. He won't get up the beanstalk now!" Paul's face was wry and empty, his camera
full.

They were at the perimeter fence of the installation by
now, bulging it in a long, slow beat. According to publicity,
the fence was hooked concrete post and twenty-four strands

of long-barbed wire, and I could hear the shrieks as they fanged themselves on it, dervishly, twenty-four briars for a tall man and uneven luck for a woman. They wailed on its wall of nails. But the fence suffered too. In the manner of crowds, the second rank were determined the first rank should have it down, and pushed, pushed, pushed. The twenty-second rank as well.

"I must get close," said Paul. He disappeared, smug and empty, into a fog of cries. The vans covered with crosses moved closer, too.

Dultie had disappeared. No, here he was in his car, alone and safe on a sea of abandoned mud. To my horror he was happy. Naïve in his way, he was unused to seeing life actually happen; he probably thought it enjoyed this pain and that the flesh being laddered on the wire was the usual jolly romp of Soccer Saturday. There were screams out front. The respectable part of my story was bleeding to death. What did Dultie care?

More to the point, where was Philips?

I was just beginning to register that Dultie wasn't alone in his happiness, that his windscreen was full of hair and the colour of corn, when Ericson hazed into me, sloshing on mud. "Do something," he said. He sounded cross, I wasn't listening entirely, I was pondering Dultie, I was fed up with Swale making things happen for Ericson who pretended to Dultie that our connection with Death was all a lie a lie a lie. I was watching the Announcer, who was wildly dishevelled but compelled by the needs of the hour to go on talking. A scream is news, if the screen can catch it escaping. Who had been roughing him up?

The camera came off him and a pair of technicians dragged at him and damaged his collar. A put-up job. Damage to Announcer at riot. Deliberate destruction of Swale's reputation: we can't get close enough to show you the corpses but meanwhile here is your own Smooth-Boy, frayed but keeping abreast of the fray.

He struggled with his technicians. This was a chance for them to be rough; the backroom boys always object to the front. One of them clubbed him, seeking to hand him a shiner in the Name of Art. He clubbed back, and the cameras got him. Obviously another friend! Boy David, leading the riot in ten million homes.

"Do something," said Ericson.

A car revved behind me and splashed me with the hard mud of chalk, whale's teeth and flints. The crowd wasn't through the wire yet. I turned and saw Philips crouched at the wheel of a Baby Morris, glued in the mud. He revved up again, and his back wheel came sliding towards us, his front in deep. Before we could dodge, he stuck in a rut and stalled.

"Half a mo!" I called, giving him my winning smile, my cheeks beaten flat by the rain. "Half a mo! I'll fix you in a minute." I leant over his front wheel. He mouthed gibberish through a windscreen of mud-drops and steam, the heavens coming down sharply now.

"You bloody fool!" screamed Ericson. "That's Philips. Away to do the dirt on us—and all you do is push."

I wouldn't mind doing the dirt on you, loud-mouth, from a great height. How is the crowd doing?

"That's right," I said, and the tyre cap came away in my fingers. Philip's front wheel evaporated in smoke, frenchchalk from inside, and his spokes hissed down into slime. I I looked at him questioningly. He was still gibbering. Mirculous sabotage—he hadn't heard it go. I went round the bonnet to explode the other side.

"Never mind that," screamed Ericson. "They're on the bloody wire!"

I looked. The fence still stood, and the riot was definitely calmer. Unless we had to compensate any local lads for losing their codpieces on the barbs we were fine. Except for the lacerated busts being conveyed under red crosses to the nearest cottage hospital. "It'll hold," I said.

Ericson blew air at me and dragged me by the elbow. "Christ," he yelled. "You're paid to be observant!" He pointed behind me. "That *wire*!"

One of the support cables came to anchor two hundred yards behind us. It rose up away from its hook, up into the static, like a white strand of light.

It was swarming with people. I gasped. The whole cable was abounce. It sagged, festooned with climbers, at least a hundred feet into the air.

"If this goes on," Ericson bawled, "they'll have the whole bloody tower over."

I hated this power—it was like Billy Graham only worse—but seeing it work always turned me to water.

Paul came past chortling, at the double.

Movietone moved up. Philips stepped out into the mud. "You lousy——"

"Well, I tried," I said.

Lightning. A long chain of fire between us and that cable, and the rain came after it like the whiplash of an electric shock, white, booming molten light, a huge rain full up with lead shot and bearings that bounced its balls back as high as the crotch. The sort of rain that springs up skirts with a scream, covered in whitewash.

The riot died in that opening of water.

Ahead, the long row of God-reaching monkeys slid back down the greased wire, some falling off, but no one from far: they wouldn't harm on the sogged earth.

The Announcer postured beneath an umbrella.

"Find out how many people are hurt!" barked Ericson. A voice spoke under my arm. It was Dultie, from the

142

lowered window of his car. His chauffeur had driven it can-
nily and kept away from the mire. "Good show, so far," he
said. "Good show. Marvellous work. I'm afraid I must be
off. Keep at it." With a wave he brought up the window,
or pressed a button to bring it up. Or simply willed it. It
obliterated itself in steam.

"Reprieved," Ericson snarled, then smiled anxiously at
the misted window.

The Rolls rolled away. "Jammy bastard," muttered Paul.

The Rolls veered suddenly, lurched, and sank into slime
like a tank, throwing up soupy spray. It came to a stop, nose
down.

"Hell's bells and Hall's balls!" Ericson said. We started
to run. "Cancel my last words!" Then, "Jesus!"

Sym from the platform, I had forgotten Sym, he was only
the catalyst of this catastrophe, not a vulnerable atom, Sym
was down and past us and running lithely to the door of
the car. Even as we hurried forward, he had it open with a
wrench of his fingers, and here was Dultie out in the rain,
dragged out by the hand, rain all over his Savile Row suit,
being grasped by a fistful of chalk.

We crowded round. It was agony. We were ready to lay
down our cloaks.

"No," Lord D. was saying, "no, I'm sorry. No. No. No."

"Do stay," I heard. "Stay with us all and feel the force
of this moment."

"Sorry, old chap. I positively can't!" And Dultie was
back in his car, tapping his chauffeur's neck with an im-
perious fist, or tickling the chauffeur's glass with a knuckle.
Somehow Dultie had a girl in with him too, one of those
who had followed him through the crowd. No wonder he
was in a hurry. She was anxiously beautiful.

The door slammed and the car revved deeper into the
clay.

"Have it your own way," Sym muttered.

Lord D. looked up in gratified astonishment, as if he could hear through all that glass: he seemed pierced and pleased at the centre of his diamond. Then his head jerked, and his stuck car lurched and went forwards. We stood and watched it move miraculously on, helped by a wave of Sym's hand. It still bore half of the landscape on its nose and it tossed up a bow-wave of water that obliterated hedges, animals, bicycles, other cars and people.

"Lucky he was here," said Ericson.

"Why?" said Paul, who had photographed it all, from handshake on, for his own private collection. "Why ever not?"

"It'll keep The Rag quiet," Ericson explained. "He and its chairman are muckers."

I realised that he had not been talking of Sym at all.

Then he looked tough. Ericson had unbent far enough. "Get this thing going," he said. He turned morosely away, the rain falling onto his sour worried face, which is the face of great newspapermen the whole world over. Because they are sour worried men.

Paul, drunk with lightning, took a flashbulb of his retreating hunched back. "Just for me . . ." He stopped. Sym was coming back to us.

Paul, a new flash in his bowl, hit him with light, but as the light struck so did thunder. He fitted another and fired and had thunder again.

"How about bending some of this lightning into a halo?" he asked Sym. "So I can take a real photograph."

Sym ignored him. "Time I go up," he said.

I pointed to a bedraggled knot of onlookers, still round the fence. The rain only added importance to the occasion for them. "They think you're already up there," I said.

The big spokes shimmered above us, needling the cloud.

144

"Perhaps I am. In a sense."

"In what sense?" I growled. I looked about me for blood, blood from the rush of feet, blood from the sharp fence. He was always blood for me. Cobbles and windows and swords.

"No one was badly hurt," he said.

"Reading my mind, eh?"

"It's not hard. You've been drinking."

True. "Well?"

"In the sense that they think I am."

"How about overtaking their jolly old expectancy, then?" said Paul. His camera pushed its nose out of its covers like a wet dog. Its muzzle beaked at us, sniffing our secrets.

"I'm doing this for *you*. Remember?"

"That's right. You're wonderful. Go on being wonderful for five minutes longer. More—have a drink!" I offered him the generosity of my hip. My breath was already holy with it.

He looked at me, then turned away through knots of people. They patted him on the back. He went through a gate in the wire manned by two men in macs. He went through puddles on mud and through pools on tarmac, watched by the bulbs and lenses, the celluloid winding at his back and the lightning flashing. He went straight to a corner of trellis, seemed to pause in distant disgust, put his hand to its knobs and bolts, and then went up into the collapsing rain, monkeywalking higher and higher like an Arab up a tree, like a speeded-up sloth, going up and up into those fireladen drops, their torturing hammer on his still bare head, the whole ladder aglow with St. Elmo's fire, his hands stitched by rain, his body shaking sometimes then stiffened to fend off the wind's pluck, he went up ill-shod and unprepared, his rope-soled shoes were still in my pocket, and disappeared into sinking cloud.

145

Quite a lot could be made of it with a camera; and the zoom-lenses on the television would be making it now—the last dangle of legs through the broth of smoke.

He was gone.

Paul patted his camera. "Perhaps his wings will come out on the negative."

It was limiting to have my intuitions derided by Paul. I didn't answer.

"Or his diamond-studded halo?"

I had a drink. Then I realised I was forgetting myself, and passed him my well-licked flask.

Paul sighed into it and we waited for time to come down, while the rain ticked in our skulls and the crowd, feeling wet and stupid, began to disperse.

V

MOST papers were front-page but hostile. We were front-page sympathetic, of course, and *The Times* didn't mention it at all—in short, it was a major journalistic success.

"Not bad," said Ericson, about eleven the next morning, fresh from Dultie. "Not bad at all. Only for Christsake let's stop being official. Don't let's do any more promoting. At least, that's what Dultie thinks. 'We're a newspaper,' he says."

"He thinks that, does he?"

"He says . . ."

"I mean he thinks we're a newspaper?"

Ericson's face became drawn and hurt. He was a hardbitten newspaper man and he liked to pretend it was a hardboiled newspaper he was running.

"What about the *Express*?" I said. "And the *Mirror*?

146

Aren't *they* newspapers? Don't they promote things—sports, and exhibitions, and competitions, with their names all over them?" What about The Rag, I might have added, but it was a painful subject at *The Post*.

"Exactly," he moaned. "Sod-all they leave us. Even if we had the money."

"They got the money by using their imagination," I said. "Our bit of imagination was this." I pointed downwards. "They left us this." I tapped Sym's face on the front page. "Don't let's make a cock of it."

"That's it," he said. "I've been having some research done." He opened Metson's *Architecture of Greater London* as if he had discovered a new translation of the Bible. I didn't tell him that I had first seen Sym climbing above an open page of that book; there wasn't time. "Now what I suggest . . ."

"You'll have to save it," I said. "He's gone away."

I was glad he didn't argue. A week ago he would have said Sym wasn't a big enough story to go away. Now he knew differently. Sym couldn't be remade or rewritten. He either was or he wasn't. Well, he had gone away. "What am I going to say, upstairs?" he asked, after a pause. Yesterday's gesture with banners had crumbled.

I went to his wall-copy of the *Britannica*, still smelling raw and unopened. Never was so much print bought by so many people and read by so few. "He said he wants to do this," I said.

I pulled down one of the middle volumes, turned over the toilet leaves and opened a glossy illustration. Then I laid it on his desk. "This, and this only."

Ericson didn't say anything for a long time. Then he asked. "That's what he said?"

I nodded. If I expected to see rivulets of sweat on his face I was mistaken. My own palms ran. But he was a newspaperman, as I've said before. And when someone tells a newspaperman that the President of the U.S.A. has been got with child by Cleopatra's Needle he doesn't have time to disbelieve it—he's too busy trying to persuade Cleopatra's Needle to write an exclusive, and then phoning up to discover what the President's going to call the baby.

"It would be another promotion," he said quickly.

"Yes."

"He'll kill himself, of course."

I didn't answer.

"That's if he even tries."

"He'll try," I said. "That's all he's ever been after."

Very slowly Ericson tore the photograph from the book. I watched him ease the one smooth page out of his otherwise unopened fifty guineas. "I'll take this to Dultie," he said. "He thinks better in pictures." He nodded at the shelf, and I put the book back, minus its moulted leaf. Our little talk was over.

I went out feeling dry and uneasy, leaving him looking down sadly at a torn-out photograph of Manhattan. I had known for ages, and of course Sym would fall.

VI

IT would all take time, of course. Weeks and then months, and then never. Meanwhile how could I live?

I thought about this in the corridor, but not very hard. I didn't need Manhattan. I didn't need Sym any more—not as a story. Once *The Post* had tied up with *him*, so many calls from cranks had come pouring in I felt I should never need a story again. That's how I'd found Milocz.

I thought about him now. He was still alive after five

weeks, so it was time he became worth more than a half-column and pictures. We hadn't bought him any insurance either: he was a Pole. "I've got a wife and daughters," he said. "Don't worry," I answered. "If anything goes wrong, I'll see they're taken care of." Would I? It depended. All the while he did statischute jumps from suspension bridges, who would insure him?

I reached my office. It had a chair I hadn't sat on and a desk I hadn't used. It had been mine for a week. Let me keep it. In theory, there was far more sensation in Milocz than in Sym. Only, his face wasn't a sympathetic story. It is hard to feel involved in the heroism of an ape.

On the unused desk was an unused phone. I picked it up and dialled him.

"Have you had any ideas lately? " I asked.

He sounded excited. "There's the Continent." He said, "Cuntinent."

"That's true. There *is* the Continent. It's been there all the time. Very expensive, too. The return fare to Paris, for example, for you, me, and a photographer. Hotel charges ditto." I didn't add that there were the Agencies, and that our English competitors could obtain a whole story through them as fast as we got it ourselves, and that the American and Continental papers would get it as a World Story if it was a World Story, and we'd lose any chance of agenting the English photographs abroad. It's best not to tell a dedicated man like a Pole that you have rivals; he might go to them. Or that you have business-interests. He might become business-like.

"You haven't heard the half of it," he said. "Not the huff."

"It's the whole of a bad story," I said. "The Eiffel Tower has been tried before. A Frenchman with artificial wings. Ten seconds later he had real wings and a hundred-watt halo. Anyway there can't be that many sensational buildings. Take away Pisa and Paris, and what's left? " Sym had told me this. "Stick to the English bridges. Someone will build a new one, soon." What about Tower Bridge? It was always news. Even with a shortened line he'd hit the road underneath, though.

"I was thinking of the Coible Railways," he said.

I caught my breath and listened.

"I could jump with a normal parachute. It would be a big thing—a free fall. It would take a lot of courage. Some of those coibles . . ."

"Wait a minute. I'll get some shorthand plugged in."

He went rambling on. In the end I felt sorry for the typist. "The Cable Railways. Now that is a new idea," I said. "That is a *news* idea."

There was a sudden silence. His modesty gloated at me.

Very firmly I said: "There's a new Cable Railway in Scotland." Then I rang off.

Before I picked up the phone to discuss it with Ericson there was a knock at the door.

Incredible. I have been in a new room alone for five minutes and somebody knocks at my door. It justified the faith in me. Swale needed an office.

"Come in."

It was a face I hadn't seen for several months, not since the Senate House, or the party the day after, to be exact.

"You remember me," he said.

"Of course," I said. "You are the Man with the Lamp."

"I thought not. The name's Bunch. I believe I mentioned it at the time."

I wrote it down on a piece of paper. One day, when I wrote my memoirs, I should be able to write "Bunch" instead of "the Man with the Lamp". Or perhaps I should give them numbers, a serial for the doers and a serial for the parasites. What was I?

"I expect you wonder why I've come," he said at length.

"I am the Press," I said. "I never wonder. I observe."

He grunted.

"Seen Sym today?" I asked.

He laughed derisively.

"So you haven't."

"Ask me some more," he said. "Ask me if I even care where he is. It's well known I worship the bugger." He tried to look dramatic and important, but I didn't encourage him. "He's got so bloody big-headed it isn't true—did you see that Chalk Hills thing? I've been a hanger-on with that lot for too bloody long. That's why I've given up."

"A great loss," I said. "You mean you don't climb any more? You've quit buildings, I mean? And all the little girls?"

"No—I got fed up with Sym. That's all. Used to mean something once—till the Press came in."

"Not entirely uninvited."

"Look at that Gaveston's write-up! Did you do it?"

"It wrote itself."

"Huh. Most of your pieces do, I suppose."

"I still haven't asked you why you came," I said. "I'm a journalist, remember? But my time is running short."

He looked at me contemptuously. He could smell how new I was in that office. His face was twitching with rage.

"Tell you what," I said. "I'm still not asking you, but if you're that jealous there's always St. Paul's. Sym won't do it. He won't climb Sir Christopher."

"He hasn't the guts."

"Well, you know about these things. I don't."

"What I came to say was there are plenty of us who could knock off buildings for you. We could keep your paper full of news."

"Not news," I said. "Not any more. Papers like variety. So do people. And they make up most of our readership, people do. Them and a few worms and crows as we blow away in the Park."

"People like skill," he said.

"You probably know about these things too," I said. "I'm just an observer, and I'm just observing that St. Paul's is still a story. A jerry on St. Paul's now—just right for the evening paper. Ornamental crested, for the sake of the long-sighted royalists."

"I'll think about it. Meanwhile, what about something difficult?"

"How difficult? The Vickers Building? The New Shell Tower? The Knightsbridge Development, when it's done?"

"Balls," he said.

"That's what I thought," I said. "That's Sym's class, though, and you'd better realise it before you make any more cracks about him."

He got up, looking pained.

As I held the door open, I said, "Don't turn your back on Sir Christopher!"

If he bit, it wouldn't even be worth half a column, but I didn't tell him that. Somehow I had to justify my continued existence on the paper, at a star salary. A column of crankery was becoming a part of our image. I also had to justify this room and this bottle and the absence of Sym and the errors bound to come. I started by looking up the train-times to Scotland. Then I remembered the food they served, and thought about a plane instead.

VII

MILOCZ was grumbling when we climbed into the cable-car and I was frightened someone would hear him. The operator stood nearby, and so did the ticket-collector. It was a proper car, not a ski-lift; but with six people on board the cable was creaking. The wind tapped the cradle.

"Why all this bleeding secrecy?" he mouthed. Ten words of English and six of them swear-words! The other passengers, a man with two girls, didn't notice, loudly. Then one of the girls looked amused at the sharp noise of Paul scratching his sock. The man disapproved, with his nostrils.

"Why couldn't you get permissions properly? I'm an artist."

You're an artist, loudmouth. In a minute you'll be painting the hills with your bad red blood. Red madder. Because a permission means being accused of promotion, means no secrecy, means no story. Do you think *The Post*, Lord Dultie, Ericson, the shareholders, are putting up all these pounds just for nothing?

"I tried to get permission. They said no, so we're being furtive." His harness was under his coat, his 'chute in an old leather grip. "Sly's the word," I cautioned, under my breath.

All which pounds? The operator moved out of earshot, to the corner of the winch-shed. The collector rolled tickets. Too many tickets on a roll; he was rolling bankruptcy. No one wanted this sort of comfort on a Cairngorm, especially now the ski-lift was working. The ticket-collector moved away. I relaxed. The other cameramen were posted.

The voice blew breath at me, heating my face. "Why not go to the Alps like I said?" There was garlic in my nostrils.

153

"A parachute won't photograph against all that snow."

Paul sighed at the lie. His fingers found his sock again.

Milocz said, "But I would. I would. I would dangle against it. Just hanging in space."

Hanging is too good for you.

"Or I could have a black parachute. It could be done. My wife has got something very similar."

The car moved into space without anyone telling us it was going to happen. I had left my gut behind, too. Even for Milocz I could be scared in this instant of moving. Or was my anxiety only Swale the Man suffering for Swale the Impresario? We went jerkily, and I worried for the three of us. I didn't want him flicked into space, before space was ready. And I refrained from looking down at it: I felt sure there wouldn't be enough.

The man nudged and the girls giggled. They clutched at one another. Milocz forgot his wife and daughters and leered. He breathed quickly, from fear, but they weren't to know this, and his rhythm was carnal.

We came over a lip of the Grampians a hundred feet below us, and then started to slide slowly across a deepening valley. There were no jolts now we had the full tension of the cable. The other car, coming in the reverse direction on the return-cable, glinted silver above us. I looked down on deer, miles below, with the sunshine prickling on their antlers.

"When the cars pass," I said to Milocz.

"Allkay," he said, his eyes still prodding a girl.

There was a movie-camera in the other car.

Milocz took his coat off and I undid the zip of the grip. I hooked the parachute onto his two belly-clips. The girls became startled. "Six hundred feet," I said, looking down. A movie: there might be some money in Milocz in the end. This was a *real* story. In the daylight.

154

Paul wound the window open, and Milocz stood up and eased himself through. The car canted and the suspension-wheel gave a fraying whine as the weight tilted. We hung on the thread of that whine.

The man jumped to his feet and we swayed further.

"What on *earth* does he think he's doing? "

"Committing suicide," I said.

Milocz was beyond voices: he was hanging outside in the slipstream like a pot-bellied monkey, his hands clenched to the sill, his toes to the aluminium, his body sliding on the varnish of the air. His deaf face turned to us with compressed eyes.

Deers, antlers, boulders, in the depths below him, rags of mist, a crag going past his shoulders.

The return-line was vibrating, sagging nearly to the same vee as ours.

"Jump!"

The girl nearest to him screamed, he put a big hairy hand back inside and tore off her brooch, and then he was gone into space, in a twiddle of artificial diamonds. There was a great jeer of triumph as he fell, the crag belled it back at us, while her scream tinkled against the rocks and went on echoing. We approached the sound of falling water.

I sat in a moment of complete shock.

All this time Paul had taken photographs from a big camera hidden under his coat, and now hooked up from his navel to under his chin. He caught the cubism of Milocz's head, the fantasy of his disappearance, and the faces of the man and girls, before and after.

The girl had stopped screaming, and the other one kept on looking amused as if she didn't believe what was happening, as if this were a dream in which a hand of cloud had dipped in through the window and snatched her friend's brooch, and as if Milocz had stepped gallantly outside to retrieve it.

"Do something," the girl was saying to the man. "Do something. I want it back."

The man was peering timidly down through the fangs of loose crags; meanwhile the great tumbled screes of the lip were coming towards us, and more falling water, and suddenly we were above them, over it, and nearly home.

At this he stood up again and said brightly, "It's all right. He had a parachute!"

So it had opened. I hadn't looked.

I had been too bloody shocked altogether.

I had watched, as he jumped, the other cable-car come past completely empty—*where were the cameramen?*—and realised that we didn't have a shot of him going down; Paul had been too busy with his entrance into space, and the mirrored horror in the vacuum faces, and there'd been no time for me to do a thing. Milocz would be annoyed, Ericson would be absolutely beserk, and I was worried about what had gone wrong. Besides, movies meant money.

We drifted to the platform, lifting noisily onto skids. We stepped out onto wooden slats into a brittleness as if the frozen air were snapping below us. We tested our feet on a piled stone eminence, a mountain-top, bald, an altitude of eggshells. One of the girls snatched at Paul angrily, demanding something. He shrugged with his elbows, and his shrug was almost an assault.

By the winding-shed stood my two photographers, a cable attendant, a policeman in an Aberdeen hat, and Philips looking oily with height.

"Tut, tut, tut," he said. "This was something I had to put paid to. You're contravening all sorts of laws and bye-laws, you know."

How did the bugger know we were here?

"You'll muck up a *Post* story once too often," I said.

"Read about it tomorrow," he said. "I'm giving you an exclusive coverage—they may even arrest you."

The Policeman took his notebook out. I saw the fivers standing up from his pocket. Paul took a flash. The Policeman looked uncertain, then buttoned up his flap.

Philips grinned at me. "Quite the big noise now." He hadn't noticed the photogenic fivers.

Paul said to him, "There's six hundred feet of space under your right heel."

Philips still smiled, but he moved. He was less than he was before the glass cut him down.

The Policeman had put his notebook away. We were winning.

I heard a cry in the valley. Milocz was hooting from the crumbled stones. We moved towards the edge.

Below us there was a familiar figure. It was Cullen. I saw the bump of his camera. A faint bird noise rose from among the rocks. He was whistling. He had snapped our story, and the Rag would be able to publish the lot.

"You made a mess of that one," said Ericson on the phone.

"It made a mess of itself. I can't help it if the Pole starts shooting his mouth to other papers. I'll find some other crank."

"Stick to one at a time. Any news of Sym?"

"No."

He didn't press the question. I fancied things weren't going well with Manhattan.

"What about putting me on something steady," I asked.

"You've got an office," he growled. "Haven't you? Well *use* it, Swale. You won't get anything steadier than that."

I put the phone down and wished Sym *were* back. Till he was, I wondered who I could get to help me.

VIII

"This is by way of a celebration," I said. "And a most belated thanks. But what with one thing and another. . . ." I moved round the table and poured some wine into Barney's glass. Looking down at him, I noticed a tiny bald spot in his brilliantined hair, and was amused by it. We were at my place this time, so when I sat down again there was no mirror to distract me. My curtains were drawn.

He was grinning at me. "I daresay you've got some other motive," he said. "But before you disillusion me by asking me a favour let me congratulate you on the excellence of your copy, Bertie. Have they pinned a medal on you yet?"

"I've been wounded often enough. All they've done is put me in an office, a new office."

"I thought people didn't have offices at newspapers. I mean, except for directors and . . ."

"Exactly," I said. "How well you express it! I nearly proposed marriage on the strength of this office. A man with an office, I thought . . . but she was more dubious. And she was right to be dubious. Do you know what I saw painted on the door of my office this morning?" I sipped my wine. Wine always strikes me as a soft drink to give anyone. No wonder he was suspicious.

"You are starting to disillusion me, Bertie. I said you would."

"*Outside Enquiries*, that's what I saw painted on the door of my bloody office. Do you know, it's not my bloody office at all—it never has been my bloody office. They just

158

didn't want Swale in the Newsroom, and they happened to have an office waiting for a signwriter, so hey presto . . ."

"You shouldn't have such bad habits, Bertie. Sure it didn't say 'Out*size* Enquiries'? In that case it's probably *your* office after all. So you reckon this Sym thing was your swan-song? "

"I do so truly reckon, so help me God."

"I liked your copy, anyway. It beat me three years ago and it beats me now just how a bloody old God-hater like you can see so much religious significance in the world."

"Find me an ad-man who believes in detergent," I said. "Oh, I can write the stuff, all right. I had a woman fall in love with my holy journalism once. Or at least, she thought that since I wrote about God so well, my Godliness must be redeemable."

"And? "

I avoided his glance for a moment, ashamed of myself for mentioning her. The bed by the curtains held another memory now.

"Oh—she committed suicide," I said. "She was holier than you are, Barney, too. She really was."

"But I don't love you, Bertie. I really don't."

"So anyway," I said, "that's where *you* come in. I want your advice. You can see my conundrum in a nutshell. *The Post* is pretty stunt-conscious just now, and all the while there are stunts in the news, it will let Bertie write them. Just supposing *they're* good enough, *I'm* there first, sober enough. . . . In short, Barney: life isn't easy. Sym has only got one more stunt in him, and it's going to cost *The Post* a hell of a lot of money for him to do it. So we wait. While we wait, I am largely unemployed. Ergo, I am redundant. There is only Milocz. Or at least, he's the only one who looks like staying close enough to death to be news-worthy."

" So? "

" And Milocz is strictly limited. So far all I seem to do is to go to endless trouble just to give Philips a story. Philips doesn't have to worry: *he's* got *me*." I tapped my head. " All I've got is what's in here, Barney."

" You're overstating your case, cock. You've got nothing in there at all. Better tell me what you want of me."

" I want a percentage risk on a bloody impossible idea," I said. " So I can take it to Ericson."

He looked at me. " You mean you want me to say that something lethal is in fact as easy as easy? "—

I nodded.

" What? "

I told him.

" He won't open his parachute, Bertie. He just won't open it. Jesus, *you've* got the background to know that. All he'll open will be his head." He stood up, and as he did so I found myself wondering whether he really cared, or whether he was just paying me back for my treatment of him last time. " It was a nice meal, and I'd do it if I could. But you can't make gold out of death."

" What about Judas? " I asked. " He was one of your boys, and he managed."

He grinned. " He didn't show a long-term trading profit, did he? Besides, you're too fat. You're not a bad bloke when you lay off the bottle and stop kicking the Bible around. You cast yourself for all of the wrong parts, cock. Why don't you sod all this and take up teaching? "

" Not you," I said. " Not another one."

He paused at the door. " Or why not the Church? "

That, coming from Barney, was a compliment, even though it was probably the most insulting thing anyone has ever said to me.

" After all," he added. " You've got the necessary hypocrisy of mind. It's just a question of applying it in a constructive direction."

I laughed so long when he had gone that I shall never despise wine again. Then I picked up the telephone. My resolution had lasted just seventeen days, but I know when I've come to the end of something.

Her voice sounded as it always sounded. It didn't sound as if it had been waiting seventeen days for the phone to ring.

"Will you marry me?" I said.

Perhaps she gasped. I'm not sure. My ears were hot with wine. "I'll think about it," she said. "If you'll promise me to chuck the whole lot in like I said. Promise me?"

"I'll think about it."

"Honestly?" She sounded eager. She was much too eager; she was giving herself away. I felt able to put the phone down almost at once. She was still speaking, but I wasn't going to be bullied. I turned back to the table and began to fold the tablecloth. Then the phone rang.

I wasn't surprised: a woman had just been cut off in the middle of something that was important to her. "Hallo," I said.

It was Barney, sounding contrite from a phone-box. Give them time, I thought, when I got over my disappointment at hearing his voice. Any true Christian will betray a principle sooner than a friend, or what do they think Christ was for?

"This thing means a lot to you, Bertie, doesn't it?"

"It means my career. But let's not attach too much importance to that."

"I mean this Miraclejack thing." His voice was impatient. "I told you I would have nothing to do with Milocz. I've been thinking some more."

"Oh! . . . Well, save it, Barney. It's the cold air."

"I wasn't lying when I said I thought you'd done some excellent reporting. But I meant to have a word about your last couple of pieces . . ."

"*Please*, Molsom. I'm practically engaged!"

"You know what I'm talking about. You want to be careful, or you'll muck the whole thing up. This isn't one of your old stories, you know. I don't care who he prays to, or what he believes . . . *Don't* goo him up with all this biblical symbolism. I'm not sure whether it's bad journalism or just plain nasty."

"Just plain nasty."

"Don't try to bring God up to date, Bertie. It won't wash. He's outside time."

"I know," I said. "Every time one of your crew tries, I realise what a bloody anachronism he is. Take the New English Bible. No, don't bother: you're too drunk anyway. Not that it's likely to intoxicate you further. It's only lemonade literature, compared with the original."

"Look, Bertie; you don't believe in anything, so you don't see when you're poaching. Even allowing for that, you must understand that the symbolism appropriate to. . . ."

I didn't hear the rest of his argument. On an impulse I put the phone down for a second and pulled back a curtain. There was no Sym, though, no Madman—even though her memory had prompted me. Just a little gush of flame a damp smoke: the meths-drinkers were dining early. I picked up the telephone again and gazing down into the darkness I said, "Suppose he's real, this Comfort of yours—and I will suppose it for a second, because it's getting late. Suppose the first four Godspreaders are telling the truth. Suppose he comes again—and it's all in the Book there, isn't it, that he will? Suppose he comes again and manages to avoid being certified as a lunatic at the instigation of his Bishops, his Archpricks, and his Popes and his Cardinals.

162

... Well then, what will he *do*? Not get himself *crucified*, anyway. What a paltry bloody gesture *that* always was ... and he's going to find it hard to outbid Hiroshima and Belsen this time, isn't he? God so loved the world that He gave His Only Begotten Son to come and suffer a little less than the least of the suffering? Oh no, Barney. I'll tell you what he'll have to do. He'll have to do something bloody meaningless and then gather all meanings into it."

He snorted. "Like climbing up a steeple?"

"If you like." One day I would show Barney this cellar-wall, and ask him what he made of *that*. "Prophets were fashionable in those days," I said. "Next time he'll be a Sportsman. I'm not sure he didn't try it before. Look at Spartacus!"

"Balls. This one'll have to start gathering his followers fast, won't he? He's only got you, so far."

"It took a few centuries of lies the last time."

"Anyway, the bloke's mad. Stark raving crackers. You've said so yourself."

"That's right. So would the Bishops. People had a greater respect for insanity a couple of thousand years ago. So've I!" So did *she* have, I might have added. Instead I said, "We're drunk, Molsom. And I'm more used to it than you are." I rang off then. It was a futile little game to be playing with words, like any religious argument. Yes, the Word was sacred, all right. It created what It expressed. But how would it set about expressing those methylated hoboes down in the pit?

Then it struck me that we'd been keeping Mavis off the line. She'd be waiting to call me back. I poured out a whisky, and sipped it slowly. It tasted horrible after wine. But the phone didn't ring. She hadn't been waiting after all.

Suppose he came back as a tiddley-wink player? Surely the tiddley-winkers would know?

IX

EVERYONE knows Helvellyn. It was designed by God in the Year Nought and landed on by an aeroplane in Nineteen Twenty Six. Either episode would have been a reasonable story for Swale of *The Post.*

I stood on its bald top with Milocz in Nineteen Sixty Three. I was surrounded by a small band of helpers. There was also a crowd. Many people climb Helvellyn in a day, of course; but not this many. The story had trickled out in advance. It was a leaky Pole, and it had leaked twice. I nearly called it off now, but I was always scared Milocz would lynch me.

Watched by the rabble, Paul sat clicking his shutter at sheep; Milocz stood swearing coldly, looking round him for somewhere to pee. There were too many people, and his impatience was increased by the noise of rocks making spatial water around us. He hopped from leg to leg. " When do we go? " he said. He jiggled. He joggled.

The air came into us sharply, full up with icicles and Cumbrian dust. The chasm vorted below. The two edges, Swirrell and Striding, writhed away from us like a giant's thighs seen from his pinnacle. They wallowed in hairy mist. The tarn, straight down under our feet, or nearly straight, was a deep pool of tar, a bruised death by drowning, five hundred feet below at the foot of time.

" Smells right again," said Paul. " Promise crammed."

" I'll need my best rural style."

" An ordinary Obituary would do quite as well."

He was right. The parachute wouldn't open. I had hoped Milocz would see that. Half-hoped. Even an idiot would have said " no "—an idiot with any life force in him, any

164

buds opening, any flowers coming out, any girls walking in his abdomen. Not he. He "thought it over". What with? His great big beating pride?

"Jesus Cripes," he said, his face blue with courage. "When—do—we—go?"

Barney Molsom, wearied to disgust, came and stood near me. He'd got himself mixed up in it, in spite of himself. I think Ericson thought his presence would make it safer. That's what comes of being an expert. I didn't mind: as I've said before, he could climb. So once more *The Post* was assembled at death. A happy band of brothers.

"Ready when you are," he said to me. Then, in a whisper, "I hope your conscience is clear."

"Ssh," I said. Was it disgust? Go down on your bones, Milocz, slip out of God, go down on your bones and break them to bits. I'll look after your wife for you. I'll do absolutely damn all for her. It will still be looking after her better than you did.

"If he hurts himself I'll heave you over too. So help me, Swale."

"Preferable to the sack." I glanced quickly beside me, but Milocz's eyes were blank with the black hills and his ears were full of hairy wax. "I'm a careerist. That gives me a different ethic. We all know that."

"This had better be good."

"Ready?" I asked.

But Milocz was gone. A murmur of amusement from the crowd signified his presence. There he was, making masculine water by a cairn of stone. By continental standards he was doing it decently, too. He had his parachute on, and a striped balaclava helmet.

He came back shaking and grimacing, and now we were ready to go. Paul framed him lovingly. The air grew thin.

The run was marked out. Elsewhere the crowd pressed

forward. Barney held a wind-vane aloft, testing for maximum velocity.

I looked at Milocz.

Milocz.

Vladimir Stanislawski Crum. Where was Sym?

He wasn't the right type for a hero, either. An indestructible ape, man's lower half: even his patched parachuting trousers, so famous to sensational photographers, gave him a baboon's backside.

The crowd took on the stillness of utter death.

"How—much—bleeding—longer?" Destiny chattered at us.

"Building-up now," chanted Barney. "Building-up, building-up, building-up." The wind-vane hummed.

The crowd sensed expertness, mystery, preparation.

Philips appeared. As I'd feared.

Well, Milocz was great good news for someone.

"Nearly at maximum," said Barney, suddenly anxious.

"Go," I said, full of dry saliva.

No one moved.

"Go!" I said, moister, and got the word out: an empty echo on the high hills.

Milocz grunted, as if unable to believe his good luck, contorted himself, and came up to our place on the lip at a frenzied run. He was counting in Polish, gibberish, something, and one step from the end he pulled at the ripcord—where was the snatch of the wind?—and jumped.

Where was the snatch of the wind? Where was the flash of silk?

I had a moment's picture of him sitting in space on nothing, in the parachutist's ridiculous exit posture—and then he was gone. As he went, he half twisted, yelling something.

Then there was the fog rising off the face, a crash of

stone below the lip, a long sliding. No chute drifted out and over towards the tarn. I just heard a long flood of rubble rolling, rubble, rocks, loose soil, scree, and tired stones, the endless snapping of shins.

Objects hit the unseen near rim of the water in distant echoes of sadness; how long it takes to fall, to roll and bounce down five hundred feet, thirty-seconds, a minute of jarring bone.

Barney sat leaning over space.

Paul turned his camera onto the crowd, who were suddenly murmurous.

I looked down, right down.

There was nothing to see; the slope was convex and it was impossible to know for more than thirty feet, and anyway the mist blew again.

Nothing except my shoes, planted on firm ground and wanting to come back from the edge of air.

Poor bloody Milocz.

Did I mean it? Yes, I meant it. I could always mean it afterwards.

The crowd pressed.

Poor bloody fool.

Paul finished with his camera. "Not to alarm them, but he's lying down there. Do you see? Left of that big stone."

A shape broken on a ledge.

Only someone had seen. So, pressing forwards, had Philips. He looked yellow, never a good man at disasters, even when they weren't his own.

A shape among a ledge of scampering sheep. Some paused one side, some the other. None of them would cross over, such was their fear of death. The sheep broke finally away on either side, leaving Milocz to the bald mountain.

A shape at which we looked.

There was a murmur of disgust. I noticed that our cine-camera stopped turning.

"Bloody *Post*. Bloody rag," I heard.

"Bloody murderers."

They could wash their hands in a word:

"All right," I said. "*The Post* has the best possible rescue team. Already assembled."

"That's principally you, Barney!" said Paul.

"All ready!" I said.

They would wait and see. They were silent again.

Barney, looking sick with contempt, got his rope fixed to a memorial stone on the summit. He backed to the edge of the cliff, looping the rope through his crotch for an abseil. Our other hangers-on fussed the rope. As I said, it was a team.

Someone I recognised as Cullen, Philips' pal with the lens, stepped forward and snapped Barney, "Well, well, well," he said to me. "*The Post* rescue team. This *is* news!"

Barney went over the lip. There was too much wind for him to be steady, and he was white-faced. There were wave-caps on the tarn, five hundred feet below him. He still looked sick.

A boulder went from under him. It wasn't a free abseil, and the face was rotten. His boulder started a small avalanche, an unpleasant moment, although there was only a corpse underneath. Smirking a little, Cullen got this too.

Give me a spectacular death. Just Milocz, nothing more than that, looked smashed but photogenic.

"Where's your camera, Barney?" called Philips. It was a nasty dig to offer a rescue-party.

Better, curse the bloody man, give me a spectacular life: Milocz, a compound fracture of the thigh and, say, a broken jaw or shoulder—they both photograph well. Let him be dragged up the face like a sack of mutton. Hero on a Crane. Christ pulled out of the Concrete.

I knew quite certainly now that it hadn't been a good idea. A man falling into space is a good photograph. But a man leaping out into nowhere, after a brisk run, and then plummetting out of sight in a ridiculous, stiff, constipated posture, is just a visual laugh. Like a Chaplin film.

Sod it.

Where was Barney? Somewhere unseen below me. The rope slackened.

Philips was standing too near to my elbow. "You boys got him well and truly belayed?" he asked, kindly. To my helpers.

They nodded.

Before I could stop him he whipped Barney's abseil off and dropped it over the edge. It left him safe enough, but helpless. There was a shout from below, as the rope fell. There are some very unscrupulous men in the profession.

He moved to the lip with Cullen to photograph the floundering.

The crowd grew intent now. I took a couple of shots myself. This was ordinary stuff, but visually it made the best of a bad job. It had photographic dignity: a crowd waiting for disaster on a hilltop.

They started to laugh.

Cullen exploded into his shutter. Philips' shoulders were shaking.

I stepped back to the edge.

Barney's rope went into space. Beyond that, nothing.

I moved to the left, nearer the crowd.

A hand, a hump, a backside hunching behind a bump that led to nothing.

Milocz was crawling up the face. He paused in full view. He wasn't even injured. He was making a farce of it. Not injured? There was more yet. Cullen clicked another and said, "Beautiful!"

Milocz was the original gargoyle. He had one black eye, soot black, with a perfect ring of bruise like a monocle; a red tulip of blood and snot dangling at his nostril; grass in his hair. His clothes hung off him in nasty pieces.

When he got near I could hear one of his teeth rattle against its neighbours as he breathed, still joined to his head by a piece of skin.

He swore. And he was funny, in spite of the loose tooth and the tulip.

Heroes don't behave that way.

We dropped him some rope and he nearly strangled himself in it.

We hauled in, jeered at by Philips.

We got him up, flashed by Cullen.

Then Barney arrived, flashed by Cullen again.

"My abseil," he said.

"Philips," I answered. Milocz was a lesser worry at present. Philips grinned.

Barney hit him, and somebody else moved out from under cover and flashed him doing it. The crowd moved in.

"They've got photographs," I said.

Barney took Cullen by the ears and tore them till he screamed. He bore down on his camera till it came off its strap, then tossed it towards the tarn, still bristling below us.

Somebody snapped him doing it.

Then Milocz got the idea and hit Philips a dung-fetcher, straight in the epigastrium.

He was snapped doing it.

Barney caught hold of the snapper.

"All right," said Philips. "I've still got my film." Cullen patted his pocket.

The crowd joined in, mainly against us.

Philips and his friend snapped this. Barney had Cullen on his back.

Milocz started to hit the crowd.

Philips and his friend. . . . But it couldn't go on for ever. We couldn't stay brawling among the windy sheep and the stones: we would have been happier in a sewer.

We took hold of Milocz and pushed our way through and looked for the path off the mountain. We had to drag him some of the way, followed by jeering cries. Sometimes, when a band of rock hid us from view, I hit him once or twice myself. He was too worked up to notice. We came gnashing down among the bracken.

"You were fine," I said to him, padding down grass to the Inn.

He expanded his chest, but his ribs were hurting.

He lost his tooth in a glass. There was blood in his first half pint.

A grubby postcard in my pocket said:

Why America? There's so much here and further South. I may be going down into Italy, and then up those new stone cities of the mind. Or I may. . . .

I touched it and paid for our beer, beneath a contemptuous mountain.

X

ERICSON was contemptuous too. He pushed The Rag at me. I knew what was in it, but I had to read it again as part of the medicine. As I knew only too well, Philips had gone to town. All over the front of it, there were pictures of us scrapping.

Inside, under the headline *Lame Bird Or Spitting Duck?*, was Milocz dribbling blood. *Cheap Exploitation Of Comic Opera Adventurer.*

"We should know better," said Ericson. "It says so here." He tapped Philips, in block letters.

"We do," I said. "All the time. That's why we're so bloody dull."

He ignored me. "What about this?——— 'Inadequate rescue arrangements . . . misled and generally maldirected by Mr Barney Molsom, whose chief qualification for leading a mountain-rescue operation resides in the fact that as a pilot he once flew over Mt. Everest.'"

"It's quite good," I said. "I like 'maldirected'."

He didn't answer. There was no need. He was going to freeze me out, and he had enough character. He was prickly with rage and there were raw places under his skin.

"Well?"

"Not very."

"Explain."

"It went that way."

"Well."

Then I was tired with the old crab. "So either I am sacked or I'm not."

He looked at me, as if I were tightening a screw on my own thumb and it was his will that I did so. Then he lit a pipe. I knew what it meant. A pipe meant that the blowing-up was over but that something was going to be discussed. My future.

"Balls," he said. "To tell the truth, when I first read *that* lot, I did think of recommending you for our paper in Iceland." He blew smoke, while I considered the niceties of my position. "But I wouldn't give The Rag that sort of satisfaction. So you're not sacked yet."

"No?"

"Not quite."

"Then there's always Manhattan."

"I wouldn't press that, Swale. I'm not."

"Why?"

"Dultie didn't think the time was ripe." He looked at me pityingly. "Would you say it is any riper?"

A girl came in with some ticker-tapes and put them in front of him.

"We've had enough stunts," he said.

She was riper. She paused, realised he wasn't talking to her, and went out.

He poked at the tapes, some of them still unmounted. I should soon be going back to the Dog Column.

Then he stiffened.

"You'd better belt down and write a story," he said.

"What for, Emperor?—the Woman's Page?"

"The front bloody page—we're empty tonight. Empty. Botch this up how you will, but get it written."

"Why don't I just resign?" I said. "I'll know where I am. That's what I am anyway. Resigned."

"No," he said. "Fool. If you were a newspaper-man you would have seen this before coming in." He pointed to a mounted ticker. "You would have known your bloody miracle-man has just climbed the effing Eiffel Tower."

Protests hung out of me. The Eiffel Tower! Who cared? I'd suggested it to him once myself, but it was a story which needed handling.

"The Eiffel Bloody Tower!"

"Don't start to tell me it's simple," he bawled. "Don't tell me it's not news. It's just created a sensation in Paris! News is what people think. Not what you make." One in the eye for Swale.

"And what about The Rag?" I asked. There was a catch somewhere.

173

"They wouldn't have the nerve to put it on their front page after all they've done to knock it down."

"It's been done before," I said. "They'll do it all right."

"If they do—and I don't think they will—I'll write a leader myself and knock them for two-faced bastards."

If you can still spell.

As if anyone'll care, I thought. The New Stone Cities of the Mind and he shins up a piece of tasteless tin.

XI

THE look of the front restored me: Sym standing tall and black, tapering down to the ankles; the Tower standing tall and shot through with light, tapering up to the top. *The MiracleJack Takes France.* A few choice words of Swale to prop up the eyes. Other on-the-spot reports inside, mostly re-written by Swale, the wog-words locked behind my best brass bars.

I got in at eleven forty-five, nearly opened a bottle, but ran a deep bath instead. I still had Helvellyn mud on my knees. There was always a future to fuddle in. Not now.

I sat swathed in ribbons of steam: me, Maggot, the Man-Mountain, as I sat on my glorious past, my medals a-dangle. The phone rang.

I stepped out onto skates of water. After all, it might be Mavis calling.

I walked into the lounge, leaving tiny glass puddles and panes, past Mavis, who had somehow got in and who was sitting on her fortune in my best easy chair. She was bound to come and see me sometime. All my ghosts have their keys.

I picked up the phone and ignored her.

"I've been thinking," Bunch's voice said. "I'll have a crack at St. Paul's. In the morning, if you're interested."

"What time?" Was I interested? A column could still twist a knife in The Rag. It was *The Post* that climbed, not Bunch.

The news-value was nil, but every time someone went up a wall, *The Post* cocked its fingers at Philips.

"About five?"

Sym would be on the newstands by then, but I didn't want to discourage him.

"At five in the morning, then. I'll make some arrangements."

I put down the phone. What a waste of sleep! As if The Rag's rag could ever be got.

Mavis was watching me. "Five o'clock! We can't possibly get up for that."

I looked at her coldly. "Oh yes I can," I said. "In fact, I doubt if I'll go to bed. There's too much to do."

I shivered suddenly. She was probably wondering why she had come back. Then she picked up the paper.

I didn't move towards her. Swale, the colossus encrusted in bath-salts, could do nothing with lust. There was too much death on his mind. I found myself some clothes, not pyjamas. As I reknotted my tie she put down her paper and stood up and kissed me.

"How often do you think of her now?" she said.

"Almost completely never." I lied.

"You're not coming to bed?"

"No, I'm not coming to bed."

"I'll stay and cook breakfast, just the same."

I tried to tell myself it didn't make any difference, but it did. It always did. That was love, I supposed. The voice from the Bush that said under my shirt and trousers I was naked

175

man, the miracle. Even me. But it needed the voice and the desert.

XII

HE was waiting for us, shivering.

If ever a man had doom written all over him, it was Bunch. His face had the loose look that comes with fear: it was flabby and unfeatured, and his breath smelled of emptiness.

"Here we are," I said cheerfully. I tasted my early morning egg. She had had no time to be elaborate: we had gone to bed after all.

Paul took a quick look around for policemen and then exploded a couple of flashbulbs at him. There was no thunder this time, only Bunch wincing. All for a few inches of newsprint.

"Tighter-lipped, please."

"Don't worry about me." His lips stilled themselves numbly against his teeth in a grimace of bravery. "People climb St. Paul's every bloody night of the year, nearly. It's a regular climb. You lot don't get to know about everything." His face loosened once more.

"We're learning all the time," said Paul. He was waiting for another flabby smile. The cabbage-head rots on its skeleton.

Still no police.

"Call it off, if you like," I offered. God, I hoped not. Mavis would kill me.

"Like hell. My girl's watching." He nodded towards a doorway, in the direction of Ludgate Circus, with terror-stricken eyes.

"Take her with you," I suggested. It was a nasty crack in the circumstances.

Paul took one of the doorway, and then walked over to her with quiet callousness. His flash exploded against the wall, bright shocks of yellow in the silver moistness of early morning.

Still no policeman.

He came back to us, whistling A woman waits for me.

A long way down, trying doors, I saw a blue figure. Bunch saw him too, his eyes hypnotic with hope.

"Well," I began. . . .

The air leaked out between Bunch's teeth and the blue figure turned down an alley towards Carter Lane and the river.

"What are we waiting for?" said Bunch. His voice was empty of air. His girl fidgeted in the near distance.

I looked up. "Which route, anyway?"

"Any bloody route!" His despair was absolute. He chewed upwards. Surely any route wasn't the answer. Some were more impossible than others.

We went up the steps devoutly, as to worship.

There was a sweaty little second at the top, when Bunch revealed himself in pullover, track-trousers, and plimsoles. Then he started to struggle up against the first big blocks.

Anyone can do it. Anyone can scrabble up that sort of wall, with luck and fingers and friction, and get up six inches or six feet, muscling up without breath, and clinging to joins and fractures. Anyone, after a time, can fall off. And fall off safely if it is only six feet.

At six feet Bunch fell.

There was a scream from the doorway, as he rolled, hurting his shoulder. I looked at him, willing him to give up. Sym had class; Milocz had courage; and Bunch, like Swale, had neither.

"Call it a day," said Paul. "I've got some pictures."

"I can call it a brave attempt," I said.

"My girl won't. She thinks Sym's wonderful." He went back to the wall, mean and determined now, and bad-tempered. Suddenly he was very brave and deliberate with anger.

He had sixty feet to go to the first overhang. He went quickly, going up with the tired eyes of London on his back.

It is true I hadn't actually *seen* Sym climb, except on Gaveston's, and that time in the cellar, but Bunch *looked* vulnerable. A man can look vulnerable on rock, of course, as I well knew; yet although this business is harder, I still felt Bunch looked more unstable than he should. He looked an amateur. As I must have looked, even with Sym to help me, and the moral support of a rope caught over projections.

Bunch hesitated, back on his heels with his belly away from the stone, in a good climbing position for a change. Evidently he had found a hold good enough to relax on.

Paul's bulbs lit the wall. His face was like wet rubber. Even Paul was suffering.

Bunch moved upwards again. Climbing slippery, among vertical columns, he got up to that first overhang, and crouched below it. How high? Seventy feet? I heard his breath now, thrown back at us by the angle of the cornice. It was harsh and dry. A car came past.

Somebody started to run up the steps behind us. It was his girl, her shoes throwing high-heeled echoes off the buildings on either side. Another car; nobody noticing.

"Eric!" she shouted, and her voice was a ridiculous voice for a man to want to impress. "Eric—come down. I believe you."

Her words flew away over London.

What she didn't know was that for Bunch there was no way down. He wasn't Sym or a cat-burglar. He was hoping to get over the top and in by a gallery window, or an inspection-hatch on the roof, or even be rescued by a fireman. He had said fireman to me earlier. I knew where the phone-box was. Firemen didn't matter to Bunch. It was going up that counted. Who was I to blame him? We all have women who want us to get up somewhere.

He tried for the cornice. It would have wanted guts by any standard. Even on a rockface as second man on a rope. Seventy feet and then those tall steps.

"Eric!"

"Shut-up," hissed Paul.

Her voice flew its echoes again, and one seemed to strike Bunch from high up. He half-turned to it, seeming to wonder from what corner of Heaven the canned voice of his girl had come from, and as he turned, in the tightness under the ledge, in the slime of the birds, he came off.

As people do, he fell off suddenly and cleanly. There was no scrabble; he was coming straight down at us, turning onto his back.

His yellow face, still somersaulting, swung over into the flash of a bulb as Paul clicked the uplifted camera automatically, and for a fragment of time the surge of the light seemed to buoy him up as it pressed against him, but it was an illusion and he fell through it and into us, the girl grabbed backwards by me, Paul jumping, no one trying to break his fall, all too fast, and he went limp arm then face-first onto the stone.

The girl ran. She didn't look or cry. She didn't say anything. She ran. She had left her face for the paper but she ran.

Bunch lay piled into himself on a step, the blood coming through his mouth quickly and freely, and through his ears slowly. He had fallen with the sort of straight stone smash that is without alteration.

"You'd better take your camera and hop it," I said to Paul. Looking white, he did.

The blood reached the bottom of the steps just in time for the first policeman.

XIII

NEWSPAPERS and policemen understand one another. They are not interested in cities of the mind, neither of them are. They both know they live in cities with hollowed-out steps, sad stone steps going down into the bowels of time, where old men toddle to lean and undo their flies.

Where Swale would toddle and lean, when all this was over, and be sick and be sick and be sick.

It was hours before they let me go home, but they had to let me as soon as *The Post* sent its part-time Legal Department round for me, its one-man solicitor.

We stood outside the Police Station together, under its numb blue lamp.

"Come and have a drink," he said. "You look as if you need one."

"No thanks. I had one yesterday."

There was a silence empty of compassion.

After he left me, shuffling off with his smug legal disapproval, I went and had one just the same. In fact, I had several in one of those city pubs that still smell of the Plague and where pale men with buboes hawk bile on the floor. But I wasn't drunk.

I didn't think I was. I should have gone and found Mavis.

Instead I got onto an Underground Train and got off it

180

almost instantly afterwards in a near suburb. The afternoon was blonde and empty, the Spring without leaf.

I started to walk. It was a story for the evening papers, not Swale. Paul would have taken care of it at breakfast time.

Reasoning this brought my mind in focus. There were men mumbling from pubs. I tried a Saloon Door. It was bolted from the inside.

The mind became sharp as its bolts went home. I tried walking. I must go back to her.

I passed a Church; High Anglican, very High, with the sun twinkling on its top bits. Repair was going on. There were workmen up there, dropping spanners, their words falling down as well, their footsteps twanging on the high scaffolding.

A steeple. Sym had been a steeplejack.

Scaffolding. Sym had been a spiderman. But don't let me make anything of it.

There were no immediate graves, but it didn't need graves to remind me that Bunch was a corpse. Who knows—I might come to face with Christ in here and be able to spit in his eye.

What I had in mind was Confessions, with the workmen padding between me and God, high overhead in their rope-soled bumpers. Outside, I had heard their nasty words, thinner with height, their laughter rocking the scaffolding as they leant on their mirth.

Inside I heard nothing. There were no footsteps to come closer.

Confessions. I liked this place.

They had a little box.

I sat in the box. After a time there was movement.

There was a hole in the box as big as a head. I only saw the ear, like a wax fruit surrounded by hair. It looked

181

like all the unpleasant things I have ever seen in my life.

"What do I say?" I said.

"Whatever you have got to say."

"Yes—that's what I mean: I don't know the drill."

The ear disappeared and an eye looked at me.

"Are you a member of this Congregation?"

"No," I said.

"Are you a member of the Anglican Communion?"

"No—not exactly."

"Then I'm afraid I can't help you. It wouldn't be significant."

"But I want to confess something."

"I'm afraid you can't. You're not resident in this Parish even?"

"No."

"Come to the Service tonight and then I'll see you on Thursday."

"No."

"Well, then there's not much I can do, is there?"

"I've just killed a man."

The eye came closer, another bubo. "I don't believe you."

I didn't say anything. The eye became frightened, withdrew into darkness, which was its courage. The voice cleared its throat.

"You'll have to take the proper steps, of course."

"I'm not legally culpable. Only morally."

"Ah, morally." It thought about the word. "Will a prayer do?"

"In a sense, not even morally, not even morally, not for this man. It's the others, the ones I didn't kill, who now lie dead in him."

"A very difficult proposition." The voice sounded thoroughly alarmed. "But if you think a prayer will be helpful."

"Yes." Then I saw I was being watched by the eye, not listened at by the ear. So I nodded.

"We must go to the side-Chapel. I don't want to turn anyone away without a prayer. Not anyone."

We each left his hole, he to come round to me, I as he thought to follow him to his chapel. Or should I go back into the sunlight? *Will a prayer do?* These people are paid to hear me say I killed Bunch, and in him might have killed Milocz, he's got a wife and kids, he was a fornicating God-fearing man and now I've killed him. He's a smear on a step, on a roadway, under a suspension-bridge, under Helvellyn, under St. Paul's, with a layer of sand on top of him. He's a bad smell of blood in a tight wooden box. Although dead he is still alive with the black eye where I tried to kill him last time. This time, although alive he is quite quite dead, front-page news, on paper only, with a multiple-fracture of his split personality. I have his blood on my handkerchief. It is brown blood. I have also blown my nose on it. It is the image I wipe off the mask of Sym, one of the million Syms, on the way to die in Manhattan.

Only Sym will not die.

Standing here, in this waiting Church, I remember. Dultie is impressed with the Eiffel Tower so much that he is also impressed with Manhattan. In fact St. Everlasting Sym has taken himself altogether out of Swale's management. And Swale in turn has been promoted. He no longer needs to think.

Where is the bugger gone? The Chapel, if this is the Chapel, is empty. My first resolve was for sunlight, the umbilicus of piety.

In its first thread, just inside the porch, I came face to face with a statue of Milocz, a cherubic gargoyle. His nose was bulbous in marble; he had dimples and wings and a residual testicle, an indecent image smothered in stone.

183

Archangel Milocz, on a plinth of choristers, rubbing soot from his crenelated crotch.

I was laughing as I stood outside. I paused by the scaffolding.

I shook the scaffolding with my hand.

A face looked over, upside down, like a dark sunspot fixed in the sun. I closed my eyes to a filter.

A great spider of tubes in silhouette, giving birth to a man's head. I looked downwards.

A white, three dimensional lens of spit smashed on my cheek, my coat, my thumb.

When I glanced up again, having wiped it off, the head was vibrating with laughter. It thought it was a Joke it had spat on, not a tragedy.

Somebody took hold of me by the shoulder.

" Are you the bloke who's been pestering the parson? "

I hadn't heard footsteps. They must have come by grass and gravestones, not gravel.

It is surprising how sober the police make me. They both wore flat hats, which meant they were from a motor-car.

" Why don't you answer, chum? "

" A bit doolally? Look—he's been dribbling on himself."

" Please," I said. " I've just had a bad shock."

" What kind of shock? "

What kind?

" Lost your money? Your wife? Your train? "

They laughed. If I wasn't careful they would lock me up and feed me boiled beef and carrots until I looked like Milocz or—worse—like the angel.

" I just saw a man fall off a Cathedral," I said.

" Too bad. I hope he could fly."

" It's in the evening papers," I snarled.

" It was on the News," said the holy voice behind me, sounding interested. He had come out to admire his betrayal.

"Well, let's all go and buy a paper, anyway; *and* make a call to Division."

We started to move.

"Sorry a prayer was too much for you," I said.

We kept on moving. They moving, I being moved.

"These gentlemen are very kindly going to see you home," he called after me.

"God bless!" I said.

We got into the car, and they called up their wireless. The car's callsign was "Whisky Two", which was intriguing. In its way, I suppose even that was a sign.

After a lot of talk to-and-fro, with words coming back to them, unlike Prayer, one of them put up his headset and said, "All right. You did see a man fall off a Cathedral."

"Well?"

"We could charge you with being drunk."

"Don't be silly."

"Want to bet?"

"Not really."

"No?—so we'll drive you home instead. But with D.T.'s like yours you're a sitting duck for someone." He laughed. "For a minute I thought you were doolally. Like I said."

I relaxed and the car accelerated away from the church with the broken steeple. Even drink made me more respectable than some things.

XIV

AT home, I filled up my glass. I knew the extent of my problem. I wanted a bottle, five-foot-four, thirty-six, twenty-four, thirty-five. A full bottle dressed in a flowered nylon petticoat and maidenform bra.

A bottle. Because you can't talk to a woman as you lie in her arms.

Or, if you do, without her purifying you in the holiness (her image) of her tears. Tasting, as always, of salt. They're always too close to awe, the human feminines. That's why God allowed himself to be born from one, instead of from a volcano or a male chimpanzee—which would have convinced even Swale.

I picked up the phone and dialled Morpath, The One Minute Prayer. I knew it was bogus as I did it; I knew it wasn't Christ but Creeping Jesus I was getting, the codpiece in gold, the holy smile on its clerical platter, but I dialled his number. Give me the Oracle, who speaks the voice of gingivitis, gonorrhea, and catarrh, I said.

A long burp down the line like a pigeon cooing.

Not a dove?

The Oracle was engaged. He might have had a word for Brother Bertram.

And Sym had gone humbly away and climbed up his Eiffel without me. While the monster had been moaning with Mavis on a couch of snow.

I dialled again. "It's me," I said. But I got nothing. Just a funny note, number discontinued. He couldn't stand living in her room any more. . . . When they cut off your telephone you are truly dead.

My finger moved out again. I prodded my living ghost. I heard her voice catch on the wire.

"Are you there? Darling, you're not . . . ? " all the sharpness gone.

Silence. The Oracle and the Ear listened to each other.

"Please. Who *is* that? "

She had connected her phone to a silence, as I had so often without even lifting it.

A gasp, almost of fear.

"Still me," I said. And she put down the phone. I heard it go empty.

I pushed it back onto its cradle and picked up a bottle with a round-robin label. I dialled her number on the label; she would be on the way over now, drawn by love and curiosity. Resist it. I can resist it with the mind. It's the body won't let me. I poured a half-tumblerful of her voice. Give it up, Swale. Forget broken Bunch. There are fat worms of gin devouring you even now as you walk doolally in your vertical coffin. Give them a little little drink and they'll leave you a little little flesh on your cut-glass bones. . . .

Let me lie on her outstretched body like a holy skyline. . . .

But if I let them eat the painful flesh off those pure bones, let the fire's tongue nibble unassuaged, I should lie in my vertical coffin a skeleton of light and be crept into by Christ the Spiderman. Climbed up in all my hungry crevices.

A tinkering cymbal.

The phone. It was the real phone ringing. I lifted it, the tumbler still untasted.

A girl's voice, I could give up all of my vices for some of their voices, said: "Mr. Swale?"

"Speaking."

"Half-a-moment, sir. I'm putting a call through for you now."

"Who from?"

"From me." It was Ericson. "Where the hell have you been all day?"

"In hell. Is there a law against it?"

"Forget it. If you're drunk, forget it. You sound horrible. And if there are any mice and elephants with you forget them."

"It's the worms. Indiarubber worms." If only I could lie with a corpse I could get rid of them, like exchanging fleas.

187

"Forget them too. So he fell on his head. Well, somebody had to. There's no summons pending, and even if there were, *The Post* wouldn't care."

I pushed the bottle away and the glass away in stone cold anger. Let the white slimy danglers, the gin-nibblers under my bones, devour me with their foreskins. Let them. "Listen," I said. "If you don't care, and Dultie doesn't care, about Bunch dying, I mean, I'm all right, am I? If the police don't care, that is?"

"They don't care. That's it: you're all right."

"What about me caring, for Christsake? Don't I matter? What do you think I've been doing all day? I'll tell you what I've been doing. I've been fucking caring, that's what."

"Well, you're a fucking fool, then."

If I could have leant on him I should have cried.

"Now get down here at once. Dultie wants you at five about that American thing. And listen—no cock-ups. If you've got the bugs, have a little drink, right now. Just a *little* one. And if you've got the drunks see you call in to a good chemist on the way here. Only for Christsake don't go up smelling of peppermint—he loathes it."

I didn't answer.

"Understand?"

"Oh, of course," I said. Smashed boy, smashed Bunch, half-smashed Milocz. Yes, I understood who the smashed ones were; I had all their faces sorted out in my head. I was back in my glass of calm; I could even tell the living from the statues. All I had to trade-in now were the ones who remained to be smashed. Those and the white worms eating my foot.

Mavis was waiting by my elbow when I put the phone down. Yes, I had the bugs, but I didn't take a drink, not even a little one.

188

"Oh, Jesus," she said. "Not again! I thought you were ill."

"So I am. But it'll only be an hour. It's Dultie—he never keeps anybody long. Not even Royalty."

She didn't believe me, but it was true. Even when he went to bed with a blonde he set a cooking-timer so he'd know when she was done.

I looked at her face. Sometime recently she had been crying. So I kissed her.

"Cheer up," I said. "I'll be back in an hour. Or under. If only I were a few years older I'd marry you."

"You crook," she said.

Not a very original thing to say. But then there's nothing very original left to be said by anyone, not anymore. I touched her hand. Even crooks are important to somebody.

XV

THE biggest crook I knew of was Lord Dultie, the proprietor. If I worked on bigger newspapers I could have known of bigger crooks still; but perhaps they would have been above sending for me. Not that I cared, as I rode up on the personal lift to the flat above Ericson's; myself and a lift girl, and my box of thirsty bugs; the worms were only as tall as grass, I would tread them down. Why should I care for any bugger who didn't live in the paper but only dropped in to smoke a cigar? He didn't even tup the typists here; he had no personal contact with *The Post* at all; except when he touched it with the tip of his pride. But Swale would be obsequious, just the same. Especially this moment, as he half-rose, pretending to meet me, and I came from the lift-gate, leaving my coffin behind me.

"You sent for me, sir?"

"I had you sent for," he said, "in order to discuss this American thing. What are your views?"

Be careful, Ericson had said.

"My views are these," he said. "This American thing is very important."

"Yes, sir." I took out my little notebook, the interdepartmental one, and wrote, my eyes shimmering: "*Lord Dultie thinks the American thing is . . .*"

"And we don't want a cock-up."

"No, sir." I wrote: "*Important.*"

"We don't want a cock-up at all. A lot of the paper's money is involved; we want the publicity; we want the advertising; we want a good story."

"Yes, sir. We don't want a cock-up."

He winced at my vulgarity. "Who's looking after things?"

"Er—I am, at present."

"Good man, good man, that's the spirit. You mean you're looking after things personally?"

"Yes, sir. I'm attending to everything."

"Well, I think it's worth leaving your other projects to your staff for the moment. Concentrate on this."

"I will indeed, sir."

"Well, bye bye then. Nice of you to give up time. That other chap who's waiting—what's his name?—Swale—was he responsible for Milocz?"

"Er, yes, sir; partly."

"And this morning cock-up as well. Nasty. I don't like back-biting at my level. It was a vulgar story. They got it back at me." He shot me a piercing glance. "Were *you* anything to do with it?"

"Only indirectly, sir."

"Yes? Well, you had plenty on your plate, no doubt. Get

190

rid of Swale, though. Let him go to one of those vulgar papers like *The Express*."

If *The Express* will employ me, I'll go. It's time I worked for a real newspaper. But they won't.

"Meanwhile, you go on looking after the America business. Keep this man off the women: we don't want him losing his head for heights."

"Yes, sir. I don't think he does."

"The spinal fluids are terribly important."

"Yes, sir."

"I've got some advertising requests here, and that's where the big money will be, of course. Look through and see what offers most, as a reciprocal thing of course. Will it pay to have him shin up a skyscraper or two with 'Oxo' on his backside, for instance?"

That was a joke, I thought. I laughed. Then the worms got me and I said, "I don't think he does, sir."

"What?"

"Put oxo on his backside."

"Don't answer now. Think about it. Take all this away and implement what you think fit."

"Thank you, sir. I'll do that."

On the way across the room I noticed the clock. It was just six minutes further on than it was when I had come in. The dial was writhing, and sections of them fell off as it ticked.

Outside I bumped into Ericson, waiting. The Editor did not like the Swales and Dogsbodies of this world keeping him waiting. As he went past me I heard Lord Dultie's greeting. "Come in," he said starkly. "I rather want a word with you." I stepped back into my worms in the hissing lift.

There was a phone call for me. I took it where it was, at

a switchboard, the wires wriggling my gaze. I kept on en-
countering her face, with its grave, dead eyes.

It was Him.

"How are you?" he said.

"Keeping."

"And are things going on all right?"

"Yes," I said. The wires were just wires now, the eyes
only marks on the wall. "Things are going on all right."

"I thought they would be. That's why I'm back."

How the hell did he know? Or feel he knew?

"That was bad news this morning about Bunch," I said.

But he had already rung off, or been rung off by one of
those pippers. Or perhaps I had knocked out a lead. Anyway
his voice was gone.

So were *they*. So was she. That's all I need, just something to hold on to and they don't come up to drink anymore. Even Bunch didn't come up, not much, with his
bellyful of writhers. He had died a whole ten hours ago.
His black name in print the phone-girl was reading was an
old, old headline. Which is all that believing in something
ever does for anyone. It helps you believe you are no longer
a shit, but of course you are. You are Morpath squared.

Discovering Sym again was quite different. But that's
what they all say, don't they?

I might just make it back to Mavis inside an hour, if the
tube was right. On the way, I started to wonder how Sym
would come into Manhattan. By first-class cabin? Or by
plane? He wouldn't be walking on the water; that much
was certain.

XVI

I LIFTED my head and looked over the sill, past the black branch and down into the bomb-site. The evening was almost dark outside the window, and the reflection of my electric-fire made a sunset through which it was impossible to see anything.

I lowered my head again, and the cat purred wickedly behind me, a broken-backed Siamese purr like a woman coming. Oh no, Sambo.

No interest: a nakedness too cool to the fingertips, parted thighs too relaxed to be inviting. Total consent. That was what marriage would be like, a corpse exchanging worms in the arms of Death.

"Tired, darling?" Sympathetic corpse. I didn't want to answer her. I longed for a final purity. A luminous jigsaw. Interlocking skeletons. Instead there was the bush cooling and her approaching anger.

I must forget all my other corpses and bring this one to life. My left hand put two inquisitive walking fingers on her ankle. She smiled. The fingers walked to her knee, and she twisted at their too-ticklish touch. I climbed upwards, and she was the ruined skyline beside me. She frowned a little as they scrambled off her thigh onto her hip, because until that moment her face had been set in anticipation, walking up the marble with those fingers. I shuffled up her stomach and clambered across her breast into the hot hollow of her neck, and there was a pulse in it. I went up across her chin, her cheek, her sloping forehead, and then off the top of her, my hand going limp into the white cloud of pillow and tangling in her smoking hair. "The Colossus of Rhodes," I muttered, still thinking of Sym.

She smiled. I was glad of that. God is a woman, I had said in reply.

Then I thought of my loose skin, my old body with the cuts in it, of her one-time disgust which might be now, and I was filled with an enormous defensive compassion; and those worms of my self-disgust—might she not find them in me? . . .

I leant from the bed and turned off the fire, and the darkness sank upon us, swallowing the red glow of her body, crumbling her bronze silhouette into old old age. And what was I crumbled into as she last looked at me? I pulled the blanket round us and kissed her, and she touched me with her fingers, and the cat purred again in the corner, and it was the whole evening purring, passion remade from the dark, as it was for Adam when his side still ached and he knew it was his own pride he kissed, blind, blind, Adam. . . . he lay close to worms in his garden, but holy ones sweet under grass. . . . And, further from Adam?

The historical climbs are all finished now, I go back in my dreams, there's nothing to be got from a pyramid, Mavis, a sexless breast in the sand, and what is this Sphynx in the Hanging Gardens? . . . a snotty-nosed little camel-scarer or the last lust of Antiquity. . . . Mavis? The Colossus of Rhodes! Sometimes in my dreams I fancy it's still standing . . . it's like Gulliver being lifted into the hands of his giant, or Man the Flea climbing God. God was a woman, I said. To come between Man and the worms in the grass. I climb up to Heaven, away from the worms in the grass.

I do a girdle-traverse round his left knee-cap, dislodging the mating seabirds, I brush their slime with the grit of their fingertips, and then inch by inch I edge by pure friction up inside of the stone thigh, sea-moss, sea-fern, ten limpet fingers, ten crab toes, five coarse thumbs, my teeth clenched on fine cliff grass . . . and then swing myself . . .

a breathtaking moment . . . as I hang free . . . and then I sit there, looking down, getting my breath back, the waves turning like mirrors, the day flashing . . . and—*what—do—Eye—*SEE?

The kitten calling, the old woman with the girl's voice, *Crucify me*, old men in methylated spirits, the cat playing ball with the birds in the burning trees, the brick wall like lines of newsprint rising faster and faster in front of my eyes as I go down falling and bring up my headlines in hospital in a heartshaped dish. . . .

Done in porcelain it was, to remind me forever of my own true love: . . . And worms do try Her long-preserved timidity. Amen.

She ran her fingers very gently through my hair, a touch older than time, and then we moved away and lay on our backs, holding hands.

My lips rehearsed, *I've got to go to America. I've got to follow what you think is my damned awful story to Manhattan*, but I said, "We may as well get married, you know. It's just as easy really."

She nodded and put her face against my shoulder, and we became very quiet.

When I woke up, Sambo was snarling as only a Siamese can. I opened my eyes and his shadow was beside me on the window-sill; he was spitting at something outside, but all I could tell in my waking moment gazing upwards was that the steep angle of glass was bleared by too many stars. Then I noticed the red flicker on the ceiling. I thought I had left the fire on, that we were on fire, that the carpet was burning—or the bed. I sat up sharply. Not stars certainly. Sequins of flame. Outside the window there was a bonfire, blowing sparks from the depths of the bombed cellar. My eyes were painful with sleep, but I rubbed them, knowing what I would see as soon as they focused through the rained-on glass and could gaze into that hot nest of petals.

The Madman was preaching. There were black shapes of people by the bombed hearthstone, not many, but a bonfire always attracts once the rain stops, and besides: the Madman was preaching. . . . Only he wasn't the Madman any longer, he was Sym. And the bare shape that rose up beside me was no longer a ghost; it had a pulse in its neck, it smelled of woman.

I pushed the window back. It was cold, bloody cold outside, and one or two sparks came in with the draught, stinging my bare chest like gnats. I'm a man, Ericson. Have a heart, I've got hair on my. . . .

The Madman was saying, or seemed to be saying, his voice came from behind me in the echoes of the room, "We go upwards . . . not the wherefore, but the Will . . . the flat plans of man hide other dimensions. Not the sidewalks and pastures only, the fat legs of sailors and whores . . . but an eggshell city. Forget the rat in the sewer, the devil in the drain. Forget, if you like, the tall places, the domes and the steeples, the beatitudes born of our flesh, the towers dreamed in our skull. We have made this haven of stone, and, inside it, Mankind lies growing . . . and his thoughts like . . . a bomb in the belly of our life . . . not an apple will tempt us anymore . . . not an apple but a button . . . and that button, each time we touch it, is the belly of God. . . ."

"God is a woman," I murmured.

"If we hatch from Her Fire into Divinity?" he went on, "shall we. . . ." but it was always too much at this point, and there was the draught at my sides and the sparks on our bare flesh, so I closed the window. What did he mean by coming *here*? He knew where I was.

When I looked again I saw the men in dark glasses with black flags embroidered with skulls and crossbones, hour-glasses, and bent clocks and scythes, and the little girl was there with a huge frame of flowers. . . .

"You don't mind this?" Mavis said. "Seeing it again?"

"No, I don't mind it."

"It's not sacred . . . the memory, I mean?"

"There's nothing sacred." Her breast brushed against me. Liar, I thought. Any sex is sacred. Even a fingered halo.

The bonfire brightened. The bush cracked with flame.

They were jeering at him now.

I had dreamed it many times before, but my dreams always follow their progress, and so do my realities. He went up the pile of rubble, and the fire rose and etched the cellar in red. He walked the ramp of brick. He climbed the crack, as fast and nimble as a flea. . . . It's the last twenty feet beyond the crack, Swale—how does he do that? But the firelight doesn't reach, I can't go beyond the crack, no man can go beyond the crack to the other side of life, there's no evidence to promote him to miracle. When we go beyond the crack, it's the clay-hole into worms . . . under stone.

All the flags go away from the cellar, all the flags, all the faces, all the flowers. They go away watched by a naked man and woman, peering above a sill with the flames catching our faces. Let me pull the blinds before we are the last attraction, we who were the first. I pull the blinds. I spend hours pulling blinds. I am exhausted by the drink and the sexlessness, by the sex and the dying. I pull the blinds, and notice how the firelight strikes differently through a different glass where the pane that the brick smashed was mended. I pull the blinds. I am mended.

197

XVII

WHEN I woke it was daylight, the blinds were still open, and the phone was ringing.

Ten o'clock.

Ericson's voice said, " What's it all about this time? "

" Ah ! " I said. My bare knee came slowly into the warmth of her thighs.

" Don't say ' Ah ! ' at me. Where are you, Bertie, saying ' Ah ! ' at ten o'clock in the morning? Sitting on the loo? Being bloody idle somewhere. So you *don't* know about it? "

Her thighs clenched my knees and she opened her eyes.

" I know it all," I said.

" So what am I talking about, Swale? I'll tell you what I'm talking about, and then you can tell me why your story's not in yet. Seven flaming factories with skulls and crosses on their chimneys—that's what I'm talking about. A bloody great wreath of flowers halfway up the Abbey. Same at St. Martin's, St. Clement's, St.——"

" Not St. Paul's, surely? "

" No, not St. Paul's. Why? "

" Ah ! "

" Pull the chain and stop making noises at me. We run an evening-paper from this office, and their editor wants——"

" Sorry, Ericson. Policy."

" What? "

" There's no God in Fleet Street."

" That's right, Bertie. There's a bloody great church with flowers on it though ! News ! Now fake something up."

" But, my dear Eri——"

" Don't say that to me, nobody ever talks to me like that !

You've been seeing too much of Paul. Get it written. Quick. Or I'll have your jack off." The phone stopped.

She pushed me with her finger. "He mustn't do that to you. I should miss it. You'd better get it written."

"I don't know anything about it."

She got out of bed and went into the shower. "That shouldn't deter you. Why didn't he let you know? Sym, I mean."

"If it *was* Sym." Of course it was. Or Sym and some others. "Perhaps he tried to. You underestimate your attractions, darling. The phone could have been ringing all night for all I knew. Come to think of it, I dreamed about firebells!" I pulled the typewriter into bed. Then I remembered what I *had* dreamed about. She was making coffee now, and Ericson would be waiting, so this was as good a place to start as any other. Not a journalist, Swale—a reporter of dreams, you bloody old gospeller. I was rapidly becoming as unreliable as the first four.

She brought me a cup and sat on the bed and read it over my shoulder. Then she looked at me and said, "I might have known she'd get into the story somehow."

"She's dead," I said.

"That's not very fair of her, is it?"

The Three Thieves

I

"No need to fly," Ericson had said. "Have a nice long rest. You can float over." I think he thought that altitude would derange me completely.

The trouble with going by boat was it meant too long away from Mavis. So I came back to bottles. The waves were my time, and after my hourly assuaging, I stood on the wet-deck of the liner looking at the seagulls volplaning from wave-cap to wave-cap, sometimes loitering disguised as small drops of ocean with feathers on them, sometimes, as far as I could tell with my bottled eyes, never rising from the ocean again, though sometimes the ocean would rise and fly high on moist drops of wings, a whole icicle of ocean in feathers of spray, and fly squawking about me and drop messages of salt in my eye.

It was a cure, nearly. When the vomiting was over I could think in crystal. I remembered her once, but it was Mavis I thought of mostly—Mavis and Lord Dultie.

Watch out for trouble, I had been warned. *You are dealing with Americans*, I had been warned. *It is true that the Great-Hearted Britisher realises that the Great Hearted American is a Great-Hearted Bastard: He must also realise he is a Cunning Great-Hearted Bastard as well.*

"In America," Lord Dultie had said, in a subsequent meeting, to Swale Resurrected, over his American Cigar, "they don't waste their children's time on Education; they make them learn things. Remember that." There was money involved. . . .

My money was involved as well. Sym had leaked into the American Press. Obviously he was scheduled to be leaked sooner or later, or where was the Advertising Value? But Sym had leaked a day or two earlier than intended by Lord Post. That was why I was wearing a new fur-collared coat. I was, in short, Taking Care of Number One at the expense of the Daily Dultie.

However, I was also taking care of Sym. The few snapshots I released with Paul's help, at the fabulous agency price fabulous pictures can bring—Sym balanced on a cloud, Sym astride the sun, Sym in a trellis of scaffolding doing a spider-dance over the Thames, Sym like a midget on the Shell-Mex Building, Sym climbing the Forking Fire—these were bound to help his cause, and they were my only transgression. For the rest—I was stone-cold sober when we docked, and ready for journalistic trouble.

There was none.

Nobody believed in Sym or his intentions, however much they liked his cat-climb photographs in their glossy magazines. And if they had heard him say what he thought he was going to do to The Empire State they would have laughed.

So should I.

Because, thanks to the amateurs who ran life for The Post, I arrived unwarned and without fuss to a New York deep in snow.

Sym, also unwarned, flew in a few hours later. I met him on a runway of ruts and scabs, with the shovels and tractors still working, and said, "This finishes it."

He looked towards Manhattan and the huge thermometers of ice.

"Nonsense," he said. "It will thaw."

204

As with everyone else who lives with the Great, I knew better than to contradict him.

" When do we start? " he said to me later, as we left our luggage at a middleweight hotel.

" First of all," I answered, " we've got to meet someone."

He looked at me sadly and I thought about Mavis.

II

MR. CARMEL WHITE sat nineteen storeys above ground in a room with no visible window. Sym had walked up ladders of stairs and I had used the lift. We sat in a breathless air.

Lord Dultie had said that Mr. White could attend to certain formalities. Apparently the Empire State wasn't ours to climb, or anyone else's for that matter. There were laws about defiling monuments, laws about emptying toilets from aeroplanes, and all sorts of other laws to apply to such vertical trespass as we now proposed. Mr. White was in advertising and would take care of those laws. He was infinitely rich because he had space to sell, infinite space. We sat in his nutshell and waited.

Mr. White's cigar smoked itself at us as if it was willing to wait. Mr. Carmel White, who was a formality to take care of formalities, had been out to us for three whole days. I was surprised by the feel of his hand : it was either homosexual or masonic. There was an ordinary erratic pulse.

" Pleased to meet you, Mr. Swale. And you, Champ. I've got six minutes. Now you boys start in and tell me something new."

I said, " I think that Lord Dultie has already been. . . ."

" Sure, I've heard from Dultie. The idea probably seemed clever in England."

"It did," I said. "It seems cleverer still in New York. Now I've seen the building."

"W-e-e-e-ll," said Mr. White.

"Never mind the formalities," said Sym. "I intend to climb that thing."

Mr. White knew how to handle a cigar. He let it hang. "*Hope*," he said. "You only hope in this climate." He stiffened it.

"He intends," I said. It sounded ridiculous.

And, of course, it *was* ridiculous. Mr. White looked at me and his look implied that we each knew what we had to say because we were sitting in the same room as at least one maniac, so let's get it said calmly. He took his cigar away altogether, and said: "Difficulty is—there are plenty of other boys right here in New York City who have exactly the same idea themselves. They might fancy they have priority."

I gasped. Clearly *The Post* was being piddled on.

"How many?" asked Sym. He was interested, genuinely.

From White's face I saw that it had been a shrewd question. He hesitated for at least one of his six minutes.

"Say two," he said.

"It's been here all this time," I said. "And they've been here all this time. Why haven't they got going before?"

"They've been qualifying. They started on the little ones and now they're ready for the big ones."

Sym listened without anger.

"'Qualifying,'" I said. "I bet they started qualifying just as soon as you received our letter."

He picked up another cigar, and then realised there wasn't time, and put it down again.

"I don't know why you're bothering to be so rude to me," he said. He wasn't even vaguely upset. "I'm just stat-

ing the facts. Plus adding the fact that we're all prepared to
cut you and your paper in—if we can get together and make
it seem right."

Sym leant forward, rather wearily. "I'm afraid I don't
understand this," he said. "*I intend to climb up that thing*
—that all. What you settle now is extra, it's finance, it's
mere irrelevancy. I'll climb up it anyway."

"Want to bet?"

Sym didn't answer.

"Thing is," said White. "Say you're all honest. *Suppose*
it. Well, *suppose* he *can* climb up the Empire State—on the
outside, I mean—and suppose, just *suppose*, he does. . . ."
He smirked; it was a fairly generous supposition, especially
as Mr. White saw it. "Thing is, there ain't a paper in town
that'll print it. And why?" He tapped his own fatness.
"Me."

I laughed. For some reason it hurt him.

"There are advertising accounts in this town that'll kill
any old story you care to cook up," he said. "You can
pickle the President's Lady in brine, and if one of those
firms said 'no' it would be no story. He would have to
marry her double." He made a quick gesture of the hand to
admit that if he was guilty of overstatement it wouldn't be
a significant guilt as far as this argument was concerned.
Trouble from Mr. White might not alarm the President
unduly, not before election time, but it could be bad for
Mr. Swale, I could see that.

"We're men of the world, I hope."

"Doubtless," said Mr. White.

Sym didn't comment.

"Well, then," I said.

"It's the clients," he said. "The Advertisers. They don't
like the idea of a Limey scaling up Manhattan. Not by himself, anyhow. No offence, of course. Like being born black

or yellow—you can't help it." He lit one after all, while Sym drummed with his peanut hands.

After he'd blown it at us, he said, "They want a race."

"Who between?"

"This boy and a couple of others."

"Can they climb?" asked Sym. He sounded concerned for them.

"How would I know? They'll be good news. Anyone who tries to get out onto that building'll be good news. Anyone who falls off'll be better news." He didn't blench at his own indelicacy. "In fact, you don't even have to go onto the building at all, not even six inches. You just have to wait until I give the word and then say you're going on, and ten million people on the television hook-up'll hear you say it, and they'll see you drink from a glass, and then they'll see a picture of a man by a bar with a little ballooon coming out of his head and inset in that balloon a little 'think' that he's half-way-up a skyscraper. . . . Get it, beer —thinks he's climbing—caption: *All my tall stories begin with* . . ." He chuckled. "I won't say the name of the beer, but I'm sure you got it. As a matter of fact we don't have to use you at all. Any old mountaineer and any old mountain'll do just as well, probably."

"Don't be silly," said Sym.

"You just get on with your *doing*," said Carmel White smugly, "and let those of us who can talk talk." He smiled at me.

"I'll have to consult Lord Dultie," I said.

"And me," said Sym. He was speaking quietly, so for the moment I ignored him. They were all trouble.

"Dultie's in perfect agreement," said White. "In fact," and his smile became suddenly warm and genuine and sympathetic, "he suggested the idea." He passed me a piece of Dultie-scented paper, stronger and more holily odorous than tobacco. I looked at it and said, "It's dated six weeks ago!" The old-fashioned English four-flushing bastard had agreed to this race before Sym or I even knew we were coming!

White felt in his pockets, searching for sympathy.

Sym stood up, and White eyed him with distasteful surprise, like a fight-promoter hearing a boxer speak without his manager's permission.

"I said this discussion was irrelevant," said Sym. "I came over here to climb. Any obligation I felt towards the wishes of other people in this matter I felt because of my connection with *The Post*. But I think that debt has now been cancelled by the behaviour of its proprietor."

White didn't look alarmed, only breathless. His idea of the story could easily dispense with Sym, I saw that.

"Anyway, I shall be on the building at dusk tomorrow evening. If anyone else is on it at the same time, that's up to them. If they think it's a race, that's also up to them. I shall climb at my own speed."

White laughed. He laughed and he went on laughing. He laughed and he laughed and he laughed, and he only stopped when Sym turned at last and reached the door across a wide deep carpet. "Climb it now? We're all frozen up," he said. "You'll have to wait weeks, perhaps months."

Then the door was hissing shut, and it breathed on its spring behind him.

"Sorry," I said, feeling hopeless.

"Don't worry," he smiled. "Like I said—News!" He put a small piece of paper in my hand. "Phone about four-pip," he said, "and I'll tell you whether he goes up, goes back home, or has a rest in the State Looney-Bin. That's final!"

Nothing to do with me!

But the paper was in my pocket as I followed Sym to the lift.

III

I DIDN'T believe there would be a thaw.

When we'd first got there, the town had been cold, frozen hard with the weather from the sad continent behind it. But the snow itself was dirty, it had been a long time fallen, and looked crumbly like the dried excrement of dogs, dusty with ashes; and the uncleared drifts, where they *were* uncleared, had holes in them, garbage holes, piddle holes, yellow rings of heat boring down to the cold centre, so the great banks boggled and grinned like mountains of skulls. The city, the great thermometers of storeys disappearing into mauve cloud, was like an old monument of tall bones.

All this time since Sym's prediction, it had been snowing, snowing from a mauve, then a yellow, then a lead sky, snowing from the great poxy bum of heaven onto Swale's uplifted glass, and I had drunk until it started snowing big fat feathers, snowing pieces of peeled skin, snowing unwrapped sunburn, mummy-cloths, white polar-bears, whole clouds and banks and fields of snow falling flat on the town.

We and the weather had gone on for these three days snowing together, snowing purity, snowing Carmelite Friars, snowing Mount Carmel itself, snowing a new crisp Golgotha of sharp ice. I toasted it. It was the white Esquimau Nell sperm of creation. I drank it. It was a whiteness like the suds of death.

When we got down from White's tower—Sym had insisted on clubbing down endless stairs—it had stopped. Even though it had been snowing on the way down.

Sym gestured towards it, his face clenched. I thought for a moment he was going to make claims for himself.

"God," he said, "look at it. It's going to take years." He

was nearly crying. All the while it fell it was possible to ignore what had fallen, but not now. "All this, and all those people against me. What am I going to do?"

He was asking *me*.

"Let's just be careful," I said. "Careful, and very, very polite."

Which one of the Swales was talking? I drink and I divide in mirrors. Or I don't drink, and I come painfully apart.

IV

SO at four-fifteen pip, here we were in a car.

According to the map The Mogashaw Training Camp was about an hour away from the city, up in the hills, and so now we sat in one of Carmel White's cars behind one of his underlings. It was a good road; it was kept ploughed, and the ice had been treated with chemical that left it caky like dung but no longer slippery. We could use a few tons of that chemical on the Empire State.

Sym sat sulky and withdrawn, like an oriental priest. White had unbent just a little; we were in a midday paper as a result of it. That paper had called Sym "The Bonze of Manhattan". It was appropriate.

At the end of our hour we turned in through a log-and-wire fence past log-gates without heading or placard. Only then did he condescend to speak to me.

"They have offered me training facilities here?"

"Seemingly."

"I don't want them."

We drew up beside a plain wall of brick, winter-eroded until it looked like plastic. The driver sat still and wordless, but a door opened in the brick, and a round, pyknyk man came bouncing down steps towards us.

Bertram Swale and the Bonze of Manhattan alighted, and were shaken simultaneously by a dry hand, palms down, contortingly.

"Great, great, great!" he shook. "I've been expecting you. This is a big thing you boys are doing. A great big wonderful thing. Come and meet the boys."

He released us and went up the steps. "Jason's the name," he called over his shoulder. "Call me Woolly." What was he—a fight-promoter, brothel-keeper, impresario? I couldn't guess.

Once through the door I knew we belonged to a nation of amateurs.

We were in a small windowless gymnasium built of glazed brick set behind aluminium parallel bars. The floor was coated rubber and the ceiling was depthless black above batons of light. It was like a futurist stage-set, with a warm wind venting round my ankles and all odour swept away upwards by fans. No sweat, nothing foetid, because the up-draught sucked it away; no ash, no vomit, no beer. No sweat, because the men trained here would be too fit to sweat.

At present the gymnasium held about a dozen men, all looking efficient, all belonging to it. Normally they would be seedy, I could tell that: the sort of men who put towels round the shoulders of champions or flick vinegar into the eyes of racehorses. At present the gymnasium purified them.

"Well, here we are!" said Woolly Jason. "Come and meet the Opposition. Or come and meet Greg, anyway." He spoke as if it was normal to meet the Opposition, as if we were all partners in the same enormous swindle. With the exception of Sym, so we were.

I followed with a lax belly. I was in a gymnasium for the

first time in years, and trained muscle always affects me with inferiority.

Greg, for instance.

A wide man, an Ape's back in a black vest and an ape's bum in black drawers, narrow and emotionless about the arse, an ape's neck crowned by pepperpot hair on a hard-boiled head, spreadeagled against the floor doing press-ups on toes and fingertips only. An umbilicus of rubber came up from his body and bifurcated into the ears of a man in a white coat. This man was the only one who didn't look seedy. He belonged to an income-group whose instinct was for well-washed fat. I smelt his scent as he lifted his arm to look at his wristwatch. One of the seedy ones was count-ing aloud: "One hunnerd un twenty-one . . . One hunnerd un twenty do . . ." *Press-ups!* I collapse after ten myself.

"Never mind," said Woolly. "He'll be through round about a hundred and eighty."

Drops of sweat, audible and regular as a metronome, fell onto the floor from a spot in the middle of the underside, I hesitate to say face-side, of Greg's head.

"What does he rate?" asked Woolly, eyeing Sym, who was muscleless.

"I beg your pardon."

"I mean: *what—does—he—rate?* How many can your boy do? Press-ups!"

"I don't know," I said. I turned to Sym. "How many can you do?"

"I haven't counted," Sym answered. "It's some time since I did any."

"Jesus," said Jason. "Don't he *train?*"

I hoped to avoid clashes of doctrine. "Well," I said——

"No," Sym said. "I prepare."

"What do you mean? You mean you just pray or some-thing?"

" Sometimes."

" Jesus ! "

Then he saw Sym's hands. When he saw those he looked more thoughtful. Sym thrust them into his pockets.

" Greg'll be through in a minute," said Jason. " Let's have a look at Al. Al is just trying his irons on, I see."

" Irons? "

Special Equipment.

There were factors here I hadn't considered. Why might Al need irons? What *were* Al's irons? Not his knife, fork and spoon, anyway.

We went over to Al.

" Al," said Woolly. " This is Mr. Bertie Swale. Mr. Swale, Mr. Shulberg. And now I would like you, Al, to meet Sym."

" What's his name? " asked Shulberg. " As for friends."

" Just Sym," said Sym.

Just Sym. Irons.

Al, who had an iron face, stopped chewing. He became manly, affronted Mr Shulberg in an instant.

Woolly looked shocked.

" Oh—Kay—Bud," said Mr. Shulberg, mainly to Sym, but he turned his back on both of us. In some indefinable way he looked even tougher than Greg. He half-turned again, not to us, but to a large pile of ironmongery on the floor—a huge man in cold blue pants, with a codpiece of stone.

Greg and Shulberg, Sym's rivals. They were born in the dark tunnels, they could climb the white towers. They made love to the statues, bending bronze and cast metal and hewn rock into accommodating postures; they clung stone to stone to the sculptures in the New York parks. What hope could Sym have against *them*? What had Sym ever clung to, Sym who did not train but prepared, except the Tower of London, Big Ben, and Shell-Mex House, those *little* buildings,

214

Sym who did no press-ups but started among spiders and steeples?

I glanced at him, but he was watching Shulberg.

"What," he asked at length, "is *that*?"

"Talks then?" asked Shulberg.

He was busy with a grasshopper of welded iron, with clamp-holes and spring-junctions and screws. Not a spider, a trestle. Two vees and a connecting spine.

"Where was you brung?" asked Shulberg, and lifted his private trestle, the iron man, without a grunt, and put the spine-piece on his back so the two vees came around him like the arms and legs of a monkey, headless and tailless, riding him. He fastened it by straps across his belly and harness over his chest, and there he was, devoured by a metal spider, jockeyed by this monkey. Not iron, aluminium perhaps, an indeterminate alloy.

It woggled at us. Shulberg the Skyscraperman.

Greg, having finished two hundred press-ups, or three hundred press-ups, came and stood by us, together with his helpers and handlers. His heart was still being listened to in umbilical sympathy, so we made rather a big circle. Shulberg sulked. I noticed Greg's skull was jocked in a wire-net: his brains had been listened to as well.

I looked to Jason for information.

"What *is* it? Needless to say," said Jason, "it is *the* Most." As an afterthought he added, "I designed it."

"Looks like an Iron Maiden," I said.

"It's a Fairy's chastity-belt," offered Greg, his heart-beats now finished. Seeing Mr Shulberg's statuesque glare he added brightly, "I wear one myself."

"Simple," said Jason. He spoke largely to me, as the publicity-man. He was ignoring Sym as I would have ignored Milocz. Unlike Milocz, Sym was impassive. "Simple."

We waited for revelation.

215

"Now the way up that Scraper can only be by an outside angle. Granted?"

Greg grunted and looked modestly at his toes, poking from beneath the feminine swell of his pectorals.

Shulberg grunted.

Sym said, "For a First Climb, yes. I've studied over nine hundred photographs of that tower, and I think it will have to be an outside-angle climb. . . ."

They all looked at him suspiciously.

"What a rockclimber would call a ridge climb. In this case a vertical ridge. Therefore I. . . ."

"Therefore," said Mr. Jason, "I have invented the Iron Monkey! All patents pending." He giggled, and slapped the ironmongery on Shulberg's back.

"Therefore," persisted Sym with asperity, "I have perfected certain climbing techniques to meet the case. No patents pending."

Greg and Shulberg looked at the nervous hands, the scarred wrists, their sneer evident. In a way, I admired them. If this was a stunt, an impossible stunt for which you enlist the aid of climbers, circus-performers, star gymnasts—what *were* they?—they were still in it to do what they could without shooting their mouth. They were going to go as high as they could for Mr. White and Lord Dirty, and what would the moneymakers care providing they went just a little way? Or fell off even? I had seen other people go high before falling off, Bunch for instance, and the smashed boy of Malet Street; and they hadn't had the Iron Monkey. These might go much, much higher. And they hadn't seen the need to boast about it yet—except with muscles like theirs, their whole body was a boast.

"Climbing an angle," pursued Jason, tasting his words, "involves *friction*. No backing-up. No incidental holds. One thousand feet of friction!"

Sym was ecstatic.

"*That* was the challenge," said Jason.

Sym let out his breath quietly, as if from a great excitement. "That *is* the challenge," he said.

"Is," said Jason. "Is, I grant you. But to a lesser degree. Now watch here a minute." He walked a few steps and patted a projection of fresh brickwork, erected in the corner of the gymnasium on a thick steel plate. "Come over here a minute, Al."

Shulberg waddled towards him, his metal hanging over and round him like a crane.

"Get on the wall, will you?"

Shulberg faced the outer corner, and pressed the rubber pad on his chest against it. Then he held out his arms along each of its two receding surfaces. There was a click.

"Locked in position," said Jason. "Pads at the wrist, and along the inside of the arms, give ninety pounds friction on a pull of one hundred and fifty. And those two claws at the fingers, pushed in by the spring across the back, give about a straight two-hundred-pound grip. Depending on surface."

"Artificial Climbing," I said.

Sym smiled.

Shulberg now lifted his two legs off the ground and straddled the angle, his thighs resting inside the lower vee of the trestle. The moment he put their weight on it there was another snapping noise and the trestle locked inwards, holding his legs against the wall. He now sat locked round the corner of the wall, three feet above the floor.

"Downward pressure locks, and clamps inwards; upward pressure unlocks," purred Jason.

Shulberg freed his hands and dragged upwards painfully, his leg clamps supporting him numbly while he did so.

The process was repeated.

Ten minutes later he was twenty-feet high, white-faced and breathing heavily.

"Take a good long rest, Al. Take a good long rest—he can rest as easy as he likes all the time he's wearing the Monkey—and then come down."

He turned to us, delighted with exposition.

"Interesting," I said. I gathered from Sym's silence that I had said enough.

Jason gestured towards the far corner of the gymnasium, and we stood there, Greg flexing his chest, Shulberg screwed to the wall, Sym tall and contemptuous as I remember seeing him outside the University Building those few months ago, while a couple of the whey-faces opened up a box.

Then, to my diplomatic horror, they came dangling the clamp, pads and straps of a brand-new set of climbing-irons towards us across the floor. *They were going to try to get Sym into a Monkey!* The bloody effrontery of it! It came from Dultie and Carmel White downwards, this assumption that Sym was a piece of News to dress-up, to manipulate— a stunt not of his own making, but theirs. I was trampled aside, knocked into by cold iron.

"Here," said Jason, his fleeciness more in evidence than his woolliness, "help the boy on with it."

And they started to lift the cage onto Sym. I tried to muscle into this flurry of metal.

"Please," he said, deprecating my assistance. "No *thank* you, Mr. Jason."

"Go on, boys," prompted Jason, the oozy impresario.

They went on lifting.

And then they stopped, somehow half-bent with a curious grunting noise in front of Sym who was still smiling, and I saw he had each of them quietly but firmly by the wrist, that they lifted not against muscle so much, one saw no muscle, but against the full weight of his authority. It was a curious touch, the scarred skin with the bone in it, as I knew from shaking his hand. It was the saint's shake, the cold flesh of lizard, and it repelled. And I remembered suddenly, but with no overtone of emotion, the way he had fended off the Teds on the bombsite.

"I don't want it," he said. "You see—I don't need it."

"You'll need it on that Scraper next month . . ."

"Tomorrow night. Tomorrow night is my time. A sky-scraper, yes. Don't shorten it—it's your own word, and it displays the right kind of reverence for the tallest tower known to man." He spoke quietly, as if the winds were howling round some curious Mustagh of the mind. "It is a great tower we have elected to climb, I and Shulberg and Greg. . . ."

Shulberg was down now, and breathing heavily behind us.

"Why tomorrow, for . . ."

"Because I'm climbing. Not racing."

Greg shouldered in. "Well—tomorrow, or when—I'll be higher than you. If you want mustard on it, you got it." He paused. "You bum. We can't go up tomorrow—it's all ice."

Sym opened his eyes. "Higher? Higher than what? I'm going to the top. I thought we were all going to the top. Or I thought you were *intending* to go. This isn't a stunt, you know."

They were laughing now. They were all laughing. I saw the whole story coming out in paragraphs of derision. All America was laughing, and I heard in that note how much more of it there would be to come.

"Bud, you're the Bonze okay," wheezed Mr. Shulberg. "You'd better carry some iron if you're going that high. What are you gonna use—magnets? In your bollocks? "

"It's a long way up," sighed Woolly Jason. "A long way up, and a long, long way down." He looked at the Monkey sadly, as if even that wasn't everything, and we left them there, packing clamps, and claws, and hooks, and trestles and springs into a long wooden box like a coffin.

V

WE had to wait hours for a car in the centrally heated fug of Woolly's office—for a time I thought we were being politely kidnapped by Mr. Jason and Mr. White; they had the weight of snow on their side, the failure of telephones, the failure of engines, as well as the cold weight of reason and the total failure of sympathy—but at last a car came, a different car but driven by the same maggot as before. It was a further half-hour before we set off.

"There's a reason for all this," Sym said. I don't think he meant anything metaphysical.

"Ice," I said. "There's ice on the wires. Travel takes time." But I worried too.

When we got back our story had been broken. I saw it dangling from the Newstands, *Limey Treads on Manhattan . . . Miracle Man With the Mouth . . . How High the Bonze?* One paper said simply, *Oh Yeah!* in high capitals; even Swale unfocused could read it across the street. *Oh Yeah!* When you go out under a headline like that you certainly think it's an unsympathetic story you have to peddle. Not even Philips said that.

Our driver had been listening in low to the car radio for some time. Now, prearranged and nasty, he turned it up. A happy voice said: "*Today, little old England, home of scientists that don't stay and cars that don't go, exported one of its tallest stories to New York. Francis Sym, a Thames-side spiderman, claims he's going to climb the Empire State. Climbs he's going to claim the Empire State. No, no, no—*

220

a third time. He says he's going up the outside of the State Building here in tiny old New York City. Well, well, well. He's lying low at present and nobody blames him for that in the circumstances—His hotel says he is out. . . ."

Thanks for the warning, I thought. We were at the hotel now and no need to listen any more. I smelt them even with the temperature at zero. We got out and I slammed the door back on the driver to stop him shouting, but they were round us in a flash. They hit us with bulbs, bulbs, bulbs. We fought. Newspapermen stink. They stink with the cigarettes of waiting, with the gum of neuroses. They also stick. They have claws.

"All right," I said. "That's him, not me." They jostled, we pushed through, skating on fathoms of cold, the New York pavement was cold as high as my crotch, knees nudged me, no pencils or notebooks, it was too bloody chilly for pencils and notebooks; besides this was the sort of story where you write what you like. We got through to the lift. They dragged me back. "All right, boys," I said. "A press conference tomorrow." They gave me the American raspberry—which is a fast one and hurts the pride. One of them handed me the sleeve of my raincoat. Nobody cheered. I followed Sym into the lift. Sym had done nothing, said nothing. His contempt hung all over us and over my arm with its torn sleeve. If I had been bleeding, it would have hung over that as well.

"Good publicity for the hotel," said the liftboy. He was about eighty. He had seen noises come and go. We rode up into the night while he chewed time at us.

The Manager met us. "Bad for the hotel," he said.

"We won't stay," I said. We left him. Stay! Of course he wanted us to stay! The liftboy sank downwards through the floor clutching a coin Sym had given him, with a dazed look on his face as if it were the new moon. Anyway, we were home. We were in our hotel at least, which was part of a building, only a fraction, a lit-up section so many storeys of dark above ground. And down there the wolves waited. We reached our room.

"Now what?" Sym said.

"No good asking me," I said. "I don't count any more. Lord D. doesn't count. *The Post* interest has been killed at birth by this comedy release of White's. You can bet the English papers will get it from the agencies the same way. And bang goes the advertising. It always goes down the drain in a comic story. Who the hell's going to care now what detergent you wash your jock-strap in!"

He got his face ready to tell me I was being vulgar and irrelevant.

"All right: you don't care about *The Post*," I said. "I know that. You don't owe anybody anything. All you want is the building. Well, you can bet they'll do their damnedest to keep you off it. After all, they've still got their own stunt up their sleeve—they want to give it time to mature. Making a monkey out of you is just part of the groundwork."

"Well, I intend to be on it tomorrow night. That will change the look of things."

Perhaps.

"Mad. They'll find some way of keeping you off it. Your only chance is by spoiling White's own story in some way."

"How?"

"Let's tell it to as many newspapers as we can. Let's tell them about Greg and Shulberg, and throw out a challenge or two. He won't dare pull against us then. You'll all *have* to climb, and the race will be on."

He sat himself down with infinite patience. "Sorry. I'm not having anything more to do with newspapers. Or with newspapermen."

"That's just what I thought," I said. "That's perfect!"

222

The sanctimonious bastard! "You think you can climb up *that* thing"—we could see it from here—"and stay out of a newspaper?" I didn't tell him they'd be wrapping his pieces in a newspaper, mopping him up in woodpulp from the ice sidewalk; I was loyal to the last. "You realise that's the way White wants you to behave? That you're playing right into his dirty little hands! You dedicated tribe are all the same."

"Please," he said.

"Oh yes," I said. "We're still friends. All I'm saying is that when you're doing something that's bloody impossible anyway why insist on starting with a handicap?"

No answer. Of course, it wasn't impossible to him. He was stark raving mad.

He watched me, imploring something. I let him see my gaze wander. He saw me look through the sheet of plate glass, our whole wall of window pressed by frost, into the acres of refracted light, the vertical ladders, the squares, the caverns and snowladen canyons, and further, deeper, into the dark bruise of sleep. If my look at those towers told him he was mad, he was right; but it told me more. It said I was thirsty, unslaked, unwatered, in a city of bone. I was dried up and done. The giants and the pygmies slumbered, their bitch-bones frozen aloft, the wide world lay under me on its back, saving its wand of Ygdrasil from the smoking hair of Manhattan. But my fertilising principle was frozen, through and through, like my wallet. Swale was sacked, bound to be now, and I gave myself up to its freedom. I should last, all right. Much better than in the old bondage. I should last. How many cigarettes would see me through this intolerable relationship with Sym, which was also my relationship with me? My relationship with me need only last until tomorrow night, then I could give

223

it all up and come into pieces. My most holy piece, hoary with failure, would sail home and redesign Mavis as a distillery.

Meanwhile I waited.

Why do people follow people round the earth's pimple? I don't mean sex, I can understand the miracle of the hot wand, the self-replenishing bottle. I mean the saintly following, the arise-and-follow-*me*. Be-my-reporter, my ad-man, write-my-bloody-bible. Why didn't one of the original twelve get up and welt the bastard with a fish?

Time passed in philosophy. I still waited.

Thirst beyond thirst because it is only the replenishment of emptiness. I am the plumed acid-trance, outside time, beyond this white window. I lick at the world in its deep crust of iced gin.

" Why don't you? " he said.

I turned back, dazed, from looking through his reflection at the pillars of Manhattan. Paul now, in colour, could have bronzed up the Bonze to a nicety. Paul, I remembered, was flying in tomorrow. If Ericson didn't stop him now this lot was blown!

" Why don't you? "

" What? "

" I'll find it for you," he said. He slid open the door of my fitted cupboard and there, don't be vague, was my haig, ten green bottles, my pillar and my nails.

He lifted one to a side table.

" It's a symbol," I said, glad of some honesty between us. " My miniature Manhattan."

He found two glasses. Two! To my surprise.

" You don't have to last much longer," he said. I was drying as he spoke. " And we may as well drink together."

He poured me a tower and I became big with the joy of it: I was a sunless shaft suddenly split open by light.

"So it makes you achieve?"

"I don't need to," I said. "After this. . . ." I poured it long now—"I don't need to climb skyscrapers. I *am* a skyscraper. It is me you climb."

"Yes," he said.

Miracle. I show him the inward mania of alcohol and he agrees with me.

"Yes?" I queried. So great was my interest in this sudden note of intensity that I poured myself more of the crystal. So great was his that he left his untouched.

"All those lives," he said. "All those lives present and past."

"Oh, quite," I said.

"It's no accident, is it? It's a pun, a divinely intended pun, like God and Dog, that it's storeys and stories I climb. Now you see the superiority of towers to mountains. It is more than mere architecture. It is the feeling that separated from my endeavour, my proximity to death, separated by a mere half-foot of stone, there is life. I have loitered outside it all, inch by inch. I have seen it all."

"The windowcleaner knows as much," I said. "He also eavesdrops on fornication. He too is God separated from Dog by a distorting glass." I refilled my own.

He wasn't listening. Do they ever?

"I once waited by a sixth-storey window to see a woman open and the child come forth."

I paused, untasting.

"I watched all night by that window. Man, the spread-eagled jellyfish. I was the star on her pane."

"Surely . . ."

"Surely it was private? Private—no: it was holy. You can't be private about *that*."

"That's what's bloodywell wrong with holiness."

"Besides, she didn't know. And I didn't know who she was. I waited for days outside that block of flats for that woman to wheel out her child, but she never came."

I smiled. To myself. He had the soul of a cat-burglar. The rest was curiosity.

He looked for conversation.

"I often wonder what St. Simeon Stylites really died of, up on that pillar."

"Constipation," I said.

"This is my city," he said. "I must know the life I am climbing."

The tower was empty. I sniffed at the cork. "Your last city of the mind?"

"Swale," he said. "Don't mock me. Tomorrow, when I've gone up that tower, they'll make a lie of me. I won't know the truth of what I do. I must go out and see it now. I want to see people."

I found myself going outside, too drunk to argue. We climbed in with the octogenarian lift-boy and he dropped us down the tower of dark as swiftly as the cage in a mine.

To my horror, when we got out there was the sound of rushing water, of leas and dregs in the drains, of gouts and gobfuls of ice shifting. It took time to penetrate: but I understood in the end.

The whole air was in endless thaw round the tall towers of light; and under all the covers the water was welling, and the huge banks of snow were already beginning to shrink.

There were no newspapermen now. They had seen enough of us to know we weren't that sort of story.

Sym let out a long breath of happiness.

"How did you arrange it?" I sneered. I was wet at

the ankles, and I made signs in the air with my forked
fingers.

VI

"WHAT'S your name, Mister. Houdini?"

"That's the guy alright, the authentic bum. I seen his
mug in a paper."

An eating-house, somewhere I can smell harbours, a room
paved in paper-pieces and peanut shells.

"What's your name, bub, and what's your friend's
name?"

They propped me up on their eyes, a circle of eyes, eyes
in bald faces, eyes like eggs in the pepper of beards. Jaws
puffed-up and tough with gum. I had lived with them for
years in the intercommunicating geography of drunk. I had
already made a speech to them, these or some others. Someone had turned my nose on full and emptied ketchup down
my shirt.

"Sym," I said. "Symposium, Synthesis, and Simulacrum."
I hicced. I hupped.

"Going up the State is he? The Empire State."

"Haw, haw, ha."

"That's right. Going up the Empty State."

"So that's what he says."

Their laughter knotted the smoke.

Sym sat motionless, holding me partially sober. I was para-
lysed there, anchored by his motionlessness.

"Balls!"

A face, several faces, one face in particular crunched up
close to me. I breathed its words. A bottle snapped under-
foot, sharpening the air.

"Balls," he repeated. "What am I saying to you?"

"'Balls'."

"Trying to find yourself a fight, eh, bub? Telling me balls?"

My nose was leaking; it must be.

"Sit down," said Sym.

I sat down, my eyes bumping down ladders of colour. I saw I had been talking to something in a sailor shirt. A sailorman. Who was about to punch me.

He punched me.

"Leave him alone!"

"He's a lousy limey."

"All limeys are lousy!"

"Well, this lousy limey is a guest in our stinking country. Leave him alone."

"For why?"

He punched me again. Then he punched the other one.

A slow drawing back of chairs, feet, tables even, the scrunch of innumerable shells. Suddenly we were no longer the centre at all; we were on the edge of a roomful of menace. People chewed silence, unwinding smoke. Their cigarettes fell, were pulled on, spots brightened. You cause all the fights, then you grin and pray on the edge, sharpening needles.

Two men crouching in the circle of us. And nobody tried to stop. They didn't say a word.

As if by agreement they each picked a knife from his clothing and circled each other. No shouts of encouragement, not a giggle or cry. It was sensed they meant to strike home.

One of them held his knife thumb to blade, and stood with a slight crouch only, the sailor.

The other one passed hand to hand, very fast, very practised. My deadly saviour.

228

They did not breathe.

They danced a slow circling dance, twitched by tobacco smoke.

Then they came into one another.

It was very fast for three or four seconds, sparks flashing, they parried and rasped blade to blade. Knuckles bled a little. They shook blood, carving apart.

The twisty one rushed. The sailorman got a wrist hold and they fumbled together, prancing, embarrassed in gesture, like girls fighting off an assault.

Then leaning from nowhere the twisty one tore free his wrist and pushed his hand to the other man's trousers, right at the top of the fly. The hand touched into the stomach and there was a knife beyond the hand, I could hear it grate on the backbone.

Then he straightened, lifting, playing the keys of the spine, the flayed breath bubbling through the stabbed man's nostrils in chords of sound, and with the front of his blade he cut the belly open and the shirt on the belly, from the fly to the tight vee of ribs.

The sailorman swayed, with the dung emptied out of him, and the twisty man rummaged inside him with his glass blade, grinning, till the sailorman started to fold on his emptied abdomen, pale flesh hanging around his knees, the sailorman started to fold and shrink.

Only if they didn't cut the emptied gut he could live. I have seen worse. I cried out in compassion. Oh Christ don't cut the gut from the man, and don't pierce the stomach or veins.

And the twisty man withdrew his blade with a red hand, spurted over, and so was his face; only his eyes were white, ogling white in his crusted grin, as he turned to us. Then he turned back to his victim.

To sever the gut?

Here was a man who would stand to the end. He made giggly little passes in the air, glinting his blade, while the sailorman, still standing, folded, his whole body a sunset dangled in chains of cloud. And the smell of death was enormous. He smelt like a rabbit opened. He stood in the fumes of his dying.

I heard the twisty man chuckle, and circle, looking for death.

He made happy, mesmeric passes, disturbing the tobacco-smoke round his victim, did the twisty man, only nobody spoke now. Sick dripped on the floor. No one had screamed at seeing a man coming apart at the waist, you only scream for a cut finger. When the sailorman had emptied himself, people had uttered vomit, a girl called "no", and then spoke her sickness onto the tablecloth.

Suddenly the emptied man struck his arm out, straight through the mesmeric passes and with a wince of gristle and bone corked the twisty man's eye with a scissor of steel. The twisty man didn't call, pierced by the sight of steel forked right into the eye; nor did he even tear forth its prong, for the fang had gone in deeply, transfixing the pickled onion of eye onto brain. And the twisty man, with his tongue bitten off by his own teeth and red on the red floor in front of him, fell dead with a crash at everyone's feet.

The sailorman dragged himself, his hands held to himself, heavily into the night.

There was a second.

There was a second, then it was all glass. A woman took a woman and bit her like an orange half an inch below the ear. Drunk, I was dreadful drunk. They smashed glass and got ready to cut one another to ribbons; they were going to circumcise each other with bottle-necks, and castrate their neighbours into fanged pint pots.

"Steady," said Sym.

But I had my chair out from under me and somersaulting over my head. A man was getting up with his back to me, and my chair was coming down, and the hammer of gravity won with the noise of bone falling.

"Get those fucking limeys!"

"Stop your bloody nonsense," I said to the whole brawling bar. "Up the Miraclejack!"

A red-haired man made a pass at my saturnalia with a broken glass, but it freckled in his fingers as I waved my chair at him, and as he shook the glass out of his palm I beat his hair into his head.

Then they bundled me.

Someone got an armlock from behind. I tried a scissor throw.

I threw myself off my feet and into the air, then I started to float towards the door, still with my chair, undulating on strong hands, and the door opened and out I went, cold air, and stars, and when would I hit the ground, what a neck-breaking throw I had been given.

Sym set me down on my feet.

The sailorman lay there like an old sausage-skin, empty to the night.

"I'm glad we had nothing to do with this," he said.

The empty man grunted.

"You'll be all right," said Sym.

The man grunted again. His saliva was still white.

We walked away from him, and the bar still smashing itself behind us.

"How do you know?" I asked.

"I've seen all I want to see of this place."

"How do you know," I persisted. "How do you know he'll be all right?"

"I just know."

231

We could hear the Police and the Ambulances arriving. With any luck they wouldn't want to find us.

VII

WE stumbled on in silence, on sidewalks paved with water. We threw up waterdrops bright with the lights of cars. Cars. I lurched. In ten minutes we should be on the State, but meanwhile we were Englishmen. We walked.

At four that morning I had been awakened by a cable from Dultie. *Do not proceed Stop Wait for White Stop Regardless of weather Stop Filmrights advertising unsettled Stop.* And at six Ericson had come in: *Lay off Stop Sending Replacement Barny Swale sacked repeat fired.* This evening I had sent, at too much expense, to Ericson and Dultie both *Balls balls balls Stop I hereby resign from your stinking fish-wrapper.* And now it was dark in the streets and dusk on the high towers. Let me get it over. I can't say the moment exactly dominated my mind.

" Aren't you going to thank me? " he asked.

Thank him? Thank *him*? Play the part, Sym.

" Why not try thanking *me*," I said.

" What for? "

What for? I watched a cat, dragging its bellyful of sex across the broken glass of the gutters. This cat and the memory of blood. He could thank me for that.

" Good publicity," I muttered.

"Do I have to thank you for that? " he mocked.

A child came headfirst and naked, covered in slime, through the greasy slot of a drain.

Not a child, a soiled bundle of rot. I smashed its head. I didn't answer.

And soon there would be one more death.

I picked my nostril, Swale's only fertile orifice, seeded by the sky, full up with the slag of New York City, cross-pollinated by London. Here, on my fingernail, glimmering like a jewel, was a bloodstained fragment of a step of St. Paul's. Here was the brickdust of Battersea, a still-open eye smashed from the skull of night, the crustaceous left-testicle of St. Christopher Wren. Flick! I was marking time. I was marking time. I saw what I wanted now. It was a newspaper stand, sick with wet. I bought one. I was still hazy with a whisky breakfast, but I could make my point.

"He's dead," I said. "It says so in here. The sailorman."

We were very close to the building and not much longer for truth. He looked puzzled.

"Look," I said. "Before you apologise. The Ear."

He looked puzzled.

"Jesus Christ," I said. "Not the swearword, the Miracle Worker. Someone gets his lug lopped off. J.C. fits it on. Plop. Miracle."

He relaxed. I tapped his chest, stumbling us as we walked. "Thing is," I said. "It's happening all the time this miracle. I reported it myself once at Dartford or Erith or Greenhithe or Hoo, one of those places. Jesus takes over a razor-fight. An old man sailor gets his ear scraped off with a bottle. In lurches some foreign, Christlike gent with a beard—a Wog, in short—and sticks it on. Complete with the spilled beer and vomit and sawdust from the floor. It adheres, this ear, as any ear would, glued by the red glue of excrement. Get me? It sticks on. Here was Swale, waltzing on the edge of this scrap, full up with beer and blondes and mustard, and what did he see? What I saw was a Miracle. I wrote it hot. I wept pickled onions for my fragment of truth. All week I was a new man: I pee'd vinegar instead of stout; I read a book called the Authorized Version; I read about Nazareth

233

and Gethsemane, Golgotha and Apocalypse. I got God. In short, I was a bloody nuisance to my friends."

He looked at me bewildered, but grateful that I was passing this tense time for him.

"On Sunday," I said, tapping the hollow of his ribs, "on Sunday, I went to Church."

The cat, was it the same cat? Cats cut themselves in the windows of sunset, they leap their dark shadow from laps that purr in ecstasy, the cat circled us, Sambo.

"On Monday," I said, and there was a catch in my voice, "the man died. He died with an abscess of the inner ear, the outer having fallen off again ages since like a leaf. Sym," I said, and I was full of piteous hope, "tell me why you said that sailor would live last night!"

If I had a mouthful of something, everything would grow calmer.

He was genuinely puzzled. "I thought he had a chance, that's all," he muttered. He mumbled as if he sensed the depth of my accusation.

I nearly wept. "And what do you think you've got yourself, tonight?"

"A chance."

"A chance—is that all you've got? Jesus Christ, why did I have anything to do with all this?"

He didn't answer. He couldn't. He wanted all of his emotion for himself, and I saw to my horror he was scared, badly scared. For the first time on this walk I let myself really look at it, instead of the cats and gutters.

It.

I could feel it almost unseen, the mainmast of the stone ship, sailing starstruck into darkness. Airless, it was too high even to lean on us. I was glad not to be writing this one. I should have to heave off my syntax of bolted brass, my Post perpendicular, and do paragraphless columns of steel.

Words.

Even sacked I was left on the edge of destiny. I shuddered. Why hadn't Paul come? Because I was sacked and they were keeping him back? We were as near as we had to be now. Nobody noticed us. People went past.

It went up out of darkness with its top in bronze cloud, the wind nowhere to be felt in these caverns. I didn't know whether the evening was normal or abnormal for this island of two million souls, this vertical city.

"God," he said. "I wish the others were here. It's cowardice, but I'd be happier with others trying."

I was reminded that he was scared, that this was still unreal and I couldn't concentrate any more. My throat rattled as if it was dice I had been drinking, iced dice. I nodded my head, which held Malet Street and St. Paul's, and now this little man going up two hundred and fifty times his own height. He hadn't even tackled the Vickers Building in Chelsea and how many press-ups could he do? Where were his irons? It's the rational thoughts that blow in suddenly, when the backside opens its eye and looks for fear in the dust. Drunk? I regarded the windy dirt with my lashless eye, and sucked up fears. Who were we?

He had his old duffel off, garments underneath expanding his bulk. He fidgeted with shoes. Mere bloody ridiculous detail.

"I'm coming with you," I said. It was a moment of crystal, the moon out suddenly in a cleft of sky shrinking with frost, and, suddenly, even with car exhausts smelling, and the town sweating from its thawed-out seams, it was growing cold.

"I'm sure you mean it," he said.

I heard a wailing note in the distance. Sirens.

Sirens? We paused. Manhattan burning? The thunderball roaring in from the sea?

235

The echoes came closer.

It was a car blowing. The car with the siren came sounding up the street, swung across the traffic, and halted beside us.

Out stepped Mr. Blanco White.

The policemen sat still. Or the actors in hired uniforms, or the ice-cream men, or the hirelings of the lemonade company, or the six smartest doormen. It's not my town and I don't want to libel anyone. To be quite fair, we were proposing to break the law. Yes, they were policemen.

A second car, without siren, gave us Greg and Shulberg, then several of the seed-merchants, followed by Mr. Jason. Somebody helped him from the car.

"In short," said Mr. White, grinning with friendship, "you can't go. We ain't ready; the boys aren't ready either. Lord Dultie ain't ready, and *you're* fired." He smiled at the policemen, all of whom looked discreetly at nothing. American policemen look at nothing with longer-sighted eyes than English policemen. "What say we all go back and talk this over at my place? Then we could go on out and eat?"

Sym smiled at him, the smile—I thought—of complete treachery, his smiles were so rare. Then he said, "Tomorrow, perhaps. You see, I must start in a minute or two."

Shulberg looked up in the air and laughed. People passing looked up, as people do. Some stopped by us. "Sssh!" said Mr. Jason, and tugged his sleeve.

Carmel White's face cracked with rage. "I absolutely forbid you to touch that building! Absolutely forbid."

Very courteously, shrugging the folds of his pullover straight, Sym handed him his duffel coat. "Listen," said Greg, from his faceless chin.

Sym was fastening his boots, cross-lacing, cross-lacing,

236

cross-lacing. Soon it would be the hessian. He didn't listen.

Greg lunged forward and hit him with both linked hands on his bowed head, as he bent to his laces, a wrestler's blow that toppled him onto his knees. We might have been fighting there and then, but it all happened in two gouts of light. Paul stepped forward, as if from across the Atlantic, fitting bulbs. "The plane was late," he said to me. "There's snow and storm coming in over the Atlantic. I hear you're fired. In good time, too!" He took in the scene with calm inquisitiveness. That made three of us, me and a queer and a maniac, but I felt better.

A thin smear of blood zig-zagged on the calm of Sym's face, and a crowd was collecting at the sound of strife, not an eager crowd, just a curious one. He stood up and reached into his bag for the hessian. Expecting Greg to fall on me I knelt down and tugged at clean pieces of cord, tightening his ankle-wraps, his shin cloths, his thigh-pieces. Greg did not fall. Paul watched the group hungrily.

'A Fairy?' said Shulberg, with more hope than disgust, looking for trouble.

Paul giggled happily and the mockery died. Fairies mustn't own up, not to manly Mr. Shulberg.

Sym was now completely ready. So White turned and gestured.

Policemen climbed out of their car, entirely without hurry, one held the door for another with Old English courtesy, and they ran their hands over their creases as they did so. Their flies were done up and their whistles in order. The crowd continued to collect on a magnet of silence, a dead pool of calm waiting for words. Paul took a bulb of the New York Police Force, Fizz.

Smirking the smile of the truly damned, Carmel White said, "I suggest you arrest this man." And he pointed dramatically at Sym with a limp finger.

The police, all five of them, caught hold of a man in dark clothes standing exactly where Sym was standing, and arrested him well. His tie tore and a button snapped off its thread.

Where Sym had been.

It was an incredible moment. In that distracted second he had stepped backwards through that throng of faces, the crowd had opened and closed as good crowds do, and Sym had vanished.

Their prisoner struggled, his clothes mashing, his patience dispersing. White cursed and tugged, and without apology they released their hold and sucked their whistles and moved into the crowd. A whistle cuts sharp in those high places. The crowd fumbled and ambled open.

"Time to duck," hissed Paul.

It was the moment Mr. Shulberg had been waiting for. "Wait a minute, Cutie," he said; and he ran at Paul with outstretched grab, like a gorilla, leering his hate. Quick as black, Paul caught him in the balls with his City of London shoes-line, then he, too, was off behind the Police Force through the shouting wilderness of Mannhattan. Shulberg, reduced to his girlhood again, lay and hiccupped on the sidewalk. The chase accelerated fast, the whistles shushing, the movement jogging and following like a train pulling out into a tunnel.

But I was too puffed and lazy with breakfast. Even as I thought about running, Greg took hold of me like steel. I couldn't struggle against two hundred press-ups and I didn't try. Young Shulberg croaked his way back through puberty on the pavement, and then stood up gasping malevolently. I was done for in a minute. I glanced up the etched shadow of the State.

Carmel White looked old and anxious, like a man taking a decision. Then he spoke into a car at a man who spoke

238

into a wireless. Then he turned back to us, hemmed by the curiosity of a fresh crowd.

"Well-done-Greg," he said. "But you can let him go." Greg's clench stayed locked in me, I nearly broke up in his fingers. "You boys better get ready to go up. *If he gets past the cops, then the race is on.*" He patted his pocket proudly —as if he kept his permission in there. I noticed Jason's face crumble with anxiety like old putty.

Meanwhile Greg let me go. There were high fumes of cloud above, obscuring the milk of a moonlit sky, and now it was dark. The longer the Police were coming back the more chance I gave him. But it was cold with the dark now. What had Paul said about the Atlantic weather? I felt the collapsing skies prickle. Meanwhile, how fast could Sym catburgle up the lower reaches?

VIII

"THERE he is!"
"Jesus!"
The police were back with us, red and sticky like old meat to report failure; *and there he was on the building.* Lit in the ordinary crossfire of lamps he dangled a hundred feet high, gesticulating upwards at the wall. There was a tinkle of glass; I saw him lash with his wrist, then the sparkle of fragments falling beneath him. Lashing? Rope? He was coming back into common sense, like the asbestos gloves. He was going window to window, using a rope and grab, bugger the glass, bugger the holy theory; he had to get high. Not all the windows would fall.

He was casting once more. His rope snaked and fell, trailing his anchor. He pulled in and tried again. Got it. He hooked on a sill, and went up twenty feet in a leanback swarm that made the whole street scream. It was abseil in reverse. It was sky-commando. It was possible, perfectly possible. But it needed the judgment to do it with a broken back waiting below, and what about higher?

I lived in a sea of upturned faces. We stirred and broke, moved by a police force that knows about crowds. It had all happened in so few minutes, this apotheosis. We were thousands now. But the police were here too in this briefness.

He dangled and lunged upwards, crouched beneath a sill of stone, climbing inside the recesses, still not up to the point where the tower rises pure from encumbrance. Still not up to the point where he would be safe. Once, twice, three times he cast again. Agony. His grabs clung at last and he tested. Firm, firm as the tower. No, it came off, and I winced to think it might have had his weight on it. I heard the claw bump below him. He hauled in.

More sirens, a million sirens, a cascade of sound. He fixed first time this throw and trusted it at once, going up as an act of instant courage, with a stone island a hundred and fifty feet under his greasy foot. If the grab slipped now. . . .

A good thing he did. It was the Fire Department blowing those sirens. He arrived and pulled in, he swung and fixed and went up again. Was he going to stay inside those grooves forever?

The Department came in on its brakes, scattering the crowd.

They put a spot on him, a blind white glare.

A megaphone hit the wall. *"Stay where you are. You there—stay where you are. We're going to come up for you."*

He slipped only for an instant, but he slipped, prised off

by the unexpected agony of words. He hung to a still by
hooked hands of fear, while they pushed rescue into his
back. "*You there—whoever you are—keep still.*"

They knew who he was, the bastards. White would have
seen to that.

He lashed upwards and failed. Then he found the ledge
above him, with his second strike. He relaxed on the rope,
almost like a man hanging in suicide. Then his voice came
clearly, but curiously remote. *You know who I am.*

A mountain of words; he waited for the echoes to stop
jumbling.

Down here the crowd was saying, "That's the guy: that's
the one. Last evening's paper." But in a silence so grave
it was like hearing its thoughts.

The voice from above said. "*I intend to get up this thing.*"
The echo said *up this thing. . . .* "*Try to get me off and I'll
jump.*" Then he went up the next swarm, scraping through
his own voice that still said *jump.*

High? He was high, but he was still ludicrously low.

The Department cursed and got busy.

They started to rumble a long escape after him. It was a
fair way up, but they obviously have them that long in New
York. A midget escape after a midget man, a fraction of the
distance up a vast tower. That bastard, White. Suppose he
jumped.

I looked round for Paul. For Greg and Shulberg. I wondered whether White was going to get them on the building.
How could the Iron Monkey compete with this, as advertising even? Did I care?

The escape reached him, a swaying island in the sky, an
insected flower-top, a snake's head of mesmerised rope. A
too-tiny trellis. Firemen figures beseeched him. It's hard to
take a man off a wall without co-operation. He went past
them. The crowd roared its approval. They wound up from

241

below and came in at him again, grim and earnest this time. Their honour was at stake.

He was nearly level with the roof of the buttress wings now. Soon there would only be the main stem of the tower above him. Only? About another eleven hundred feet. I felt sure he would come off soon. I felt him cry and plummet inside me. This rope business was too vulnerable.

The crowd pointed.

Something was happening up on those buttress roofs in the floodlit night. Were the police up there, trying to persuade him across to them as he drew level? Ridiculous. Why were they doing it? The wind started to blow, coming in from the Atlantic. Pinned against the stone by it would he feel the wall sway? It was supposed to move four feet a gust. Four feet over cloudy gulfs of vomit. The sky had already thickened.

It started to rain, a cold rain that turned the night to grease. I saw the high firemen crouch, pierced by its needles. Down here girls shrieked, became sexless mouths, old women of misery. The cloud was all on us now, illuminated by spot-light, nearly halfway down the tower. Sagging and drooping it tore apart, hurling down spears. It was hail, impossible hail. I saw Sym clench on a window, the cloud coming down at him, exploding fistfuls of gravel.

Somebody screamed, up high. Wordless, wordless. Not Sym, surely? A face at a window? Who dare disturb concentration by uttering fear? It was a man screaming too, not a woman.

Then I saw. There was a figure clamped on the wall above Sym, on the angle, above one of the buttresses, just near where we had been pointing. A man with his legs held stiffly. *The Monkey!* Greg or Shulberg. Everyone saw him now. For a second I wondered at the speed of it. Then I realised. That bugger White, or that smoothie Jason, had got them on from the roof of the buttress. One was up here and the other must be round the back of the tower. They must have gone through a hatch there. That was the huddle I had seen earlier. It was cheating, but it might be a winning cheat in the end.

Now he screamed, savaged by nails. He couldn't have been ready for this! Press-ups don't count when the brambles come. I fancied it was Shulberg, but I wasn't sure. I felt ill; I had nearly died on a wall myself. Sym made no sound.

He crouched in a hump of water, in a hump of bouncing crystal. He was probably safe—they were good ledges. If any ledge is safe in a storm, with nothing to tie you on, and the air dropping down to zero.

And God, it was cold now, with the ice falling.

I couldn't look up into the hail, not properly. The stones would black eyes. We crunched on marbles. The crowd didn't move, couldn't move perhaps; there were crowds beyond the crowds to hold us still, and eyes beyond the eyes. There were cameras here, and movies, and telecameras too. We were boxed in by cars. There were police megaphones calling. But in the cold, as the cold fell, this great crowd became numb and holy.

The hail stopped, a last dumb fistful of rivets. A framework opened itself high up in the wall. Sym, with gargoyles ogling behind him.

I saw they were trying to get him through the window. The firemen were down, but the window was opened behind him. Someone was wrestling him in. Not firemen, either. They wrestled high up, scuffing on the airy terraces.

Jason and partners, no doubt. Drag him in and that leaves Shulberg a winner. Drag him in or push him off. You heard him say he would commit suicide rather than give in—well, he committed.

243

Shulberg riddled by water hadn't moved. If I could find White now I should choke him to death. The wind was too cold to shout.

Sym fought free and got along the sill from trouble; it was long, but he still wouldn't have time to cast—they were following him too closely, lurching, beseeching, edging him to death if need be.

They jostled, on the verge of hope. One, two, three figures, and then Sym. They snatched. They crooked at him. They punched home. A weighted line fell, casting a ruled shadow. Sym had lost his rope! Surely this was the end of him!

He stepped off the sill, far above our stilled breathing. There was a gasp. He came back along the twenty-foot inset, away from the window. He was coming out onto the glazed face. What would he cling to? They grabbed at him, madly, skating, treading on marbles of ice. They jostled. One fell.

Was it a liveness falling? One minute there were three, then there were two, still falling now, he fell so slowly down the huge building. He screamed in the air for perhaps five seconds, waving at the ladders of glass, clutching handfuls of space, and then he hit flesh on stone and the scream went on boring into the earth's centre. Up high, they shuffled on the frosted ledge. They were pulled back in, defeated by death.

Sym reached an outside angle. No one could get him now, not alive. He could come off, of course. The wind plucked him. But somehow, once he climbed without his rope, he no longer seemed vulnerable. He clung to his own dynamic; he was moving up now, glued to the mystery. Straddling the corner he fumbled for finger-blocks. I wondered what holds he found there. What half-inch flaws, what inset perfections? A building rocked by the winds like that one must

244

have pitted and fractured a little. Just a stud for a finger-tip. I gave him my hope.

It was then, as Paul had said it must, that it started to snow. I saw the white darkness fall, meandering slowly, the building measuring its downfall from Heaven. Shulberg, a midget man, awakened to despair, and clawed at the iron on his thigh. But the iron seemed locked and immovable. Sym still moved upwards. At what height? Four hundred feet? Impossible to estimate. The next instant the cloud smoked down, I saw nothing but a vanishing wall and a million illuminated falling feathers, diamonds at first, in the light, then dove-white, then dove-grey, then blotting out all illumination completely. I was the uplifted eye on which the vulture sits.

IX

BY two in the morning it was a World Story and they all must have been dead for hours. The streets were refrigerators, the snow fell heavily and thick on the emptied side-walk, not feathers any more but huge grey plumes from the cloudy chasms between the towers. The crowds had long since gone back to their wirelesses—if they were interested, but mostly, since death will keep until breakfast, to their beds. The Press were here, there were police, there were fire-department, two ambulances, there were even movie cameras on trucks, but nothing much moved for them. The vehicles drifted deeper into whiteness, the Press into anything we could find open in the triangle between Thirty-Fourth and this side of Broadway.

I think I lost emotion quite early. Paul found me and got me in to hot food. There was a re-employment cable from

245

Dultie, but what did I care? Anyway, the agencies found me long before then. I signed several papers in the excuse of daze and shock, and I persuaded Paul to sign, but it was the excuse of dollars, really. Then I sent a cable *Still Balls I stay resigned*, but I relented a few minutes later and pushed off some sort of story. In my sense of compassion I had a long talk with Jason. It seems Greg was a circus high-cat, and Shulberg just a bum with muscles. Compassion? No, not compassion: we both knew that if we played it cautiously we played it rich. Apparently Woolly was a bona-fide designer of artificial climbing-aids, étriers, and stirrups and so forth. He had hoped to patent the Monkey for use on rock-pinnacles before White found him. White! He and Dultie were the only ones I hated. With Sym dead up there I knew what *I* was, but these were the people who paid me to be it.

Dead up there? I looked out: Greg couldn't fall, nor Shulberg, not from the Monkey. But surely Sym would have fallen by now, dead or alive, into the muffling swallow of snow? There were lights on all up the tower, I knew that, even though they were invisible about two floors up. I had tried up above, myself, on endless elevators and escape stairs, flashing out lamps, but I knew it was hopeless.

Towards breakfast we saw all the papers. We saw them: and saw it all over them, but there didn't seem to be much point in reading them.

Only, as dawn broke, and the binoculars got busy, and the stretchers trudged round the building and prowled on the buttress-roofs, it became clear that the biggest release was to come.

Greg was there, so was Shulberg, frozen stiff and still up the wall, little midget men in their unkind armour of ice.

But Sym, where was he? His body had quite disappeared.

246

They dug in the snowdrifts for ages, but he just wasn't
there.

X

DID THE MIRACLEJACK MAKE IT? . . . .
??? HOW HIGH THE BONZE ???
The Evenings buzzed with speculation, in large square
type. *Body disappears*, the rawrub of truth, was only added
as an afterthought. Paul and I discussed a pile of them in
an Italian restaurant, sixth generation, in midtown Manhattan, where we only had ourselves and the smells of a
season's cooking to contend with. We were waiting for our
television appearance in the evening.

"I'm a rational man," he commented, after he'd read
through the lot. He curled spaghetti round a battered iron
spoon as lovingly as he would have wound a spool of
film.

"He probably got there," I said. Did I believe it, or was I
just rehearsing?

"Visions, cock—visions and delusions of grandeur. Ordinary men have indigestion. You have visions. You know
where visions come from? Bottles."

"It's a matter of instinct."

We were both of us drinking something insipid from
plastic cups. After a while he tapped his pocket, which
bulged with more cuttings. "I believe *The Post* scooped."

I looked at him sourly.

"And Lord Dirty scooped, and the British Press scooped,
and Carmel White scooped. And the American Press, which
knows how to scoop, it scooped. And the New York Police
Orphans scooped. And Mrs. Dead Shulberg scooped—she's

holding a cheque and a frozen corpse. What a funny shape to die, they'll have to break him for the coffin. This is *the* story of the year, isn't it? Even Mrs. Greg says so. Another curious coffin in that family."

"All right," I said. I was fed up with being surrounded by people who behaved as if Life was my fault.

"The only problem is—when do we scoop?"

"We don't," I said. "We're making plenty as it is."

"Balls. People who are fortunate enough to be at martyrdoms always scoop. They flog souvenirs. And when there is no martyrdom handy they cook one up." He stared at me and fished in his pocket. "That's your case, of course. Not enough deaths in the world so we promote them. Now all we need are the souvenirs." He handed me an envelope. "That's not exactly the pig's bones, even. It's the dear old Pardoner's testicles in the hog's turd."

I took out his photographs. The first one was Sym leaning backwards into space in an avalanche of snow and stars.

"Where did you. . . ."

"From the top of my own private ambition. Living for kicks in a world of bricks."

"But *where*?" The next one was miracle, unbelievable miracle, a crowning apocalypse. It was Sym on the top of the radio-mast on the top of the tower, thrusting up through a sea of cloud, his arms outraised in a living cross. It was incredible and beautiful, as incredible and beautiful as the spinning sun of Fatima, as the statue weeping. It was as true as the inscription of lichen on stones. I looked at him speechless.

"Officially," said Paul, "I took that from a helicopter."

"Who flew it, for Christsake?"

"Barney, I daresay. He ought to get something out of this story. There's ten thousand quid each for us in that picture, if you write the words properly."

"But this thing is going to have religious significance for people. I can't muck around with *that*! "

He grinned. "I daresay it will be an official miracle for some of them. I faked it so well, old cock. Unofficially I took it in a dark-room. As a matter of fact, I'd prefer not to have the Vatican examine the negatives—they're rather cautious about those. Nor the Press Council."

"You mean they're *faked*! " The picture said so much to me that I didn't want to know it wasn't genuine. And yet it *had* to be faked, of course. It was just that miracle seemed a better explanation.

Paul looked at me unadmiringly. "You're very naïve for one who has come so far and cried so cynically at every step," he complained. He looked at his watch. "A long time to go yet! "

I knew what he was going to do before this television interview. He was going to find me something to drink, and I was quite powerless to stop him.

XI

THERE was a cable from Morpath in my pocket. It read: *Congratulations Stop There is no liar like a holy liar Brother Bertram Stop.*

I carried it with me. Brother Bertram stop.

What did Sym do and say in that blast, that is the question. What did he do and say and think, nailed by the icicles, tented by the black spear of wind? Did his breath freeze into thorns, his sweat drip from a halo of frost?

"To where did his body go? " A problem unanswered by *The Post.* Did it whirl away like a helicopter, frozen into

249

its own aerofoil; did it fly like a frosted sycamore seed into the murk of the East River?

My friends, I will let you into a secret.

I met him again.

I was famous, mind you. Three days later I was television famous. I was famous because of Sym, and with Paul I was famous because of his miraculous photographs. There was no need for me to climb the Empire State upside down. I just had to be drunk and agree. After we published that photograph I was even on speaking terms with a bishop. . . .

I had just been speaking with Mavis, transatlantic cable, when I met him. She was in love, all right. She was in love with the success on my back. The toad would never need to creep out from under his stone again. He was wearing a white plastic topcoat, and he came from an alley I was walking past kicking paper-cartons and boxes, and scuffing up snow.

I couldn't speak. All my lies knock me down in the end.

" Have you been drinking? " he asked. He sounded urgent about it, as if our whole conversation hinged on it.

" You should know." I felt belligerent. How I hated him for all this!

" Yes," he said.

A real voice, flesh and saliva.

He had wounds. I didn't hear what he said for a minute because of them. He had wounds that went right into the crevasses of memory. His face was all frostbite, his chin sunk in cloth.

" You bastard," I said. " Where the hell have you been. Letting me carry all this."

" I saw you on T.V." he said.

" Well, you heard what I said. The Christ of Manhattan some paper called you." I suddenly felt beseeching, earnest.

"Tell me, Sym—is it true? Did you really get up there?"

He smiled, mad and wise. "I've been in hospital," he said. He wasn't going to answer.

"That's nice," I said. "That's bloody nice. You've been in hospital, lying low. How the hell did you get there?"

He smiled. "I'm finished," he said. He moved his hands suddenly. The finger-ends were wrapped. The palms were compressed under a transparent bandage.

"Go on," I said. "Tell me."

He lifted his trouser-leg. His ankles were gored by stone. Gored to the bone. Or so he told me. I saw the white bandage.

"I tore a vein out," he said. "I tore a vein out on a bolt." He looked up. "My blood's up there."

"The other two didn't bleed," I said. "They just froze. They were stopped at the twenty-fourth and twenty-fifth storeys, just above the buttresses. They were locked on the wall and they would still be there if the fire brigade hadn't taken them down."

"I underestimated them. I didn't realise they'd climb from the buttresses. I came down inside and when I climbed out I couldn't find them."

I was incredulous.

"You mean you went out onto their angles."

"I went out, yes. But it didn't do them much good."

"Then you went back inside and right down the lift into hospital! How come nobody knew you were there?"

"Doctors don't talk. It's sheets that they wrap you up in, not newsprint."

The wind got keener. Men don't stay talking in this weather. You could lean on the wind and rest on it, it was so solid; but it would be like resting on broken glass: it cut the kidneys out of you.

"Let's have a coffee," I said, but he didn't answer.

I believe he went back into the alley; it was snowing again.

"Who was that, Mister?"

A reporter; I knew he was a reporter: I could smell him. He had my smell.

Another one of them. "Who was that you were talking to?" They looked about themselves suspiciously. Snow fell on my shadow.

Why should I lie? I got money if I lied. I got money if I told the truth. I was the man who knew Sym. They followed me everywhere now, in case it was all a trick and I alone knew the answer.

"That was Sym," I said.

They peered into the alley. It wasn't like an English alley. It was just as dirty, but it was newer, and that meant it had become just as dirty in less time, and that made it different. It was a transatlantic alley.

One of them even stepped into it.

A transatlantic step.

It made an alleyway noise, the stone coughing echoes up the high blocks. The snow wouldn't settle very much in here, only drift.

"Cheese," he said. "Don't kid me."

Or was it Jeez?

"Don't kid me," said the other. "That was a hobo."

"That," I said, "was what it was. A bum."

They looked at me. We prickled and shuddered in the glass wind. Paul was waiting somewhere.

"Come and have coffee," I said.

Coffee is the same the whole world over. It is bad. As I drank it I saw they were watching me furtively, as if I were some sort of madman. Then I remembered the words

I had shouted as she had left me. "You can't expect me to compete with God," I had said. "He's got more experience than I have." The mistake I had made was in supposing He confined his attentions to women. Well, I wouldn't break now.